THE
PERFECT
GIRL
FRIEND

THE
PERFECT
GIRL
FRIEND

HAYLEY SMITH

Bookouture

Published by Bookouture in 2023

An imprint of Storyfire Ltd.
Carmelite House
50 Victoria Embankment
London EC4Y 0DZ

www.bookouture.com

ISBN: 978-1-83790-266-8
eBook ISBN: 978-1-83790-262-0

For my parents, who taught me to read.

Black is the colour of my true love's hair
Her lips are like a rose so fair
She has the sweetest smile and the gentlest hands
And I love the ground whereon she stands.

TRADITIONAL FOLK SONG

PROLOGUE

She crouches and listens. A torch beam flickers between the trees, the crack of twigs showing he knows she is there and he doesn't intend to let her go. He will be stalking, scanning the ground for signs of her presence. He will be following her desperate trail.

There is a smattering of stars above the canopy of trees, but she cannot work out which direction leads to the edge of the forest, to the road where she can let her lungs rip open and scream for help.

She can't afford to be reckless. Every movement matters in this cat and mouse situation. The longer it takes for him to find her, the angrier he will be. They are past the point of kissing and making up now and she knows for certain that death will be the only outcome. Slowly, cautiously, she gathers the skirts of her dress and stands up, keeping her eyes pinned to the wavering beam of light. Stepping silently towards the nearest tree, then the next, she ignores the pain from every stone and thorn that embeds in her bleeding feet, her mission only to reach some place of safety.

'I know you're there! I'm going to get you, however long it

takes!' His voice rings through the trees, bouncing on every trunk like a pinball.

She waits again, her heart hammering, forehead pressed against papery birch-bark.

Then the torch goes off. Where is he?

Nothing. Stillness and blackness. Then the rustle of undergrowth, the flap of an owl above. Sharp quick breaths and footsteps.

Should she run for it now? Should she stay? She twists and turns her head to listen, trying to decipher the direction he's coming from, but she can't hear anything above the bashing of fear under her ribs.

Suddenly he's there, behind her, his fingers clutching at her sleeve.

'No!' She tears away from his grasp and sprints clumsily through the trees, stumbling in rabbit holes and whipping her cheeks on tendrils of overgrown ivy.

'Help me!' she shrieks to anyone who might hear, but she knows that it is futile: the nearest houses are over a mile away and even the most committed dog walkers don't come out at three in the morning.

Ragged sobs escape her as she runs pointlessly like a trapped animal. Is this it? Is this how it is going to end? His booted feet thunder behind her and all he will need to do is reach out and his hand will be on her neck...

CHAPTER ONE
AUGUST

We get together at a music festival. I watch him weave through the crowd as I stand behind thousands of others in a summer shower, waiting for the band to start. He is wearing a polythene bin bag and a pair of shorts, and holds a pint in each hand. He isn't my normal type, but as I observe his journey a tiny smile nudges the corner of my mouth and I even stretch up on tiptoes at one point to keep him in my line of vision. On and on, he zigzags diligently between groups and couples and discarded camping chairs and hairy blokes wearing saggy fairy wings. Ironically, he arrives at the space in front of me.

He stops. I examine the back of him: chestnut mussed-up hair; facile wiry frame; muscular mud-spattered calves.

I lean in a little and seize the moment. 'Love the shirt.'

He turns and grins. His wet face is tanned and stubbly and his green eyes speak of countryside.

'Hey,' he says. He pushes one of the pint glasses into my hand and shakes my other one. 'I know who you are. You're the fiddle player from Cuckoo Spit. I saw you on Stage Two yesterday.'

Flattery does a lot for me. I am a temporary member of a mediocre folk-punk band that plays mainly support gigs.

'My playing must have made an impression.'

'Nah,' he says. 'I thought you were fit.'

Two hours later we are rocking his campervan. Rain thrashes at the roof and baked bean tins rattle in the cupboards.

'Don't let me stop you from seeing the headliners tonight,' I say when we lie tangled in the fusty bedding afterwards. 'They're supposed to be great. Sort of traditional songs with layers of dance beats. Big hipster following. And they've won loads of music awards.'

'Yeah, I know,' he says. 'I love how they fuse the two styles – I'm a big fan. Their new album is so good.' He reaches over the driver's seat and switches on the CD player.

'*Black is the colour*' – the words sing out from the stereo and the music drowns out the rain – '*of my true love's hair.*'

He looks deep into my eyes as he runs his fingers through my dark, tousled tresses.

He kisses me desperately. And I consume him, drink him, breathe in his subtle cannabis scent. I want him. More than anything, I want him.

* * *

He is called Jason, but prefers Jay. He works on some historical estate in Nottinghamshire doing forestry stuff: coppicing and conservation. He plays the guitar and likes all sorts of music apart from country, rap and swing. He has a motorbike, an old black Suzuki that is forever breaking down, but his best friend, Rick, is good with engines and always gets it sorted. He hasn't seen his father since he was a nipper, and his mother has gone to live in

Spain with a bloke who runs bingo nights for Brits. He brews his own beer and grows vegetables in his garden. He'd lived with his last girlfriend for seven years – even been on the verge of marriage – but it had all gone pear-shaped. He doesn't want to talk about it.

I tell him about me, about my previous job as a school violin teacher during term times, a session fiddler in the holidays. I tell him about my parents and how they love real ales. How they seek out micro-breweries and beer festivals and are dismissive of the government's recommendation that people should only drink fourteen units per week. I tell him about Lou, my extravagant elder sister who shops her life away while her husband works all hours. I talk about all sorts of things, things I have to make up just so that I can continue the momentum of information trading. But of course I don't tell him the important things. I have to know everything about *him*. I don't want to scare him off.

He tells me he's been waiting to find someone like me. Our meeting is fate, destiny, a blissful coincidence. He can't believe his luck; he thinks all the planets have aligned to bring us together.

And I have to agree. Destiny. It really looks like it is.

There are two days left until all the tents are bundled into back seats and car boots, and people change out of their tie-dye clothes and leave their stamps of yellow grass alongside broken camping chairs and empty cider cans.

'It's been a good festival,' I say as we sprawl on a muddy tarpaulin, the damp, earthy smell rising to a coaxing sun.

'It's been the best,' he says, winding my hair round his hand and pulling my face towards his.

I laugh. 'We missed most of it.' We didn't even see the head-liners. We stayed in his van, listening to the CD instead.

He looks at me. My chest suddenly hurts. It is as if neither of us can speak of afterwards.

'I'm at another festival next weekend,' I say. 'We're playing in Devon.'

I pick at blades of grass while he ties his bootlaces.

'Hope the weather's better than this. I'm not sure my tent will stand up to another soaking.' My words hover, like a party-goer on the edge of a clique. He scrambles to his feet, wiping his muddy hands on his jeans.

'Let's get some food,' he says. 'I'm starving.'

Sunday night comes. The last band has finished and people are heading back to their blow-up beds through the misty drizzle. We sit in his camper in a fuddle of dope, half clothed, half unbuttoned as if we are in the middle of playing strip poker. Tea lights in jam jars blush because the interior lights don't work.

'Where are you going after Devon?' he says, suddenly, flicking ash into the sink.

'Home, I suppose.' The words are out and my heart thumps. 'Back to sunny East Anglia and my flatmate, Rachel.'

He turns to me. His expression is weighty.

'Don't,' he says, passing the smouldering spike.

I close my eyes and suck. My body tingles. He leans over and kisses my bare thigh.

'What do you mean, *don't?*'

'Come and live with me.' He hugs his knees up to his chest. His body looks small and thin. There are patches of dried-up muck on his feet that snake between his toes and I am aware of his vulnerability.

'What would I do?' I say.

'Do whatever you do now. Just do it with me instead.'

It is a momentous point, the opportunity I am waiting for. A chance to get my life sorted out. To find out everything I need to move on. He undoes the rest of my shirt buttons and nestles me into the dank folds of the oversized duvet, and I let his love smother me.

* * *

'He's got a cottage in the countryside,' I tell Rachel as I squawk coat hangers along the wardrobe rails. 'With a wood-burning stove for cooking on.'

'What? An Aga?' Rachel feigns interest.

'I think so.' I envisage a gleaming green and chrome beast in a beamed-ceiling kitchen with a white Belfast sink and a waxed pine dresser.

'Hmm, a bit *Escape to the Country* then?' She can't hide the snootiness in her tone. 'You should've got a picture of him: he must be on social media. *Everyone* is on Facebook.'

'Apart from me,' I interject. I haven't been on Facebook for years. When you've had an *inappropriate* relationship for most of your life you keep secrets rather than updating a public status. And Facebook is about having 'friends', isn't it? The few I've had have all blocked me in real life, as if I am the one at fault. It seems unfair, when Martin is still on social media, uploading pictures of family events, commenting on posts about local crime and sharing judgemental opinions about celebrities and royals.

Rachel grimaces. She knows the score. 'He sounds like a proper hipster, though. They do all that stuff, don't they? Growing things. Keeping bees. Has he actually *got* bees? Didn't I say that a hipster-type would be ideal for you?'

'I thought hipsters had to have big beards and tweed jackets. And the most expensive phones. He might be lacking a few characteristics.' I laugh as I slot pink stilettos into my holdall. I can't remember if he said he kept bees. 'I know he's not my normal type, but, you know...'

'It'll be good for you,' she says. 'After all that's happened. Didn't I say you should break the mould? Find a new bloke. Get your head sorted out. Try something new. And having the chance to move away means you get a completely new start.'

Break the mould. Keep away from men like Martin, that's what she is thinking. *Get your head sorted out.* Get back on the rails, stop all the grief and accept what's happened. *Chance to move away.* Get out of the spare room where you've been dossing around paying virtually no rent. I am good at reading between lines.

But really, Rachel is right. Although she isn't a best friend – no one could ever fill *that* slot – she had reluctantly taken me in when I had been at my lowest point and not even my family wanted to know me. We'd had a long and tearful talk back in April, where I had promised her that I would sort my life out properly. Break out of my cycle of negativity. No more dead-end relationships and one-night stands. No more blazing conflicts with everyone who tried to help. No more endless days in bed, hungover, thinking about slitting my wrists. I needed to get out and do new and exciting things. 'Do it for Nell,' she'd urged me then, and that had been the catalyst for me getting involved in the band – standing in for their fiddler who'd had a serious accident and would be out of action until autumn. I had ended up on their spring and summer gig schedule, playing grotty venues, supporting big names in arenas, and gathering new fans at festivals.

'I know it seems a bit sudden,' I tell Rachel, now, as I remember his warm, rough hands, and the way they had touched me. 'It was just a chance thing, but I'm so looking forward to having something – *someone* – to focus on so that I can leave all the bad memories behind.'

'You can always come back to visit,' says Rachel. Her voice is tight. It is obvious that she wants me away because she feels tainted by me.

'Everything should fit in my car,' I say. 'One trip will do it.'

I imagine pulling up outside his cottage with my meagre possessions: dragging my wheelie case through to the bedroom to unpack. I think about what his bed will be like. Black, wrought iron, scattered with rumpled pillows and crinkled white linen trailing onto a polished oak floor.

My heart flutters with anticipation. My head reminds me to watch my back. After all, some dreams turn into nightmares, don't they?

I am taking my clothes, shoes, a few books. The expensive stereo system that Martin had bought me two years ago. My musical equipment that fills the car boot and most of the back seat: two fiddles, amplifiers, leads, effects pedals. My old photograph albums where, sadly, the skewed snapshots of me and Nell have been eradicated: I had implemented a tactful memorial bonfire beside my tent at the Devon festival until a steward told me to get it extinguished.

Rachel gives me a modest hug. She closes the door before I've even got my seat belt on.

'Goodbye,' I say to no one. I flap my arm out of the window just in case Rachel is watching from somewhere.

The car moves out onto the main road and slips into the stream of traffic.

I am utterly alone, between two worlds.

CHAPTER TWO

I arrive under a cherry sky as the sun drops onto the horizon. There had been no houses for miles apart from an old gamekeeper's cottage. I saw the landmarks Jay had described in his directions: the dense edge of forest; the signpost to the quarry; the disused slag heap in the distance. Then the final left turn, marked by a sign denoting a no through road.

I push down my indicator and turn cautiously into a lane full of potholes and puddles. Two ivy-clad cottages pass me by, fenced in by five-bar gates and vivid gardens of tall, quivering flowers. A dog yaps at my tyres as they crunch along the track. A chimney pushes out whorls of smoke, and a narrow bend in the lane reveals another stone fantasy. Surely, I am close now. The map is imprinted on my mind. But now the cottages are left behind and the road grows thinner. I check the directions again; he'd told me the satnav wouldn't recognise the postcode so it was pointless trying to use one.

The road becomes a thin strip of gravel and grass. Brambles snatch at my wing mirrors and a ridge of turf scrapes the underside of my car. Then, suddenly, the end of the lane is visible in the distance. I can just make out a figure scrambling to his feet at the end of the track: Jay, waving his arm high in the air, running towards me, pulling the roll-up from between his lips and flicking it away, a huge smile unlocking his face. I shiver as I reach for the handbrake.

He pulls me out of the car and crushes me into his arms, pressing dry, smoky lips onto mine, his tongue between my teeth.

'I've missed you,' he says, rubbing his face into my hair. 'Let me take you to bed.'

He tugs my hand and I follow him up the crumbly concrete drive.

The cottage is not as I had imagined it might be. It is a small, brick-built fifties-style bungalow. The only door is at the side of the house: a blue panel of wood, heavily veined with layers of paint. I glance towards the back garden up a side alley of rusting engine bits, mouldy carpets and a small, broken trampoline. He pulls me up the step into the kitchen and kisses me again.

But it isn't the house I have come for, it is him. I will look later and take it all in. In the meantime, I just let him lead me through it, into a tiny hallway with an unexpected wooden staircase stretching into an open square in the ceiling.

'Up here,' he says, dropping my hand and leading the way to the room above. I follow him and the bedroom is divulged with each step.

A bare Velux window frames the glowing sunset. A clock radio on the bedside cabinet flashes *eight eight eight eight*. Jay has his shirt off, his belt undone, as I squat to untie my trainers. A dusty full-length mirror, oblique against the opposite wall, glances at my uncertain figure. I recognise the duvet as the one from the campervan.

It is dark when I awake. A flurry of stars hangs over the roof window. I turn towards the warmth of Jay.

'Hello,' he says. I hear happiness in his voice. The clock is still throwing its eights into the room, as if no minutes or hours have passed, as if we have devoured each other's bodies until we are breathless and running with sweat in a parallel world.

'What time is it?' I whisper.

'I don't know, might be around midnight.'

He sits up and swings his feet out onto the carpet. I remember it is turquoise.

'D'you fancy some food?'

I say that would be great, and he disappears, down the hole in the floor. I lie in the intermittent blackness, listening to the sound of pans and cupboards, cutlery, and the suck of a fridge door.

The aroma of frying bacon drifts upstairs. The clatter of crockery, more cupboards opening, then Jay emerges from the floor again, jabbing a switch and flooding the room with white-bright light from a bare bulb. I blink and struggle into a sitting position, my back touching the cold wall.

'What d'you think of the place then?' he asks, passing me a plate.

I've hardly had the time to take it in. I pause. Bite into the bacon sandwich. Exaggerate my chewing while I think what to say. 'Well, I've only seen the bedroom so far.'

And there it is, all around me, the brilliance highlighting everything to find wrong with it. Wallpaper edges gaping like new wounds. Fifty-year-old furniture. A room that looks like something from *Homes Under the Hammer*.

'It needs a bit of work,' he says. 'I've not really had chance to do much.'

'I don't mind getting stuck in. Think I could be quite good at interior design. I love watching all those kinds of programmes.'

'There might be limits, though,' he says. 'What with it belonging to Rick's mum and that.'

'Oh, I thought it was yours.'

'I'm renting it. It used to be Rick's grandma's until she died.'

In my mind I see a small white-haired old lady sitting where I sit, surrounded by the dark furniture and gaudy carpet, propped up on an unyielding bolster pillow.

'So where does Rick live?'

'Oh, he lives with his mum. She's a GP, so they've got this massive posh house, next village along. She looks after him: he gets decent food and his clothes washed. He wouldn't be able to fend for himself.' Jay gives a snort.

I finish my food. 'I ought to bring my equipment in from the car. My fiddles at least.'

'Hey,' he says, leaning over and kissing me. 'I'm looking forward to doing some music with you: we'll have a jam tomorrow and I'll get the old guitar out. There are some other good musicians round here, too: it would be fun to get them round at some point.'

He gets out of bed and steps into his jeans, rummaging through my pile of clothes for the car keys. 'Stay here and go back to sleep. I'll bring your stuff in.'

I watch him disappear down the staircase. A starting point is what I need. Somewhere definite that I can refer to where this new life begins. I reach out for the clock radio to set the time.

* * *

I wake under a fresh scrap of sky to an industry of bird chorus. I reach out to Jay. He is still asleep, his dark lashes smiling, his lips slightly apart. I study his face, wondering what he dreams of. If his dreams are as dark as mine. I creep out of the warm enclosure and pull on my clothes. Barefoot, I pad down the narrow staircase.

The small hallway holds three other doors: flat white slabs mottled around the handles with dirty fingerprints. One is an eyeful ajar, inviting me to push it so that it shushes over the brown carpet. The living room: a feast of off-white woodchip walls. Gold satiny curtains and beige Dralon suite. Brick fireplace. Dark wood sideboard under the window. I sweep my eyes around, and quickly draw the door shut, aware of a gentle stickiness on the handle.

The next one is the bathroom: a long thin room with mustard walls and an avocado suite; the plastic bath dull and sheenless, its plug hanging on a slimy tug of string. I look around and wonder how it can all be put right.

Lou would be horrified. I know I need to make up with her, but there would be no way I could invite her to a place like this. I visualise the sneer at the edge of her lips, see how she would open a door with an elbow, politely refuse a drink with a note of disdain in her voice.

'Lauren.' Jay's voice reaches down to me and I close the bathroom door swiftly as he skips down the stairs. 'Having a nosy round?'

He takes my hand and kisses the palm. 'Best place is outside.'

I follow him through the kitchen and slip my feet into a pair of his old trainers by the door. The frayed insoles scrunch under my toes.

Outside, the morning is resonating with birds, their dark bodies mottling the cloudless sky. Traffic noise doesn't exist here.

'You'll like this,' says Jay as he leads me through a trellis fence woven with honeysuckle.

I'm not sure if I gasp.

Jay says, 'Ta da,' and holds his arms out in a flourish.

The garden is there, acres of it: sweeping, sprawling, with clumps and swathes; fruit trees dripping with crimson apples and purple-black damsons; leeks growing in manicured rows; the orange tops of pumpkins showing through carpets of leaves.

'Wow,' I say. It's all I can think of.

I allow myself a brief moment to dream about a perfect life here, where there's a barbeque – a big half-barrel – hissing and spitting, pushing smoky meaty smells into the air as I chat, with a glass of chilled wine, to well-dressed friends and acquaintances. Fairy lights strung through the trees – right down the garden – to give a sense of the length and space of it all. Spotlights in the flowers, picking out the architectural ones: I've seen all the garden design programmes. Nice hardwood furniture, a swinging bench, maybe a hammock. My fantasies are futile, though. Who would accept an invitation from me after all that has happened?

'It's like something out of *Country Living* magazine,' I say.

Jay laughs. He wanders across the grass and I tramp after him, his trainers slobbing on my feet. We brush through more shrubbery, breaking out dewy-armed into a stone-flagged area with a bench and sundial. Jay flops down and pulls me onto his lap.

'I could have you on here,' he says, slipping his cold hand up my T-shirt.

I grab his wrist. 'Show me the rest of the garden, then you can.'

He pulls his hand out. 'Go and have a look around. You'll appreciate it more if you see it on your own. I'll wait here.'

So I follow the narrow gravel path. It winds round lilac trees, clumps of lavender, rosemary, and an old, padlocked shed. Further on, there is an orchard and another vegetable garden with wooden compost bins.

At the end of the garden is a low stone wall. Beyond that, the edge of the forest – Sherwood Forest I assume – with a perimeter of waving saplings receding into dense trees. I breathe deeply and the leafy, loamy spoor washes the stress out of me. There are no visible paths to lure me into the dark woods but I have a sudden foreboding sense of how it feels to be in its core, hidden within the gnarled, ancient sanctuary.

But I brush the feeling away and lean on the rough wall for a long time and think about everyone I have left behind. I think about the people who have left *me*, have been *taken* from me. This opportunity is fate, it's serendipitous. I've only been here a day, but this place feels like it can heal me. It has everything I need. Including Jay. He seemed like such an effortless catch! I close my eyes and linger until I am aware of the sun glaring on my head and Jay calling my name through the sighing garden.

* * *

Jay's best friend, Rick, turns up in the afternoon. He has a goatee beard and tiny ringlets of silky, black hair. A dangling raindrop of gold hangs from his right ear.

'So, you're the fiddle player then,' he'd said after walking in without knocking.

In the living room I perch on the arm of Jay's chair. Rick sits in the middle of the sofa, his short legs splayed apart, his polo shirt straining across stacked rolls of flesh. He rubs his face a lot when he talks, and pokes at his ear.

'So, what's on for this week?' Rick asks Jay.

'Not much until next Wednesday. A bit of cutting back, preparations for the hedge-laying, you know.'

'I could do with sorting out some work for myself,' I say. 'I might ring round a few schools, perhaps check out any local studios now that my time with Cuckoo Spit is over.'

'Good fun while it lasted,' Jay says. 'But you're here now. And there's plenty to do in the house and garden so you won't get bored.'

Rick glowers and shakes his head, pointing a finger at me. Already, I'm finding him a bit weird. There's an uncomfortable pause, so I offer to make tea.

In the kitchen I fill the old enamel kettle and set it on the range. There are no dials to adjust the heat, so I look around the room as I wait. Dead flies on the windowsill; black mould on the net curtain. I open the cupboard under the sink. Engine oil, washing-up liquid and two scrunched dishcloths, hard like cardboard. I make a mental note to buy bleach.

Rick and Jay go out at seven o'clock.

'We're on a mission,' Jay says, but when I ask if the mission includes me he winks and kisses me. And out of the corner of my eye I see the tiny dart of Rick's look towards Jay, and wonder what it means.

But I welcome the time alone so that I can explore the house fully. I check the rest of the kitchen cupboards and drawers. Cutlery, carrier bags, the grater attachment for a non-existent food processor. Mugs, saucepans, crockery: everything you'd expect to find. A reasonable store cupboard of essentials. I search the sideboard in the living room. Bank statements, the most recent one ninety pounds overdrawn. Ashtray, pack of cards. Five pint glasses, slotted into each other. Set of guitar strings. A bunch of assorted-sized keys. A stack of CDs: Levellers, New Model Army, and both Cuckoo Spit albums, neither of which feature me.

I try to open the door, the one that I haven't looked through yet, but it is fitted with a lock that won't let me in. I return to the sideboard for the bunch of keys and try each one in turn, but nothing fits. I go outside and peer through the dirty windows, blinkering my eyes with my hands, but see nothing. I return inside and unpack my clothes. Lay my T-shirts beside his in the fusty drawers. Hang my fabric-conditioned frocks next to a green army shirt in the wardrobe. I leave my shoes in the holdall.

· · ·

He is back within forty minutes, alone and with a bottle of red wine.

'Oh, a treat,' I say. 'Something to drink and you all to myself.'

He proposes lighting the fire in the living room, but I suggest sitting outside on the bench in his heavenly garden.

Instead, we take the brown duvet outside and spread it on the flagstones still warm from the day's sun. We stab candles into the dry soil of the surrounding flowerbeds, and we lie there like we are on a beach with the nearby forest splashing its sound softly, and us drinking our wine and whispering and kissing, and the sweet night smells of the garden turning the evening into some sort of perfection.

CHAPTER THREE

Monday morning. I've had no contact with anyone: my mobile was constantly coming up with *no service* and Jay had thrown his head back and fell about when I asked him about a wi-fi connection. There is no phone line, no sign of a telegraph pole anywhere near the house.

'How do you manage to keep in touch with anyone?' I ask, incredulous.

He says he's got his motorbike, his campervan, his legs. He doesn't do virtual stuff.

I had tried to text Rachel on Saturday morning, to let her know that I had arrived safely. That the house was nice. And each time I tried to send I got *message failed*, even though I had gone upstairs to the bedroom and held my arm as far as I could out of the loft window.

'Don't worry,' Jay had said. 'It's just the pit tip getting in the way. No phone signal. No internet, no 4G or anything. It's always been a blackspot round here. You'll get used to it after a while and find that it's so much nicer being out of the social media loop.'

'A proper off-grid kind of place,' I'd remarked. Perhaps it

was what was needed. 'Let's see how we survive in the real world then.'

The house is starting to feel familiar now, not just like temporary holiday accommodation. I make a snagging list of all the easy fixes I could turn my hand to: walls I could paint, areas that could be rearranged to work better.

I ask Jay about the lock on the dining room. About where the key is.

He laughs and looks sheepish. 'Ahh,' he grimaces. 'Bit of a cock-up. I put the key in a safe place and now I can't find it. But I'm sure it will turn up somewhere. It's just that the room is unusable in the meantime.'

'Idiot.' I give him a friendly punch on the arm and remind myself to check carefully for the key before throwing anything away.

It is cloudy and cold outside. A stripe of white is trapped between grey sky and the horizon. Jay says he wants to clear up some of the fallen apples, cut a few courgettes. He'll take them round for Rick's mum to keep her sweet.

I focus on the pile of rubbish beside the kitchen door. 'Could we get rid of some of this junk? Is there a local tip or something? It might look nicer if I start doing some tidying up.'

'Yeah, whatever.' He walks off towards the orchard shaking a carrier bag from his pocket.

So I shift some muddy bottles to the front of the house. An engine-looking piece of metal looks heavy. I drag a wet rug out of the heap. Its underside is lined with clinging slugs.

Jay returns with a bag full of produce from the garden.

'Looks like you need a strong man to do that,' he remarks as he sees me tugging at the engine-thing.

I point at the broken trampoline in the middle of the pile. 'Something for Rick's grandma to keep fit on?' I laugh.

'It's been here ages.' Jay hauls the piece of engine into his arms and kicks at a flap of carpet as he walks steadily down the path.

The rain starts. It slants over the forest and sweeps over the garden, flattening pumpkin leaves, throwing soil over the lettuce. A stream of water runs down the kitchen window from the split guttering above.

'Aren't there any pubs we could walk to?' I check my phone again and try resending the text to Rachel.

'What, in this weather?' says Jay. 'Probably about two miles away, the nearest. I don't think it even opens on a Monday. Anyway, if you want beer you should try my home-brew.'

'It's not even half eleven in the morning and you're offering me home-brew?' My phone beeps and says *message failed*. 'I tried some once. It was like cats' wee.'

Jay starts to riddle ashes out of the kitchen stove. 'You haven't tasted mine, though. Mine's as good as anything you've had out of a beer tent this year, I bet. Your parents would love it. And it's all part of a self-sufficient lifestyle.' He scrambles up from the stove and goes into the living room, returning with a book. 'Look, this is what you need to get into.'

The Complete Book of Self-Sufficiency. On the front there's a man drinking beer and a woman preparing a feast from bread, eggs and vegetables.

I raise my eyebrows at Jay as I open the front cover. A message is scrawled inside, balancing on a row of kisses, but Jay reaches over and flicks to the middle.

'There,' he says, tapping a page. 'Chickens. A little coop like that in the orchard. Half a dozen to peck around and lay eggs for us. Sell what we don't need.'

'Hmm.' I look at the different designs of poultry arks.

'It would be great, wouldn't it?' There's a shine in his eyes. 'You and me here, living the good life.' He scoops me into his arms and presses his hot mouth on mine.

* * *

I'm alone again. Jay had shoved the carrier bag of apples and
courgettes into an old rucksack and said he was going to drop
them off at Rick's.

'Can't I come?' I asked.

'I'm taking the bike,' he said. 'I've only got one helmet.'

'We could go in my car,' I replied, but he was already
fastening the strap under his chin, flipping the visor up.

I watched him straddle the bike, stirred at the sight of denim
tightening over his backside as he kicked the machine into a
roar. As soon as he was down the lane I made my way past the
stack of junk and back into the dingy kitchen.

I don't know why but my hands are trembling. I open the
self-sufficiency book and look at the inscription: *For the rest of
our lives together, with all of my love, R.* Plus nine kisses.

I try to think of names beginning with R. Rachel, Roxanne,
Rosie. I try to remember if Jay mentioned anyone's name when
we first talked at the festival. But no, he couldn't have. I would
have remembered. Rebecca, there's another one. I close the
book, press the front cover down and put a mug on it so that it
can't spring up and display the message. Is R the ex he said he'd
been on the verge of marrying? And if so, what happened?
Where is she now?

I pick up my phone. No messages. Ruby, that's another
name. I decide to go for a drive, find somewhere I can get a
signal, communicate with people, frazzle my brain with calls.

My car keys are not in my bag. I rummage, poke into the
corners past the disintegrating tissues and accumulation of bric-
a-brac. Nothing. I tip the contents onto the carpet. No keys. I
search the bedroom: the wardrobe, drawers, bedside cabinet.
Nothing in the kitchen either. I wonder if Jay has put them on
his keyring with his bike keys. I shiver, feeling trapped. But I
won't let it deter me. I will still go out, explore the area.

I take my phone and step outside. A fresh, washed smell infuses the air and there is a lull in the rain. The door will have to stay unlocked. I set off, briskly, down the lane past the brambles and endless hawthorn hedges towards the posh houses with the oak kitchens and beams and ceramic sinks. I didn't realise that our neighbours were as far away as this.

People look at me, but no one speaks, apart from an old man in a garden near the end of the lane who nods 'oreyt' and holds his hand up. If I turn right I will end up on the busy A road again and miles away from civilisation, so I turn left and walk towards the abandoned pit tip. Perhaps there's a village around the other side of it.

I follow the narrow road. Swells of nettles and rosebay willowherb jiggle beside me. A patchy sky tries to hold me back. I check the time: it has taken me fifty minutes to get here.

I turn a sharp bend. My phone beeps. Text from Lou:

OK, so it's good that you've started dealing with stuff, but doing a runner with some bloke we've never heard of is a bit random. Don't you ever switch your phone on? Did Rachel kick you out? When are we going to meet this man? What's your new address?

Her questions suffocate me and I can't reply. Pictures of her spotless, five-bedroomed house pop into my head. Glossy marble worktops, unnecessary en suites, remote lighting, stainless-steel appliances, huge white freestanding bath you could drown in.

I dial Rachel's number. She answers on the first ring, her voice low and whispery. 'Hi, sorry, I should be on silent, I'm in a meeting. Call me later, bye.'

Mum's phone rings out for ages. She doesn't have an answerphone facility and rarely replies to texts. I wonder if she's still avoiding me, if I'm still the black sheep, the family embarrassment even though I've moved away. I give her twelve more rings before giving up.

I'll walk to the village anyway. See what's there. The road thins even further and a sports car rushes by, top down, booming bass. Over a hill I can see urbanisation: a council estate, speed bumps, the roof of a primary school. I cross the road to walk on a clipped grass verge, avoiding the dog turds.

Then, suddenly, he's there. The oncoming bike, slowing; familiar thighs clenching the machine, rough hands flicking a switch on the handlebars, kicking down the stand, pushing at his visor to lock me to those green, green eyes.

'I needed to get a signal,' I say, holding up my phone. 'Where are my car keys?'

He shrugs. I look at the keyring in the bike ignition but mine aren't on it.

'You'd better get on,' he says, patting the space behind him.

And there I am, with no helmet, no coat, rain spits starting in a half-arsed way. I've never been on a bike before. But I swing my leg over and snuggle into his back, circling my arms around him, pressing my face into his jacket that smells of damp wood and smoke and danger.

'Keep your head down,' he shouts. 'I'll take it steady.'

We cruise back over the hill and now my phone is ringing in my pocket. But I'm clinging on to Jay – can't let go – and as we turn the bend and approach the spot where Lou's text appeared, the signal is lost and all I can hear is the throaty purr of the bike engine.

CHAPTER FOUR

It turned out my keys were in Jay's pocket, left there after he'd unloaded my car when I first arrived, so I made him add an extra hook next to his on which to hang them. The stove wasn't such a challenge: Jay had shown me how to twist newspapers into tight sticks and layer with kindling, then small logs. He'd shown me how to use the hotplate and adjust the air flow in order to raise the oven temperature quickly or maintain it on low. And *I* thought you just had to throw wood on.

We went to the nearest B&Q to buy stuff for the kitchen. Tins of emulsion, paint brushes and a new roller blind. I'd paid for it all, saying that it was my contribution towards living there. I didn't mention that I'd seen his bank statements. Didn't mention that I had over three grand in a savings account for emergencies.

I'd caught up with everyone. There had been a good phone signal in the shop and I'd had polite conversations with Mum, Dad, and Rachel, to let them know how great life was. Harped on about the stove, the fantastic garden, the self-sufficiency thing. I could tell from their responses they were glad that I'd gone, glad that I was no longer the top subject of local gossip.

Rachel mentioned that she'd spotted a red wine stain on the spare room carpet and was it anything to do with me? I denied all knowledge and cut her short. It was one of those conversations that could have set me off, but Jay was milling around and I wanted to keep things diplomatic. I texted Lou to say that things were amazing, lovely cottage but crap phone signal and we really should get together soon to try and put things right.

* * *

'So, who's R then?' I say.

'Give me a clue what you're talking about.' He looks flummoxed.

'Woman's name beginning with R? Is it a previous relationship?'

He doesn't flinch. His chest rises and falls steadily. He blinks, slowly, and I can't read the expression that flashes over his face. He rubs his nose. 'What d'you mean?' he asks.

'The inscription in that book,' I reply. I keep my voice bright. 'You know, that self-sufficiency one you showed me. There was a message in it but no name. Just an R. And loads of kisses.'

'Oh,' he says. 'That. It was just from a charity shop. No one I know of.'

* * *

Jay says he is going to work this morning. Pulls on a pair of combat trousers and a brown fleece. He takes muddy boots from a bag out of the wardrobe.

'You had them on at the music festival,' I say. They have a fungal smell and bits of the laces are growing white fur.

'Yeah, I'd better scrape some of this muck off,' he says, hooking them onto his fingers and carrying them downstairs.

I wonder if he's been to work since the festival. Wonder what sort of job lets someone have three weeks off and then turn up after half ten on a Wednesday morning.

I make a start on the kitchen. I throw the net curtain in the bin and begin painting. I'm full of energy, wanting to do it right, and I don't stop until I've finished the area along the top of the cupboards, when the sound of Jay hustling his bike onto its stand outside makes me check the time. Three twenty. He opens the kitchen door, sticks his head round and grins.

'Do you want the good news or the good news?' he says. He sidles in and he's holding something behind his back. He's still beaming.

I jump down from the chair, then he does this magician-like movement – a sleight of hand – and the thing behind his back is on the kitchen table, brushing against the paint lid. It's a dead rabbit, a massive, muscular creature with its eyes open and its shoulder crushed, bits of bone and blood sticking to its dun fur. I shrink away from it, shocked at its sudden appearance.

'Roadkill,' says Jay. 'Have you ever tasted hare?'

'I haven't,' I say, although I'm not sure if I want to.

'You'll love it,' says Jay. 'Dark meat, like succulent beef. It's a fantastic road down here for roadkills: pheasants and everything. I even picked up a deer once.' He looks at me and sees my apprehension. 'Don't worry. I'll do all the skinning and gutting. I'm used to it.'

'What's the other good news then?' I ask.

'Party time. I've invited a few friends round tonight. Thought it would be nice for you to meet everyone, get to know my mates.'

He sees me looking at the hare on the table.

'Don't worry,' he says. 'I'll move it.'

* * *

His friends amount to two: Maria, whom Jay described as 'a cracking percussionist', and an accordion player called Kevin.

'Hi,' says Maria. She approaches as if she's going to hug me or something, then changes her mind. 'Bit of a get-together, then. Have you met Rick yet?'

'Yes,' I smile. 'Last week.'

'Ah, he's such a sweetie, isn't he? And really good fun. He has me in stitches every time I see him.' She smoothes down her tight T-shirt over her stomach and pushes her breasts out.

Rick follows her in. 'Lolly's gone for a run around the garden,' he says.

I assume that Lolly is a dog, but it turns out she's the ten-year-old daughter of Maria's boyfriend, Phil, who will be arriving later.

'I hear you're something prominent on the folk scene,' Kevin says to me. He's got long, thinning brown hair and a flamboyant thumb ring. 'Fiddle player with Cuckoo Spit?'

'Well,' I reply, modestly, proud that Jay has shared this information, 'it was only a temporary position. But great fun doing the big gigs and festivals.'

Maria has settled into Jay's armchair by the fire. A wine glass sits on her heavy djembe drum at the side of the chair. Her legs are very brown and she's wearing a faded denim skirt that's much too short. Her hair is short too; spiky with cerise porcupine-prongs high around the crown. Jet kohl eyes.

'I like your skirt,' I say, but she doesn't reply, doesn't even change her expression. 'I used to have one like that and ended up giving it to a charity shop and then regretting it.'

I hope that she doesn't think I'm trying to say that it's unfashionable. Perhaps she thinks I'm trying too hard to talk to her. Perhaps I am. I bite my lip and look away.

Kevin raises his glass.

'Well, here's to Lauren,' he says sincerely.

'And all who sail in her,' Rick retorts.

Maria giggles and chokes on her wine.

'It's really nice to meet you all,' I say. 'I don't know anyone else around here, so basically I need all the friends I can get.' I laugh at my own joke. Maria is still looking over and laughing at Rick.

Jay is on the sofa with his guitar, strumming a riff already. Then he looks up; winks at me. 'Give us a tune then, Lauren.'

I start an easy jig, slowly, to give the others a chance to join in. Maria picks up the beat and Kevin and Jay play around with the chords. It sounds good. We smile at each other and I tap my foot in time, and before long we have moved on to the next tune. All this newness, this getting away to a new life: my chest surges and I absorb the music and the atmosphere into my body like a tonic. Jay's eyes are closed: he must be feeling it too.

Rick is sitting behind me in one of the armchairs. I turn to look at his reaction and his eyes meet mine.

'*Go*,' he mouths to me silently, a steely expression on his face.

I jolt and miss a note. 'What?' I glance around the others to see if he was maybe communicating with one of them, but they are all still engrossed in the music.

And when I turn back to Rick, he gives a little shake of the head before looking away.

CHAPTER FIVE

'Lolly's a bit of a weird name,' I say to Jay. 'And she seemed strange.'

'Why's that?' Jay pulls a Rizla across his tongue.

'Well, she was outside all night, just walking round the garden. And did you hear her doing those murmuring noises? But she never smiled. Never spoke to anyone.'

Jay shrugs. 'She doesn't talk. There was a trauma type thing. Anyway... She just doesn't.'

'Amazing hair,' I say. 'Like an orange football. Such stiff, tight curls.'

'If you thought you might have a kid like that, would you get rid of it?'

'What d'you mean?' There's a sudden constriction in my chest. Surely, he can't know... How could he?

Jay flicks a crumb of ash into his coffee mug. He stares at me with a fixed face, sculpted into a look that is empty, yet full of something, I don't know what.

'Only joking,' he says. He jerks his eyes away from mine and picks at a curry stain on the table.

· · ·

Jay seems to spend all day sorting out the hare. He beheads it and skins it, burning joss sticks around the sink to get rid of the smell. He pulls out the guts before washing the meat, picking off bits of fur, rinsing, turning, holding it like a father bathing a baby. I have to leave the room.

He joints it up and gets bottles out of the cupboard: red wine, balsamic vinegar, olive oil. Tugs handfuls of thyme from the garden, and chops it roughly. He crushes garlic and peppercorns and juniper berries. He puts everything into a dish and mixes with his bare hands.

'We'll leave that to do its magic,' he says, sliding it into the fridge.

Later, he sears the meat until it squeals, then tips in the marinade and adds tomatoes from the greenhouse. He slow roasts shallots with fennel and chunks of squash. The smells nudge their way into every room of the house, making me want to capture them in a bottle and give them to Lou to sniff. Only I wouldn't tell her it was hare. Or that it had been picked up off the road.

We eat at the kitchen table. Candles are pushed into empty wine bottles and spindly shadows bounce around the room. Jay takes my hand alongside the steaming plates and bows his head to kiss it, like we're on a date in an expensive restaurant. I stare at him through the turbid light. I can't take my eyes off him. He's my obsession. But I need to know more; I need to get right inside his head.

Jay grins. 'Waiter, waiter, there's a hare in my food.'

I raise a smile slowly and pick up my knife and fork.

The food is sensational: a palette of flavours. We eat slowly, commenting on each mouthful, each perfectly cooked vegetable bursting with sweetness and how it works so well with the hare.

Then, I take a deep breath.

'Tell me about your last girlfriend,' I say. I've had enough wine to be able to.

'I thought we'd done all that sort of thing at the festival.' He stabs a shallot on his plate.

'We didn't really say anything about previous relationships.' There. I spill it out.

'There's nothing much to tell.' He looks at me before pushing a hand through his hair. Reaches for his wine. 'I'd prefer not to talk about it really.'

'But you were with someone for a few years. It must have been serious.' I'm pulling in my stomach, controlling my tone of voice.

'I'd rather not talk about it, though.'

I ease the meat away from a thighbone and slide it onto my fork. Jay reaches for the salt.

'It's not like I want to know intimate details,' I try again. 'Just basic facts.'

He stares at me with his face scrunched.

'I just mean like what her name was. What did she look like? Was she fatter than me? Thinner than me?' I reach out and move the pepper pot an inch to the left. I look at my plate. I can feel his eyes on me.

'I just don't. Want. To talk. About it.' He speaks calmly, firmly.

I feel like I've pulled a scab off something. I hold my breath and look at my cutlery, not knowing whether to continue with this tricky line of questioning.

He slides his knife and fork together and pushes his plate away. He's left half his vegetables.

He goes and sits in the living room and puts the television on, flicks around the channels, but he's not really looking at the screen.

I lean in the doorway and watch him. 'Why are you being like this?'

He switches to Channel 4. There's a naked couple thrusting away on a bed.

'It wouldn't kill you to answer some of my questions,' I say.

There's a wildlife programme on BBC Two. Cameras zoom in on an ants' nest. Ants are crawling all over each other. David Attenborough says that although their movements appear directionless, the ants have a purpose.

'What's wrong with telling me stuff like that?' I say. 'Like was she tall or whatever?'

The ants are coming in and out of the nest. A group of them are carrying a dead ladybird.

'Like what colour hair did she have? What's wrong with me knowing that sort of stuff? How can that hurt?'

He points and squeezes the remote. The television goes blank. 'She had black hair,' he says, still staring at the screen. 'Long black hair.'

I pull the door gently into the frame and go to bed.

He comes up later, in the dark, undressing quickly and quietly. I hold myself still, breathing deep sleep breaths, facing the wall. He doesn't touch me: he's on his back, face to the ceiling. A bedspring is pushing into my ribs, trying to bully me into moving, but I won't stir. He might think I'm making the first move. Apologising. The spring digs further in, like an accusatory finger. Jay turns. I can sense his warm breath on the back of my head. The moment is fragile: the snap of thin ice on a winter lake. Suddenly, he has me scooped in his arms, he's burying his face in my neck; I feel his teeth, his wet mouth. He's gathering my hair, winding it round his hand as he's mumbling something, I'm not sure if it's *sorry*, or *I love you*.

And all I'm thinking about is long black hair.

*

Purple really suits her, really goes with her colouring. The dress fits perfectly, clingy in all the right places. He shakes down the skirt, pulls the sleeves into place, tweaking the lace cuffs. She looks gorgeous and he's desperate to get started with her.

But he needs to brush her hair first, smooth it all down so that it's sleek, glossy, spilling like black silk across his hands.

Her wrists are tied with rope, arms hoisted up to the hooks in the wall. She's semiconscious: smiling and helpful at times, but her head lolling and weighty at others and that's OK, he can work with that.

He puts his tongue into her luscious cleavage and licks up, up, up to her neck where he nuzzles for a while before it all gets too much and he sucks, bites, then finally spins her round on the rope to face the wall.

Tugging the heavy fabric up around her waist, he spanks the hairbrush onto her pale buttocks and thighs over and over and over; each red sting blooming like a ripening strawberry. She flinches and moans but he knows how much she enjoys it.

'I love you,' he says. 'I love you so much.'

He spins her round again and kisses her full on the mouth. 'Do you love me?'

'Yes,' she says. Everything is beautiful, heavenly. 'I love you.'

CHAPTER SIX

SEPTEMBER

Summer fizzles out. The campervan waits in the drive for next year's festivals. Money is tight now that I no longer have gigs with the band, and I realise that I should start contributing somehow.

I shove kaftans and flip-flops to the backs of drawers, bring out jeans and jumpers, pull on thick socks. We go out foraging, picking field mushrooms to fry up with garlic; trawling the hedgerows for sloes and damsons. I gorge myself on blackberries and my fingers are stained purple for days.

The sky is washed out, diluted to a thin cobalt by days of pestering rain. Chimneys down the lane trickle wood smoke, and reluctant dog walkers wrap up in green wax coats and sturdy boots. Organised minds slide towards Christmas. Mine is stuck in the past. With Nell. With Martin.

I sit in the library. I joined this morning. My email account has been locked and it is not possible to sort it out via my phone, so I have booked a computer. An old lady sits at the next monitor poring over pages of search results on Ancestry.com, a notebook displaying a sketchy family tree open beside her keyboard.

I work my way through the *Retrieve Email Account* process. Pages ask me for authentication numbers and passwords, making me type in encrypted codes (I attempt five of them before getting on to the next stage). Finally, it tells me that the retrieval has failed. No reason. I want to scream but have to be satisfied with sighing loudly.

I set up a new webmail account with a different provider. I email all the people whose addresses I can remember or guess: Rachel, Lou, Trish who plays the mandolin in Cuckoo Spit, the agency who managed the tour, and an education provider who booked me for a fiddle workshop in the past. I write a standard greeting, copying it to everyone:

Hi, hope you are well. Just wanted to let you know my new email address, however I am only able to access it a couple of times a week as my technology is not fully up and running yet. Will be in touch soon. Cheers.

It seems a pathetic attempt at communication and I feel a pang of concern that I have so few acquaintances.

I look at websites for jobs. There are no vacancies for violin teachers. My qualifications seem inadequate for anything apart from ancillary work. I note down a couple of schools advertising jobs for teaching assistants. My mood dips. I check if anyone has replied to my emails yet but there is only a hollow welcome message from the webmail provider. I browse around the website of the festival where Jay and I met. Next year's dates have already been announced and there are some photographs of the bands that played this year, but I don't seem to be on any of them. I zoom into the crowd scenes to look for me and Jay, but we're not there, we're probably in the campervan swathed around each other. A box pops up on the screen:

Please save your work. Your session will end in sixty seconds.

* * *

When I get home Jay is finishing painting the kitchen. I move across the room to take over from him but he grabs my hand.

'Let's have a wine break. Come on, I just fancy it.'

So we take a bottle to sit in the living room and talk about plans for the garden, about festivals, about music, about how I don't need a job just yet. How we could get a band together and look for paid gigs. Our enthusiasm reminds me of the times when me and Nell would talk about our duo act and plans to travel around Europe. We had songs already written – I can still remember them but there's no way I could sing them now without breaking down.

'By the way,' Jay says suddenly, 'I've sold your stereo.'

'What?' My mind spins: the wine placates my reactions.

'It was just that an opportunity came up and we've already got mine, and I knew you'd be OK about it because you think the same as me, and we'd talked about getting chickens and obviously need money to buy them.' He reaches into his back pocket and takes out a folded wad. 'Eighty quid. I thought it was a good deal.'

'It was a quality system,' I say. 'The speakers alone would cost double.'

'But, like I said, we've already got one. And you'd much rather have chickens than a bit of equipment doing nothing. It's that sort of thing that I love about you: how you're not a materialistic freak like everyone else, and how you don't give a shit about not being able to be on Facebook or having the latest brand of trainers.'

He laughs and ruffles my hair. I'm uncomfortable and puzzled and flattered.

'You're my soulmate,' he says. 'We're perfect for each other.'

He puts on a CD, a trippy, wordless drone. I shouldn't worry about Jay selling my stereo, really. He's right: we don't need two systems. Cohabiting is all new to me and I need to learn how to make it work. We return to the discussion about the band and the music fills the blank spaces in our conversation and squeezes the ideas out of us. In the kitchen the paintbrush goes hard like driftwood; under it a thick skin covers the clean new colour.

* * *

Jay has found out where we can get chickens: a specialist breeder that sells day-olds, growers, pullets and all the equipment you need.

'This is going to be fantastic,' says Jay.

He spends four days building a chicken coop. Rick brings him rolls of wire mesh and old shed panels from an allotment. I go out with cups of tea periodically, asking questions about the design, as Jay taps and screws it all into place. He paints it green, and then we put it in the orchard and fence it off from the vegetable area.

'Good work, that,' Rick says to Jay, later, as we all stand and admire the construction. 'It's what you've always wanted, isn't it?'

There's this look between them. Only a split second, but it contains so much knowing. It makes me dig my fingernails into the palms of my hands.

Jay spots a hole in the fence and goes to sort it, leaving me with Rick.

'You don't know him like I do,' he tells me.

'I realise that,' I say. 'But I'm working on it. Obviously, things are in the early stages but everything is good.'

'Everything would be better without *you* here, more like.'

I'm stunned, unable to reply. Why would he say such a thing? Jealousy? I bite my top lip and go to see what Jay is doing.

. . .

Later, I drive out with Jay into Derbyshire, through Matlock
Bath with its cliff edge and bikers and faux seaside vibe, to a
poultry farm with rickety sheds and a lofty, ginger-haired man
in overalls.

We get five Light Sussex chickens and a Rhode Island Red
cockerel. According to the book of self-sufficiency, this is the
dream-team of poultry.

'They're dual purpose,' says Jay. 'A cockerel and five
chickens of these breeds will give us lots of eggs, but we'll be
able to breed and hatch as well, grow them on for meat.'

'I thought we only wanted chickens for eggs,' I say, thinking
of the plucking diagram in his book.

'Well,' says Jay, 'think free range chickens. Think organic,
no food miles. How much would that cost you in Sainsbury's?
It's got to be good.'

He wants this sort of life, he really does. And the way that
I'm getting drawn into this kind of mindful existence has been
the best therapy I could possibly get.

'Go on then,' I laugh like an agreeable parent. 'But *I* don't
want to wring any necks.'

He kisses me, a mad swoop of wet lips on mine, a crush of
arms and breasts and thighs, right in front of the man who's
standing there waiting to be paid.

* * *

Kevin and Maria are here for another music jam. Jay has put
bowls of crisps and nuts out which Maria says she can't have
because she's just had her tongue pierced and the salt's a bit of a
bitch. Then Rick arrives and Jay is all over him, offering him the
snacks and rushing to get him a beer from the fridge.

'Preferential treatment or what,' says Maria.

Sometimes I like her. She just turns my mood downwards though when she struts in wearing her tight T-shirts and skirts up to her backside.

Rick sneers, reaching for the crisps. 'It's because I know where all the bodies are buried.'

'What?' An icy tendril brushes the back of my neck.

'Don't talk about the bodies,' says Maria in a fake horror-film voice. 'And definitely not the one in the quarry.'

'Shut the fuck up with all that.' Rick makes a slashing motion against his neck. He rolls his eyes towards the kitchen where Jay has gone.

I don't know what's going on between them but the room prickles with tension.

Kevin looks uncomfortable as Jay comes back into the room. 'Why don't we try that set of Irish tunes again?'

'Good idea,' Jay says, picking up his guitar.

Rick looks at me. It's an expressionless look, more of a stare, three seconds, four seconds, and I end up turning away first. I rub a finger across my eye like I'm trying to get an eyelash out.

CHAPTER SEVEN

Jay brings me coffee in bed. The thump of a headache tells me we shouldn't have had that second bottle of wine last night.

'Haven't you got a hangover?' I croak.

He smiles. 'I'm running at about eighty per cent. It's worth it, though. Remembering what we got up to on the rug in front of the fire.'

I try to open my eyes but a rare sun is burning into the room.

'I've got a meeting with the estates manager at ten,' says Jay. 'You stay in bed if you like.'

He kisses me, a short, tender press of lips. He smells nice, of something lemony, and I notice that he's shaved off his stubble.

* * *

I fidget in bed between sips of tepid coffee. Try to remember that weird part of last night, where Maria and Rick had joked about dead bodies. What was all that about? My stomach feels queasy, but it could be my hangover.

Eventually, the brightness drags me up, into old leggings

and a baggy T-shirt. I lumber to the kitchen and use a slice of bread to scoop coleslaw out of a tub. I drink a glass of water after it's run icy from the tap. Break off a piece of cheese to nibble as I return to the locked dining room. I try the bunch of keys again but they still don't work.

What could be in there that needs locking away? My head throbs. I return to the kitchen and swallow two paracetamol. There is a torch in the cupboard with the tablets and it gives me another idea. I take it and go outside, to the front of the house, to the locked room window.

I press my face to the glass, cupping an arm around my eyes, shining the torch at the blackness. It's as if the windows are boarded up on the inside.

There's a crunch of tyres and a car pulls into the drive. I spin round to see Maria getting out of the driver's door.

'Hi,' she says as she looks at her watch. 'I'm really sorry to have to ask, but I've got a bit of a problem and wondered if you could help?'

''Course I can,' I reply quickly. Sometimes I wonder if I try too hard with people.

'Phil's gone to work, leaving me to drop Lolly off at school, and when I get there it turns out it's an inset day and the bloody thing's shut.' Exasperated, she taps Lolly on the back of her springy red hair. 'I've got a job interview at half eleven and wondered if she could stay here for a bit.'

'Yeah, 'course she can,' I say, smiling at Lolly, even though she's not looking; she's in her own little world staring at the sky.

'Great,' says Maria as she turns to go. Her lack of gratefulness bristles me a little.

'What time,' I begin to ask, 'are you picking...?'

But she can't hear me, the gravel is too crunchy, and I don't want to chase after her with Lolly standing in the way: she might become alarmed or something.

'You can play outside if you want,' I tell her. I speak loudly and slowly. 'You've been in the garden before, haven't you? Only don't go into the chicken run, or open the gate. We don't want them getting out. Or you can watch television if you'd rather.'

But she shakes her head and trots onto the lawn. I leave her and go back into the kitchen, peering at her through the window for a while. She's engrossed in her own game, skipping up and down the path, touching a red rose, then a peach rose, picking up a piece of gravel and skipping along the path again. She doesn't look up. She doesn't see me watching.

I go outside with a packet of crisps later. Lolly is sitting on the damp grass in a circle of shredded rose petals. As I approach, I see her lips shifting into shapes, see her wagging her finger at nothing.

She turns, startled by the sight of me, and clamps a hand over her mouth.

'Have you been picking my flowers?' I ask, but I try not to sound fierce.

She shakes her head and touches two of the petals.

'That's OK then,' I say. I crouch down and offer her the crisps.

She takes her hand away from her face. '*Toys?*' she mouths silently, like a fish.

'What?' I say. 'I don't know what you mean.'

She puts a hand over her mouth again. 'Toys, in the shed.' It comes out as the tiniest whisper, and I am not sure at first if I have heard her words or just assumed them.

She points a finger to the shed. '*Can I play with the toys?*' she mouths.

'We haven't got any toys,' I say kindly. 'We haven't got any children in our house.'

'*There's a bike.*' Her lip movements are exaggerated, her eyes intense.

I stand and gaze at the shed. The window is blacked out: a

bin bag is taped over the inside. I walk towards it as Lolly opens the crisp packet and dips into it with a licked finger. I tunnel my eyes with my hands around the edges of the window but there are no gaps. And the window is too high for Lolly to see through anyway. There are padlocks on the door.

I go back to Lolly who is still picking crisp crumbs out of the bag. My stomach pivots at the sight of her wet, greasy fingers and the bits hanging on her chin.

'There are no toys to play with,' I say firmly. 'And the shed is locked. You can't get in.' I leave her sitting in the petal circle and go into the house, into the living room, to open the side-board and see if that bunch of old keys is still there.

Maria returns just before three. Her lipstick has worn off and she smells like she's been drinking.

'Did it go well?' I ask her as we gaze across the garden, and a film of vagueness slips across her eyes before she says that yes, it seemed OK, they will let her know next week.

'I gave her a cheese sandwich and some crisps. I hope that's all right, she's not allergic to anything.'

'Oh, she eats whatever,' says Maria, flapping her hands. 'I hope she's behaved herself.'

'She was trying to tell me something earlier; I did my best at lip-reading, but, you know...'

Maria frowns. 'Sorry, she can be a bit weird. I should have mentioned it. It's like a traumatic stress thing. She hasn't spoken to anyone for ages, apart from imaginary friends. It's a bit of a nightmare at school. There's been a psychologist involved.'

'What happened?' I ask.

'An incident. I can't really say.' She talks to me as if I'm prying too much and I wonder if Lolly has been abused.

Suddenly, Lolly skips down the path. She slips her hand into Maria's and presses her cheek against the shoulder of her smart black jacket. The edge of Lolly's mouth leaves a slug trail of saliva on the linen.

'Urgh, get your gob off me,' says Maria, pushing Lolly away roughly. 'Scruffy cat. Why can't you be normal?'

Lolly looks at me sadly, and I give her a quick, sympathetic smile.

'This is what it's like when you take on a bloke with a kid,' says Maria, brushing her jacket with a tissue.

I bite my lip. The bunch of keys is warm inside my fist, inside my pocket. I glance towards the shed.

'Thanks ever so,' says Maria.

I wait until I hear the car pull away before I take the keys out of my pocket. I try each one in turn until I find the key that fits both padlocks. Inside, among the garden tools, between the lawnmower and wheelbarrow, is a small red bicycle with stabilisers. On a shelf sits a scrunched-up shell of a paddling pool. At the end, a pair of children's plastic golf clubs.

I know what these things mean, these garish pieces of plastic. Jay has a child. I look at all the things and begin to think that there is a lot I still don't know about Jay.

I lock the shed up again. My mind is twirling thoughts around. How old would the child be? The bike looks suitable for a four-year-old, possibly five. I should go into the house and double-check the bank statements. See if there are any transactions that look like maintenance payments. As I stand and wipe my hands onto the front of my jeans I hear the sound of Jay's motorbike on the lane. I hurry down the garden path curling my lips into a smile.

I choose my moment carefully to ask Jay if he has a child: I want to sound casual and conversational, as if it wouldn't bother me if he has.

'What makes you ask that?' he says, and I know my face has gone red.

'I found some toys in the shed,' I say. 'Lolly came round for most of the day and she told me they were in there.'

'How come when she doesn't speak?' he says sarcastically.

'Well, she did, and she said that she wanted to play with them. I unlocked the shed, and there's a bike and stuff in there. I wondered if she might have been here before and played with them.'

He's frowning, eyelids crumpled around his green eyes. 'Where did you get the keys from? I've been looking every-where for them.'

'The keys were in the sideboard,' I say, but I begin to feel that he's leading me away from the subject. 'Jay, the thing is, why is there a bike in the shed? Whose is it?'

'Probably kids who've lived here before. Like the trampoline that we took to the tip last week. I don't know.'

'I thought Rick's grandma lived here before,' I remind him. 'Why would she need a children's bike?'

'How the fuck should I know?' he replies. 'Stop going on at me like a nutter.' He twists around and picks up the soap at the side of the sink. Rubs it onto hands that don't look dirty.

'Why don't you get rid of all that stuff then? There's no need for it to take up room in the shed.' I can't see his face as he wraps hand over hand around the soap, under the running water, splashing onto the new paintwork that I don't like to mention.

'I'll get rid, then,' he says throwing the soap into the sink instead of putting it on the holder, and not shutting off the tap properly. He strides across the room pressing his wet hands across the tea towel and not the hand towel hanging next to it on the rail of the stove. 'Yet another tip trip,' he remarks as he goes through to the living room. It's as if I'm being unreasonable. I put the soap back on the holder and switch off the tap. I straighten the creases out of the tea towel and re-hang it so that the front and back are the same length.

* * *

A current of schoolchildren swirls around a large-bosomed woman. She stands in the middle of the heave, grey plaits, swathed in flowery vintage fabrics, asking them to sit on the story carpet. Some of them comply. A teacher and two librarians get involved. I push past the waist-high surge to locate a computer.

There are several emails to open. It feels unusually delightful to see the bold black addresses there waiting to be accessed.

Rachel tells me that Steve, her new man, is moving in with her. She has got rid of the bed from the spare room and converted it into an office. She doesn't mention anything about visiting or meeting up. I send her a polite response, knowing that she's telling me I can't return, that my emergency refuge is now closed. But some friends are only for a season, aren't they? And anyway, my life is looking up. Things couldn't be better.

Lou has written an essay. She's trying to make it seem like nothing went wrong between us. She tells me everything about the clothes she bought last week (four designer tops and three pairs of jeans); about how she's worried about Dad – his blood pressure is still high despite the medication; about her neighbour who has been seen being picked up by a young, tanned bloke every Thursday afternoon (she's wondering if he might be an escort); about how she's thinking of getting a new fireplace, one that you can operate with an app on your phone.

She doesn't mention Martin. She doesn't mention Nell.

But there's a PS on her email. Her and Dominic are planning on having a few days in York at the beginning of December and thought it might be good to call in on us for an afternoon, drop off the Christmas presents, catch up on gossip, meet Jason.

Fuck, I'm thinking. Oh fuck. Then, for a brief moment, I'm back in our teenage years, back with her in matching skirts and crop tops, back to that first time in the reclined seat of Martin's car while Lou and her friend, Maxine, were at the disco that I wasn't old enough to be allowed into. I tried to tell her what had happened afterwards, but it was like she thought I had made it up, like she thought her friend's father would never do such a thing. 'Maybe stop wearing short skirts,' she suggested. 'Or don't talk and smile so much, because it can come over as quite flirty.'

But now is not the time for reminiscing. I have to be focused: stuff needs sorting. I can't let Lou see the house in its current state. The kitchen is done although I still have to fit the new cupboard handles. Then there's the living room that needs a miracle. The walls. The carpet. The furniture.

I go home via B&Q.

CHAPTER EIGHT

The chickens strut and scratch in the orchard. It's easy to while away half an hour just watching them enjoy their environment. I can lean on a tree trunk and imbibe positivity and mindfulness, feeling my spirit reach a sense of calm.

There are five beige, dappled eggs every day now, snuggling into the scratchy straw. The chickens know me when I take bowls of scraps into the orchard: leftover pasta, dry bread, cornflakes past their use-by. They run to me, a bundle of dashing white feathers, jumping around my feet for treats, letting me stroke them and pick them up. I use their eggs to bake quiches and cakes, whip up omelettes and tortillas and pancakes. I fry them, poach them, boil them, scramble them. I have even made my own mayonnaise.

We sell them now and then, to Kevin and Maria, two quid a dozen. But Jay gives them free to Rick. 'They're for his mum,' he says every time he sees the look on my face as he packs them methodically into an old ice-cream tub. Rick never even says thank you.

* * *

The kitchen is finished. Fresh white cupboards with black handles. Cream walls. The Rayburn scrubbed clean, its chrome hotplate lids shining like mirrors, set into the terracotta wall. Hanging above the stove are bunches of herbs from the garden. The old floor tiles, although some of them are cracked, have been restored to a satin sheen. It's my favourite room in the house: so clean and new. In October I will decorate the living room, in November the bathroom. The dining room key still hasn't turned up so I will discuss with Jay about breaking the lock off.

* * *

Rick calls for Jay, like they're a pair of nine-year-olds. He would normally walk straight in, not bothering to knock, but it's early and the door is locked.

Jay had said for me not to get up, to have a lie-in: it's only eight o'clock. But I felt there was something going on that I didn't know about and if I saw him off I would get a sense of what they were up to.

Jay is in the bathroom. I hear Rick's car pull into the drive and I give him time to get to the kitchen door. I watch the handle move down and up, down and up. I wait for four seconds after the frustrated rap, then carefully turn the key in the lock. Rick shoves the door open.

'Where's Jay? I thought he'd be ready.'

'He is ready,' I reply. 'What're you doing today, then?'

If I speak brightly, keep my tone friendly, he might think I already know. He might let his guard down and tell me.

'Special mission,' he says, tapping his nose. He winks at Jay who strides into the kitchen running wet hands through his hair.

'So, what's this special mission?' I ask Jay. They are giving each other secret signals: there's this look in Jay's eyes as he communicates with Rick over the top of my head.

Jay holds his palms out. 'Just work. Bramble clearing, some new saplings to put in. General maintenance.'

I shrug my shoulders at him.

'What do you think we're doing?' he says. Then a glance towards Rick, who scratches his nose and smirks as he looks over the floor tiles.

'You don't normally work with Rick,' I say. 'I thought you did it on your own.'

'It's a freelance contract. I can do it with anyone. It just makes it easier if there's someone else to help carry stuff. Tools and that.'

'So I could come then?' I watch his face for more signs.

He blinks slowly. 'Don't be daft. You'd get scratched to fuck.'

'Come on,' says Rick. 'I've got everything ready.'

'Gotta go,' says Jay. He kisses me, darting a tongue into my mouth. I can feel the upturn of a smile on his lips.

* * *

'It's a concrete floor under this,' Jay insists. 'So no, we can't get the carpet up and varnish the floorboards. There aren't any.'

'Well, OK, we could put laminate down then. I can make this room look fantastic,' I tell him. 'It wouldn't cost too much. Anyway, we should be going busking. All the days that you don't have to do forestry stuff, we could go out and make some money. One of the musicians I worked with says he regularly used to do over a hundred quid in less than two hours.'

Jay's face is changing, I can tell I'm talking him into it.

'We fritter a lot of time away,' I say. 'Sure, we play music, but we could just as well be doing it in a marketplace somewhere. There are plenty of towns within easy driving distance.'

'Come on then,' says Jay, picking up his guitar. 'What're we waiting for?'

'Hang on a minute,' I say, flicking open the Ikea catalogue. 'Just tell me if you think two two-seater sofas would work better than a three-piece suite in here.'

'I thought you just wanted to decorate,' says Jay. 'Don't go mad, it's not as if we've got royalty coming.'

He doesn't know that Lou will be here in ten weeks. And he doesn't know Lou.

'It's for us,' I tell him. 'Doing up this place together, how romantic is that? It's going to look perfect.'

He sighs and smiles and winds his arms around me and kisses my brow. I close my eyes and feel the beat of his heart against my breast. I wonder who the last woman was he touched like this. And what happened between them that always makes Jay so prickly and guarded about her.

* * *

Rain is hammering on the roof window and I press my face further into the pillow, pulling the duvet around my shoulders. Voices are murmuring in the distance and I can't work out if they are real or part of the haze of my half-dream. I stretch my arm towards Jay, but there's just cold space where he should be.

I tug myself into consciousness. There are voices down-stairs, men's voices, a woman. I open my eyes as I hear footsteps on the stairs. A ginger mop of hair bounces into the room.

'Hi,' waves Lolly, coming to stand at the side of the bed.

I peer up at her, holding on to the bedcovers. 'What are you doing?'

'Dad and Maria are downstairs.' She breathes quietly through the fingers that she has clamped over her face. 'Did I scare you?'

'Not really,' I say. I blink long and deliberately to try to make her go away.

'Nothing scares *me*,' she whispers. 'Not even ghosts.'

'Right,' I reply. Jay is laughing downstairs. Surely Maria and Phil will wonder where Lolly is, they wouldn't just let her wander into someone's bedroom?

'Can *you* see ghosts?' she asks, louder this time, before sitting on the end of the bed.

'No, not really,' I reply dismissively.

'I always see the boy in the garden. He has a red jumper on. And there are others,' she says. 'Because people have died around here.'

This is creepy. This is not the sort of conversation I want to be having with some abnormal kid the moment I wake up. It could set me off if I'm not careful.

'Would you go and ask Jay if he'll put the kettle on for me?' I ask her in a soft voice, even though my heart has started thumping.

She makes no attempt to move, gazing around the room as if she's sensing something, gauging something. Then she stands, and holding herself exceptionally tall and erect, she steps down the stairs without holding on to the rail.

I lie in bed for another fifteen minutes. Then the back door shuts, vibrating through the walls, and a car engine starts. I get up and dress quickly and go down to find Jay at the kitchen table jotting figures onto the back of an envelope.

'What was all that about?' I ask him.

He beams and leans back in his chair, spreading his arms.

'Good news,' he says. 'It could mean a bit of regular money for us. I'm going to set up an organic box scheme.'

It turns out that it's a trendy, ethical type of thing to do. Maria and Phil want to buy a box of fresh vegetables every week, and they have other friends who would like to do the same.

'Fifteen quid a box,' says Jay. 'We pick a variety of stuff from the garden, plus we've got plenty of stuff stored to put in as well. That's extra cash for us and veg not going to waste.'

'Great idea,' I say. 'Will there be enough to keep it going?'

'I'll just keep planting as much as we need,' he says. 'Dig some of the lawn over if necessary. We could expand it gradually.'

I like the notion of the boxes. It might mean that Rick gets to take less away.

'Lolly came upstairs when I was in bed,' I tell him. 'Just wandered in and sat down.'

Jay shrugs. He's making a list.

'Her name's Collette,' I say. 'I asked Maria. But Lolly has always been her nickname.'

Jay writes *apples, onions, carrots, eggs, courgettes, lettuce, tomatoes* and *plums* in small capital letters under the heading 'Week One'.

'Lolly says she can see ghosts,' I say. 'She says that people have died around here.'

There are exactly four seconds of silence. I hold my breath.

Jay puts his pen down. 'What?'

'That's what she said this morning.'

'So, you're trying to say that you're the only person she talks to? When her own family can't even get a word out of her.'

'She does now and then,' I say. 'I'm not making it up. It's a strange thing to say though, isn't it? What do you think she means?'

Jay doesn't say anything, but there's movement, and I'm not sure if it's a shake of the head, or a shiver through his body, but he looks away and picks his pen up again to write 'Week Two'.

* * *

Another morning where I can't find my car keys. I search all the usual places: my hook, pockets, bags, behind cushions, shelves – but they are nowhere to be found. Eventually, under a bundled pair of Jay's jeans, I find a set of keys for the campervan in the bottom of the wardrobe. I will have to use that. I hope my insurance covers it.

The library is quiet today. There are no other people on the computers, and in the main area only a couple of white-haired ladies are browsing the romance section.

Just one email this time. I reluctantly click on the bold type that says 'Lou'.

She wants to know a date for visiting so that she can book their holiday in York. My heart sinks immediately.

I shouldn't feel like this about her, I tell myself. She's my sister. But my sister's personality has been fabricated from the pages of *Hello* magazine; a lifestyle created from *Homes & Gardens*. A perfunctory calendar of shopping and beauty treatments and aerobics classes and lunches that never get eaten.

I stare at the screen, wondering if I can think of an excuse to put her off. Remembering how we left everything.

The last time I saw her she gave me some white gold earrings, an intricate Celtic knot design. I still have them in a drawer somewhere. A tiny sticker displaying the eighty pounds price had been left on the underside of the gift box.

It was the day I got sacked from my job. Apparently, I had let down the Year Sevens too many times by being hungover and turning up late. Apparently, I'd had a fortnight off without authorisation. Apparently, the school's Talent Evening had been expecting my input and dedication but I had been found having a raging phone argument in the cafeteria when I should have been introducing the string quartet on stage. Apparently, complaints had been made against me by staff and parents and students. My fate was inevitable. The head escorted me off the school premises just before the lunch bell and I stood, wretched, in the car park with no one else to call but Lou.

She took me to a coffee shop in town, and we sat with cappuccinos in front of us. She stroked a spoon across the froth and I waited for the I-told-you-sos.

'What's this for?' I asked, dejectedly, when she gave me the box, a twist of white tissue paper around it.

'No reason, really. I've just not had time to see you much lately.'

But there *was* a reason. And that was to give me advice about my life and what I needed to do to stop everything going wrong and get out of my endless cycle of bad decisions.

We sat for a while as she ranted at me, and I drank my coffee: she left hers. She hugged me when we got up to go. It's not something she does often. I said a meagre thank you for the earrings. She probably expected me to try them on but I pushed them into my handbag.

'You need to get a new life,' she said, summarising all the ranting into one final speech. 'Get away from here, like miles and miles away, so that you can't bump into people any more. This – now you've been sacked too – is like the last straw. You won't be able to get a reference. And how can you afford your rent now you're unemployed? You've got to get motivated and put your troubles behind you. Find somewhere else to live. Get some help dealing with Nell too, because your head is seriously messed up with everything.'

My *troubles*. That was how Lou described it all. My best friend took her own life. My boyfriend dumped me. I went off the rails with a series of one-night stands and was then dismissed from my job. *Troubles!*

But in the end, I did take her advice. Because I had nothing left to lose.

And now here I am. Sitting in the library trying to think how to reply to her email and rebuild our relationship.

But my mind isn't functioning properly, so I log out of my account. I will wait for a while and see if she changes her mind about the visit.

I take out a book, *Bottling and Preserving*, a hardback with a tacky cover that looks like it has been in the library for fifty years. Even if I don't read it, the sight of it will please Jay, will signal that I'm with him on the self-sufficiency thing.

In the car park, I reverse the campervan out of its space and follow the one-way system to the exit. Suddenly, a car pulls out right in front of me and I stamp on the brake pedal to avoid hitting it. A woman with long dark hair and a contorted face starts shouting through her open car window. She's clearly angry about something: aggressive eyes, gesticulating with her fist. I wind down my window to tell her that it is my right of way.

'Perverted bastard,' she shouts.

'What?' I lean further out of the window. I might have heard wrong: it could have been 'reversing faster.'

'You drove straight in front of me,' I say, and the woman suddenly looks embarrassed.

'Is this *your* van?' she asks sheepishly.

'Yes,' I reply. We've pooled our assets now: we share the vehicles, the house, the CD collection recently arranged in alphabetical order. It's what cohabiting couples do.

'Oh, I'm so sorry.'

'Right,' I say. 'Can you move then?'

There are three cars waiting behind the camper but she seems to want to explain herself.

'It's just that I recognised...' she begins.

I indicate the queuing traffic behind me and she winds her window up and pulls back into the parking space so that I can drive away.

CHAPTER NINE
OCTOBER

We wipe the dew from the apples as we pack them into cardboard boxes. Jay has two hundred cartons folded flat in the shed, bought from a local packaging firm yesterday. Then we put in onions, courgettes, beetroot, potatoes and eggs.

'The chickens aren't laying as many eggs as normal,' I tell Jay. 'It could be difficult keeping up with this box thing.'

'Maybe they're moulting,' he says. 'Or perhaps it's because they're getting less sunlight. We might not be able to supply eggs every week.'

'Just cut down on Rick's quota,' I say without thinking. 'Then we'd be able to manage.'

Jay folds his arms and stares at me. I regret the words immediately.

'What have you got against Rick?' he says.

'Nothing,' I reply. 'I try to be nice, but he doesn't seem to like me.'

'I don't know why you think that. He's been more than accepting of you.'

'Accepting?' I query, in a voice that has risen slightly, and I can feel the crackle of an argument pressing around us.

'I've known him a long time and this sort of thing matters to mates. It affects group dynamics. We've been a close bunch, you know, Maria and Phil included. But you're not the easiest person to get on with. You've got to admit that you're a bit standoffish, you're not that friendly. Like avoiding people, staying in bed when they come round. That sort of thing.'

'Did your friends prefer your last girlfriend? Is that what you're really saying?' I grip onto the egg in my hand.

'What's that supposed to mean?'

'Well, you never answer my questions. It just feels like you're hiding something.'

'I don't need all this crap on a Monday morning,' he says. He grabs the egg from my hand and flings it onto the kitchen floor, where it shatters its slimy white up the front of the stove. Then he picks up his tobacco tin from the table and stomps out of the kitchen door.

I bend and scoop up the mess, then wipe the stove and floor. I go into the living room, slump into the sofa and switch the television on, pretending to watch *Homes Under the Hammer* in case Jay comes back in.

I love being here, I really do. Feeling cocooned in nature: walking barefoot on the grass in the morning; getting my hands deep into the dark soil; cooking and eating meals fresh from the garden. I cherish the mindful task of running a paintbrush across a wall, of bringing a room into a new lease of life. And there's the sex, the music, sharing a bottle of wine, doing everything together. This experience is so different to how my previous relationship was conducted; it feels so *right*. And I can handle that he's a mysterious character: arresting, enigmatic, precarious, his green eyes drawing anyone that peers into them to be smitten. So I really don't want to spoil things by giving the impression that I'm a jealous, nagging type. But all these secrets keep eating away at me. I just want to know more about him. I *need* to know.

He comes back in, quietly clicking the door open, not making eye contact. I notice how his hair has grown since we first met: how the tangles of dappled chestnut lap around his neck. I realise that I am the only one who has known the extra inch of hair closest to his scalp, that whoever was with him before me has had no involvement with that small piece of him.

Jay sits down beside me and takes my hand.

'Sorry,' I say.

He sighs and stares at the ceiling.

'Talk to me,' I whisper. Suspense hangs like fog. 'Tell me about your life. About when you were young.'

'All right,' he says, after a long time.

Then he starts to tell me what he can remember from his childhood, his earliest memories. His father a miner, hated for being a strike breaker, and his mother, abandoned first by his dad and then in turn abandoning him. I listen as he tells me about the police and the pickets, the fights, the poverty that the village suffered. How the family were shunned and spat at, how they returned from shopping to find bricks through the window and dog shit on the carpet. I empathise, remembering my own experiences of being frozen out within my family and community: how my hairdresser refused to take an appointment, declaring in front of a room full of clients that they didn't do *homewrecker styling*; how my own parents would only eat out publicly with me in restaurants well away from our home town; and how other teaching staff deliberately deleted my name from Christmas party events.

But all this new knowledge about Jay: it's like the brief moment when a pear that has resisted for so long surprises you with the suddenness of its give.

'Dad eventually took redundancy and buggered off,' he tells me. 'Mum got some of the money towards paying off the mortgage and they got a divorce. He couldn't handle staying there with no friends, not being able to go out. He'd always been a sociable person and just couldn't live like that. So, he went to start a new life. Last I heard he was working on a holiday park. I got a couple of birthday cards with a fiver in, but he hasn't been in touch since I was about seven.'

'How sad,' I say. But I recognise completely now how leaving people and the past behind and starting a new life can often be the only solution.

I sit and let all this new information seep into the cracks of me and feel the emotions it brings, thinking about how the person that is Jay has been shaped.

'It sounds like your family had a hard life,' I say. I'm truly full of sympathy and pity.

He brushes it off. 'Everyone round here had a hard life then.'

I look at him and realise that this is the beginning of knowing him.

* * *

A thin pool of sunlight runs over the kitchen table. Jay is out with Rick on the estate, tidying up the paths, checking the hedges. He needs to put time in while the weather is still good.

And here I am, making a shopping list: flour, cheese, minced beef and washing powder are already in my neat hand on the paper. I start to think about all the things I don't know about Jay, and all the things I need to know, and then it's like I'm possessed by a desire to write everything down: suddenly there's another column on the paper – a line scored down the middle – and on the right-hand side I find myself scrawling *Rick, ex-girl-friend(s), locked room, child,* and the words are nowhere near as neat as the groceries next to them.

I gaze at the words as if there's some sort of sequence to them, and I stare and stare until all I'm doing is seeing the words. There's something not right. The relationship between Rick and Jay – and even Maria – is too intense, like something is being covered up. And the secrecy around Jay's last girlfriend is weird, too. It's not normal. They are hiding something from me and I won't be satisfied until I find out what it is.

CHAPTER TEN

I asked Lolly about seeing ghosts. The ghost stuff had been on my mind, one of those things that popped into my head daily. I've never been a superstitious person, but it just seemed like... I don't know. What she said about someone dying around here kind-of got under my skin like a splinter.

Lolly came with Maria last night for another music jam and went into the garden with a tennis ball she had brought with her.

The others were in the living room while I waited in the kitchen for the kettle to boil. And through the window I watched Lolly, in the dying light of the day, bouncing her ball around, attempting clumsy catches and scurrying after easy misses. Compelled to go and speak to her, I slipped outside and followed her along the path.

'Hi, Lolly,' I said in a loud, sing-song voice, because I wasn't sure if she knew I was there. 'What are you playing?'

She jumped slightly, shrugging guiltily.

'It's OK,' I said. 'I don't mind you playing with your ball up here. Just remember what I said before about not opening the chickens.'

She gawped, holding her body rigid while she pulsed her fingers around the ball. I realised that she was looking past me and I turned to see what she might be staring at. There was nothing but trees.

'What is it?' I said. 'What did you see?'

She shrugged again.

'Is there a ghost in this garden?' It sounded ridiculous after the words were out.

Her shoulders lifted and dropped. Quickly she clamped a hand across her mouth.

'I thought you could see ghosts,' I said. 'That's what you told me.'

She closed her eyes tightly and turned away from me.

'Lolly?'

She obviously didn't want to communicate with me on that occasion. And then, suddenly, Jay was shouting me, over and over with urgency in his voice, and so I ran down the path, but he was only shouting because the kettle had been boiling – whistling like a steam train – and they had all been wondering where I'd gone.

* * *

We busk in town, on the main pedestrianised street up to the marketplace, our backs to the dirty window of an empty frozen food shop. It's a Wednesday: a tepid morning encouraging pensioners out for bargains at the fish stall. Young mums with buggies shove twenty pences into their kids' sticky hands, wheeling up to us, so close that we can smell the curry they had for tea last night, before prising the cash out of their toddlers' fingers to drop into my fiddle case.

Jay smiles and says, 'Thanks.' He's a natural: he has a good way with the public. He moves with the tunes and people notice him. He knows how to charm old ladies with a wink and a grin, upgrading their fifty pences to pounds.

We run through our full list of folk tunes that Jay has sell-otaped to the back of his guitar, playing to the dinner-hour punters who are off to The Unicorn for their pints and lasagnes. Some people look at us like they've never seen musicians before. They stand and listen with folded arms, leaning on litter bins for ten minutes or more, before walking away without putting any cash in. Occasionally we get an audience, circling and clapping at the end of tunes. Sometimes there is no one and it seems like we are only playing to the window of the shop opposite which has a scrawled sign advertising a sale on bras up to 48FF.

By the time we finish, my finger ends are feeling the strain. Jay tips the money into a carrier bag and tucks it into his guitar case.

We wander through the market stalls arm-in-arm, like tourists. Jay has a grin stretching across his face. He's a good-looking guy anyway, but a smile on those full, seductive lips just adds an extra gorgeous element to him.

'What are you thinking?' I ask.

'Yeah, I've enjoyed it today. We should do it more often.'

We stop and buy olives: a huge tub of succulent, oil-smothered green ones marinated with chunks of garlic and herbs. It's an extravagance we're not used to.

'They'll go with a nice bottle of white when we get home,' says Jay.

The sun's not even out and I've got a feeling close to elation. We're only walking through a car park and it all seems right, it all seems to fit. I slip my fingers through his and he winks at me.

When we get to the campervan there's a piece of paper on the windscreen, an A5 flyer with some kind of newspaper article on it.

'What is it?' I ask, as Jay rips it off and screws it up without looking.

'Nothing,' he replies. 'Just junk.'

But none of the other cars have one, and the casual way he tosses it into a nearby bin makes me think that this has happened before. Makes me think that it's something intended for him.

Jay counts the money as soon as we get home. It's the first thing he does, before he takes his jacket off.

'Forty-seven quid, plus a handful of coppers I can't be bothered to count. Not bad for a couple of hours' work. That amounts to' – he screws his face up – 'twelve pounds an hour, nearly.'

He forgets about petrol money, car parking, the fact that we put three pounds in the box ourselves to start it off, and that we actually played for over two and a half hours.

We drink the wine and eat the olives, talk about music, drink another bottle of wine. It's something that Jay made last spring, something before me. We discuss festivals and which ones we want to go to, maybe even ones we could play at. I think about bringing up the subject of Christmas, and I look at my watch and find that it's ten past four. Jay reaches over to unplait my hair and array it around my shoulders, then unfastens the top three buttons of my dress, telling me that I look like a stunning wench.

We put music on – some chilled-out dub vibes – and feed off each other's laughter, talking about how we first met in the rain with Jay wearing the plastic bin bag, and try to recall how many times we had sex in the van, then the talk starts to make us horny so we go upstairs, peeling off our clothes quickly, then fucking urgently without kissing, coming almost together, and falling asleep minutes later.

It's dark when we wake: soon the clocks will be altered. We dress and go down to the kitchen but the stove is cold, neglected by our afternoon of indulgence. Jay lights the fire in the living room and we stick floppy slices of cheap white bread onto forks to make toast. There's a film on later, so we light candles and snuggle together on the lumpy sofa.

And every time I consider my new life here and how it's going, I feel like bursting inside. Today has been heavenly. I wouldn't have been able to do any of this kind of thing with Martin: our domestic arrangements and all the necessary subterfuge prevented any typical relationship activities, and it's only now that I realise how much my heart has been yearning for this sense of normality. Why did I consider us to be a couple for so long? Why did I not recognise the abuse to which I was being subjected? I was so blind, so conned, so shielded from what I could have been having all along. A proper boyfriend and our own house to enjoy together. The knowledge that I am the priority in someone's life rather than a secret add-on. Security and routines and every night together instead of illicit snatched moments and lies and finding myself alone in a double bed at each sunrise.

Times like this with Jay make me thankful. It may have seemed initially like a rushed, rash decision to leave everything behind and move in with him, but my God, it really has been worth it.

'It's been a great day today, hasn't it?' says Jay, echoing my thoughts. It's like we're even telepathic sometimes.

But he's right. It has. We haven't seen Rick all day. He hasn't even been mentioned all day. And apart from the note on the windscreen of the campervan it's been an absolutely perfect day.

CHAPTER ELEVEN

There are four texts and a voicemail from Lou. She needs to know if they can come on the fifteenth of December. They'll just pop in for the afternoon, bring the Christmas things. Wants to know why I haven't got back to her. Thinks that surely you can get a phone signal somewhere around the house in this day and age.

I imagine the house and how it should look when she comes: laminate floor, freshly painted walls, leather sofas, soft cream rug, crackling fire, like something out of *House Beautiful* magazine.

I scroll through and delete all her texts.

'Got friends?' says Jay. He's driving us to Chesterfield in my car. The busking bug has hit him and he's desperate to go again.

'Big sister,' I say. 'Reminding me about Christmas.'

'What about it?'

'Well, they might like to drop in. On their way to York or something.'

'Whatever,' says Jay. 'They could kip down in the living room. Have a bit of a session, there's plenty of home-brew.'

He has no idea what she's like. She doesn't do kipping

down. She does guest rooms with crisp white linen and bathroom facilities. She doesn't do sessions, especially on homebrew. She does dry, chilled Chardonnay, but never more than one glass because she might end up letting her hair down and having a laugh.

'It's probably best if they just call in,' I say. 'Perhaps nibbles, or lunch.' I think of the sort of things that Lou would eat: white seedless grapes; small cubes of cheese, usually medium cheddar; little cherry tomatoes; prawns; strawberries, perhaps even with tiny meringue nests and a teaspoon of clotted cream.

'Nibbles.' Jay laughs, and I guess that his idea of nibbles are pork scratchings, salted peanuts and sausage rolls.

Saturday morning. Jay has gone out to deliver his vegetable boxes. He wanted us to go busking again, pleaded with me, said that it was the best day for shoppers, we'd make more money than the rest of the week, as if I didn't know already. I told him my fingers were sore, that we had been twice this week and made a good start: almost a hundred and twenty quid altogether. He left me in bed, thought I was wanting a lie-in. But as soon as I heard the kitchen door close I was up, pulling on old clothes to make a start on the decorating.

I get the scraper, a bucket of hot water and bin bags.

The woodchip waits. I sponge water onto the paper, working my way methodically from left to right.

I dig my scraper underneath the soggy wallcovering and it comes off in a concertina mush. The wall is yellow underneath: a faded, daffodil wash, still shiny in places. The task becomes easier as I carry on. I reach the middle of the wall and suddenly find writing on the yellow paint underneath. Thick, black marker pen. Huge letters, a foot high: 'l o v e s'. I stand back to look at the word. Try to work out what's missing.

Then it registers. My body seems like it's been knocked off-balance. I need to strip above and below.

I push my blade at the wet paper above the word. Yellow wall, black marker slash, yellow wall, black curve, yellow wall. It takes ages but it's seconds really.

'J a y' it says.

I step onto the floor, crouching to lash away the wrapping from its secret, the name revealed letter by letter. 'R u t h i e'. That's what the black marker tells me.

Jay loves Ruthie. The girl with the long black hair.

Jay gets home in the afternoon. Just strolls back in with a dopey smile on his face. Slaps ninety quid on the kitchen table like he's playing Snap.

I'm ready for him. In these sorts of circumstances I don't crumble, I'm rock hard.

The discovery this morning was a turning point. I now had the name of his ex. How did I feel? Deceived, to some extent. Angry. Why hadn't he told me when I asked before? Envious: she had been here first, putting her stamp on the house, the garden. Suspicious. Definitely suspicious. Did she still live locally? Was she still in contact with Jay? *Ruthie*. Things had gone up a gear, and the situation now was that I needed to know everything about *her*, too.

I had a bath to settle me, to reduce my anxiety: a bubbly, steamy tub full that emptied the tank and left the taps cold. I soaked the thoughts out of me. Hot oil treatment to make my hair look fantastic. Legs and underarms shaved. Perfumed with Chanel. Make-up that brought out my eyes, eyelashes, full lips, cheekbones. Silk thong (for later) under skin-tight jeans, clingy but casual T-shirt.

I've been here before. When you're ready to confront someone you need to look stunning. You need to have prepared so that you can assure yourself you won't break down. It's a hardening process, like firing a pot.

So now I sit here at the kitchen table, looking fantastic – the perfect girlfriend – pushing my breasts out at him, saying nothing, just knowing he desires me. I pull my glossy black hair over my left shoulder.

'Wow,' he says. 'I bet you know what I'm wanting.'

'I bet I do.'

He comes over, stroking the hair down from the top of my head, smoothing it over my left breast, letting his cold hand linger.

'But *I* want something first,' I say calmly.

'What's that then?'

He pulls me up from the chair but I push him to arms' length.

'An explanation,' I say, and he starts to look puzzled.

He takes both of my hands and I sense his face starting to colour. He tries to kiss me but I dodge his lips.

'Come in here,' I say, worming my fingers out of his and leading the way. I lure him into the living room.

I don't know if the first thing he sees is the mess of wallpaper on the carpet or the unexpected yellow on the walls, or if it is indeed the very words that I am requiring an explanation for.

I watch him as he stares at the writing. Does he remember the moment he scrawled it on? Does he remember how he felt at that point, how he felt about someone else? *Her. Ruthie.*

He stands there and looks for only a second or so, then casts his eyes around the piles of soggy paper at the edges of the carpet.

'Ruthie,' I say slowly, exaggerating the syllables to show what a stupid-sounding name it is. 'Tell me about her.'

Jay groans. 'Not all this again. I just wanted to come home

and chill out with you and instead I get in and there's mess everywhere and you getting ready for the Spanish Inquisition.'

'Sit down and tell me,' I insist in a firm, level voice.

And I don't know if he feels threatened that I've discovered a secret, but he sort of freaks out and grabs me by the shoulders and puts his face right up to mine, like he's going to headbutt me or scream or spit in my eye.

'No, *you* sit down.' He pushes me into the sofa and stands over me. 'Don't think that you can go snooping around to find things out and use them against me.'

He reaches towards my neck and pins my head back with the cup of his hand. I can smell the sour sweatiness of his watch strap. A lock of my hair is pinched under his thumb. His eyes are mad: all the love and goodness have vanished from them.

'Stop it, Jay,' I whimper. 'You're scaring me.'

He takes his hand away suddenly, stumbles back to drop in the armchair.

'Sorry,' he says with his eyes to the floor. 'I'm sorry. I didn't mean to.' He rubs his face; plucks at the worn Dralon of the chair. 'OK. OK, I'll tell you about her.' He meets my eyes.

'Go on then,' I say.

'She was a few years younger than me,' he begins. 'We went out on and off for a few years as teenagers, then she went off travelling for a while before going to uni. She wanted to be an architect. She'd only done a year of her course when she came home for the summer and we got back together.' He takes his tobacco tin from his jacket pocket. I'm sure his hands are shaking a little. 'When she went back to uni in autumn, we found out she was pregnant.'

I knew it. The toys in the shed.

'She dropped out of uni the following spring and we got chance for this place...' He tries to pull out a Rizla but they are stuck together.

'So where is she now?' I ask. 'What happened to the kid? What about maintenance?'

Jay stares straight at me, like he's easing up a little.

'Everything fell apart,' he says. 'Everything. She's gone. And there's no maintenance. We lost the kid. End of story. And now what you really need to do is trust me and stop asking me stuff. Because I don't want to talk about her any more.'

He lights his cigarette. I keep my mouth shut. Maybe that is the end of the story; maybe it is true. I rub my neck. Erase the memories of his hostile fingers.

After Jay's revelations about Ruthie, he seems to move into a phase of exuberance. Perhaps it's the relief. Perhaps he's happier now that I know. Only an hour later he has a bounce about him, like some children do when they've been drinking blue pop; he puts music on – some gypsy fusion techno stuff – and pulls me around the room in an attempt at dancing.

'Got something for you,' he says. 'A special kiss. For a special girl.'

He presses his lips on mine and pushes his tongue into my mouth. And as I give myself up to his kiss, he slides the tiny bitter pearl into my mouth.

'Mmm?' I question, but he puts a finger across my lips and whispers,

'Swallow.'

And although I don't know what it is, I do it for him, and we dance and kiss and his hands are up my top and down my knickers, and twenty minutes later I'm reaching a level of euphoria that I have never felt before. We go upstairs – I'm not even sure if I walk or if Jay carries me – and we are all over each other and I can't work out if time is moving slower or faster as the music booms below us. And later I won't remember if we dance or make love or go back downstairs again: all I will remember is the elation, the joy, the incredible high.

Eventually I find myself lying naked, uncovered, shivering on the bed, sore like I've had my brains shagged out. My arms are heavy; there is a red weal on my wrist and my hair is all over the place. The house is silent. I have no idea what time it is, what day it is either. Jay is sitting on the end of the bed, watching me.

'Back in the land of the living?' He laughs.

He kisses me and tells me to stay where I am. When I ask why, he says to trust him. I stay, and listen to him as he moves around downstairs for thirty minutes, forty minutes, perhaps even longer, until he returns and says I can go into the living room.

He has painted the wall, erased all trace of his name with *hers*, created a clean, blank space.

I stare at the wall and stare at Jay. Am I supposed to feel like this? My heart bursts and I am blissfully happy like I have never ever been before.

*

'Arms up,' he says, pulling off her T-shirt. He unclips her bra; drags down her knickers to kick across the floor.

Then he dresses her like a doll, arranging the velvet skirts and deftly fastening the delicate silver buttons. She's compliant, smiling, humming along to the background tunes.

'You're looking fantastic,' he tells her, threading his fingers through her hair. 'We're nearly ready now.'

He leads her down the stairs, through the door to where the candles are already lit and tossing arcane shadows at the walls, dancing like ravers. She patiently lets him knot one end of the rope around her right wrist before he threads the other end through both of the thick wall hooks. Lifting her arm, he knots the other end around her left wrist.

'I've got you now,' he says, moving in and kissing her neck. 'You're captured.'

She laughs and sways a little to the music despite being tethered. His knee is between her legs, shifting the velvet dress up and up, and he takes her by the buttocks to lift and press against the wall. Frantic for her, he can't hold back any longer.

Violent, lip-splitting kisses that leave them both with blood and saliva on their chins.

Mouthfuls of her hair, biting it, tugging at it, imbibing the smell and length and colour of it into him.

Fingernails in her thighs, pulling her apart, letting her cries of pain warm him like oak-aged brandy.

Lovebites on her breasts like crushed, smeared blueberries.

He licks her face and whispers 'baby, baby' over each closed eyelid.

'I love you, Ruthie,' he says. 'You're my everything. I'll never love anyone else like you, ever. You love me too, don't you?'

'Yes,' she replies.

'Say it again, Ruth. I need to know.'

'I love you.'

He unbuckles his belt and flips her round on the rope to face the wall.

CHAPTER TWELVE

'Hey, this looks awesome,' Maria says as she lugs her drum through the living room door.

Awesome is overdoing it a bit. There are gouges in the plaster that should have been filled before painting. Some of Jay's haphazard brush skills are evident around the window. But it all looks better than the awful woodchip.

'Thanks,' I say. 'Me and Jay got it all stripped and painted over the last couple of days. But it's a work in progress really.'

When Rick gets here he looks around with his nose turned up, and says, 'Hmm... different.'

'Don't you like it?' I ask.

'I thought it looked all right before.'

I won't be drawn in. He wants to push me, to goad me into an argument, to make me look stupid in front of everyone else. He thinks he's lord of the bloody manor just because I'm living in his dead grandma's house. But I will make an effort to be friendly, to coax information out of him which might be useful.

'Jay did most of it,' I tell him. 'I think he's done a good job.'

'Painting's all right. It's just the colours.' He nods at the aubergine wall. 'It's what my shit would look like after eating a jar of beetroot.'

I smile as sweetly as I can. 'Maria likes it anyway.'

'And I've got taste,' says Maria. 'I watch all the property programmes.'

Kevin intervenes with the announcement that Patryk has just turned up. He's another acquaintance of Jay's: a tanned, ponytailed man in his mid-forties, who can play the bass guitar.

We jam out some tunes and Patryk makes a big difference to the sound. He has a good ear for the bass lines.

'We're getting a great band together,' says Jay as he gets up to put the kettle on.

'Two sugars for you?' I say to Rick.

'You've got it,' he replies, and something clicks, something feels like progress.

I ask if Rick is his real name or just a nickname.

He flinches, off guard.

'It's not a trick question,' I say. 'I just wondered.'

'His name is Hugh Janus,' shouts Maria.

'Ha, ha,' Rick says. 'It's actually Ivor Biggun.'

'No, come on,' I say. 'What is it really?'

Rick taps his nose.

'It's Rick the Dick,' says Maria as he smiles and nods.

'It's Richard,' says Jay as he comes back into the room carrying four overfilled mugs of tea. 'But everyone has called him Rick since infant school.'

'I'll call you Richard if you'd rather,' I say.

Jay guffaws and picks up his guitar. 'Ooh Richard,' he says in a posh, feminine tone.

Then Rick looks at me with that evil eye again. 'That privilege is reserved for special people.'

'He means his mum,' says Maria.

I don't know why I bother trying to be kind. And I don't know what it is that Rick despises in me. But I will find out.

* * *

I go into town to use the library computer again. It's my once-a-week office now. I finally email Lou. I tell her it will be great to catch up and see the family, lovely for her to pop in (although we are in the middle of renovating the house – we have spent most of the time sorting out the huge gardens first). I send love to Dominic and tell him not to work too hard. I weave in subtle eccentricities of my new life (the joy of chicken-keeping and the pleasure of soup-making with home-grown ingredients) so that the shock won't be too much when she arrives in December. I hover my curser over the *send* button for far too long before I click it.

In town I browse around the shops for Christmas gifts. I ponder over the choice of either perfume or a bracelet for Lou. I think about buying a Christmas tree: a real or artificial one? And where to put it: under the window or in the alcove by the fire? I think about the locked room again and wonder whether to force it myself or insist that Jay opens it. My face is twisted into a grimace as I nibble the inside of my cheek, then a hand taps me gently on the arm.

'Hey, don't look so stressed.' I'm pulled away from my thoughts by a smiling man, thirtyish with close-cropped blond hair and blue eyes. He's dressed smartly in suit trousers, shirt and tie.

'Sorry.' My face is flushing; I can feel the warmth. The man is still smiling.

'I remember you. You're the fiddle player, aren't you?' he asks.

It's like déjà vu without the festival field.

'How do you know?' I ask.

'I saw you busking on the high street last week,' he says. 'You were underneath my office window, the solicitors. I heard the music and looked out.'

'Did my playing impress you then?' I had to ask. It's not just a chat-up line.

'It's not really my thing, the folk stuff. Although you must have a lot of talent to play that style,' he replies. 'But I thought you had lovely black hair.'

I touch it instinctively.

'Hey, could I get you a coffee or something? I'm on my dinner break.' He slips the book he had under his arm onto a shelf. I read the title: *The Abs Diet and Workout Book.*

He sees me looking. 'Oh, it's not for me, I was just browsing. Wondering whether my brother might like it. Actually, I'll admit it did look quite good. I've always fancied a six-pack.' He taps his flat stomach.

'I've got to go,' I say.

'Sure I can't interest you? There's a lovely coffee shop just up the road.'

In my old life I would have been tempted. No, I'll be honest, I would have gone. Definitely. Clean, good-looking, well-dressed, well-spoken professional was my type. But I have left that behind with the rest of my failed life. Now I'm in a much better place mentally I have realised that you can have a perfect relationship without having to be with someone who looks flash.

'Sorry. I'm really busy.' I walk away, tripping on someone's pushchair wheel.

'Play under my window again,' he shouts behind me. 'Tomorrow.'

I smile and flick my hair over my shoulder. It's good to have admirers, though, whatever type they are.

* * *

'I've said hundreds of times that I can't find the key.' Jay lets out a long sigh that makes his nostrils flare. 'And I really don't want to damage the door by bashing off the lock with a hammer.'

'But I can't believe that you would let an entire room be wasted just because the key is missing. It could be an extra bedroom.' I must convince him.

'We don't need an extra bedroom,' says Jay. 'Unless you're wanting Rick to join our drinking sessions and have somewhere to sleep over.'

He has me with that one.

'OK, music room. We could have a PA set up, perhaps do some recording in there. Then we can have some demo tracks to send out if we want a chance at playing any festivals next year.' It's a good argument. I can see him considering it.

'Hmm,' he says. He stands up and opens the kitchen door. 'Let me think about it. I might be willing. But don't nag me.'

I smile as he goes outside. It's a victory of a sort. But I know that he won't want me to look inside it. He will wait until I'm at the library or something, and I will get back and the door will be open and all the evidence gone. I need to make sure that I'm around to see what's inside.

I fill the kettle and watch through the window as he strolls towards the shed. He's unaware that I'm watching him. Scanty clothes hang around his vulnerable body. Shapeless, faded T-shirt, jeans with oil stains on the thighs and threadbare on the left buttock. His bare, sinewy arms swinging, the tanned skin fading to a lighter shade now. Something surprising claws my insides – lust, compassion, love. It catches my breath, jumps into my heart and makes me want to hug him and fuck him so I can return to that level of euphoria I felt the other day after the wall was painted.

* * *

It's the next day, and I seize an opportunity while Jay is at work. A sudden impulse takes over me when I see the axe cleaved into a stump of wood outside. I yank it out and take it with me into the hallway, knowing that I will have to act quickly before I lose my nerve.

I swing the axe at the lock. My ears ring with the metal-on-metal reverberations, and a gap opens in the wood. I force the blade of the axe into the gap and use it like a crowbar. The frame splinters. A spring drops from the mechanism and bounces across the carpet. I launch the axe at the lock again, feeling like a trespassing teenager.

I pull the lock from the door and poke at the apparatus buried in the wood, and a metal bolt slides back.

It's done.

I open the door and look inside.

It is too dark to see anything because the window has been blacked out. I flick the light switch and then it's all there: more woodchip walls, more cheap carpet and a window frame boarded over with plywood. But there's nothing to see, apart from two rusty electric fires with fraying flex and a wooden clothes horse. A small stack of newspapers is wedged into one corner: a black bin bag sits on top of it. A snake of blue nylon rope sleeps on the floor. The room smells of damp and soil and cannabis. I notice odd hooks in the wall, some of them clutched by straggly knots of garden twine. Two of them are heavy duty, the type you could hang a pig from. A pull-out laundry airer is fixed to the back wall.

The contents are puzzling yet appear familiar. Have I been in here before? I ask myself what I expected to find and now I wonder. Evidence, of some sort. Photographs, boxes of letters. Personal things that would give me clues about Jay. Expose his mysteries. Let me know him completely.

I look again at the disappointing elements. It doesn't add up. I wonder why I'm disillusioned. Did he have the key? Had he been in the room before and cleared it out? I walk around, trying to fathom it all. I pick up the bin bag, peering inside to find a scrunch of purple velvet. I pull it out. It's a dress: long, low-cut with a beaded bodice and a heavy skirt. I hold it up against me: it's just my size.

Was this hers? I think, even though I have the sudden, baffling thought that it might be mine. It all feels so confusing.

I turn and stuff the dress back into the bag. Scan the room again, shove the thought of Ruth and the dress from my mind. Another trip to the tip. Another session of paper stripping and painting. But the carpet might be OK once it's cleaned. And with Heritage Green walls. I can picture it already.

CHAPTER THIRTEEN

NOVEMBER

The laminate flooring goes down a dream. If I'd known it would be that easy, even for a non-DIYer like me it would be in every room. It hasn't been quick. Clearing the furniture out and rolling up the carpet was the most labour-intensive bit, especially as I had to do it on my own: I picked a day when Jay intended to be out for most of it on the estate, so he could come home and it all be done and I could cover his eyes and reveal it at the right moment.

My knees are stiff and sore and one of my fingers is bleeding from a sharp fragment, but I am delighted with the results. It's a transformation, especially with the new colour scheme. The room doesn't need anything else apart from new curtains, some throws for the three-piece suite, and a big mirror above the mantelpiece.

Jay was angry about me breaking into the dining room. I apologised and tried to show that I hadn't done too much damage: most of the woodwork could be repaired with filler and paint, and although the lock was broken the handle still worked.

He paced around, touching the hooks and kicking the rope underneath the pile of newspapers.

'It really needs airing in here,' I said. 'We need to take the plywood off and open the windows, get rid of the smell.'

'It's only weed.'

Then it suddenly dawned on me what had been happening in the room.

'Have you been growing it?' I asked.

'Bit of an enterprise,' he confessed. 'I used to grow the plants in propagators until they were sturdy enough to put outside. Then me and Rick would take them to the estates land and plant them in there, in their woods. No public access, it's a doddle to hide stuff. At harvest time we'd bring them back here and dry them out. Bag it up ready for festival season.'

'But that's so illegal. You could get done big time for that sort of thing.'

'It was strictly festivals,' said Jay. 'No local dealing. No chance of getting tipped off. Anyway, there's been virtually no harvest this year, crap spring weather, I think. There are a few plants left I need to pick up, but hardly enough for occasional personal use.'

'Why didn't you tell me about that before, when I was asking about the room?'

'You never asked about the room. You only ever went on about the missing key. Anyway, it's open, now.'

It was. Ready for my special touch to transform it into a perfect new space.

* * *

Later, I ask Jay what the situation is with the rent. This is after he has suggested that we sell my car because money is tight.

'Well,' he shrugs, 'there's no formal contract. I don't really pay much.'

'How much?'

'It's hard to say.' Jay tucks a long strand of hair behind his ear. I suggested to him last week that he should tie his hair up into a man-bun, like all the trendy, beardy blokes do, but he rejected the idea quite forcefully.

'Well, surely you could give an estimate.' I try to hide the frustration in my voice. 'How much has it cost over the past two months, say?'

'Nothing. Although I've taken loads of veg and eggs and stuff,' he says, shrugging.

'But it's not like two months' worth of rent. Not like fifteen hundred quid or more which is what it would cost if you were renting something properly, through an agent.'

'Rick's mum doesn't mind. She's loaded, anyway. She's glad that the place is being looked after, and that we do the maintenance.'

'Why didn't she just sell it when the granny died?' I'm finding it hard to get my head around the situation. It just seems too good to be true that there must be a catch.

'I don't know. Perhaps she just can't be arsed with dealing with estate agents and that.'

'So, when did you last give her any actual money?' I ask.

Jay scratches his head. 'It was probably June or July. Two hundred quid, I think. She's OK about it. Don't stress yourself.'

I sigh deeply. It worries me that we're in a situation where we don't have proper tenant's rights. I couldn't bear to have to leave the place that I am so attached to, so invested in.

'The thing is,' Jay continues, 'how do we find money to run three vehicles? We don't need three. And seeing as it's your car's tax and insurance that run out at the end of this month, it makes sense to get rid. Raise some cash.'

'Why not get rid of the camper?' I argue. 'It's falling to bits. It will cost a fortune to get through the MOT.' My car is the only link to civilisation that I have: it gets me to the library to use the computers, and to the elusive places where a phone and internet signal might be around this patch of wilderness.

'Rick can do the welding, that's no probs. And what d'you think we're going to sleep in at next year's festivals?'

'Well, can't we just live a bit cheaper?' I ask, immediately regretting my question.

''Course we can, if we don't bother with all the bloody grand designs projects. OK, the floor looks nice – well all the room does – but it wasn't necessary. We spend hardly anything on food; the heating and hot water is free; the rent can't get any cheaper, so what do you suggest?'

I'm stuck. I don't want to tell him about the rest of the money in my account and I realise that I don't contribute anything apart from my fiddle playing in the busking trips.

'I could look for a job,' I suggest, weakly, knowing that no one would ever give me a decent reference. 'Or go on the dole.'

'I'm not being funny,' Jay says, 'but all that Jobseekers crap is a nightmare nowadays. You have to jump through hoops and prove all sorts of stuff. Go to interviews everywhere. And if they caught you busking you'd get done for fraud. Thing is, we're trying to live off-grid.'

'Make our own electricity?' I laugh.

'You know what I mean,' he says, somewhat irritated. 'Out of the system. Not claiming off the state, and not contributing to it either. And yes, we could look towards electricity. A twelve-volt system that Rick could rig up with a turbine and an alternator and batteries.'

He's off into self-sufficient dreamland. And thinking about it, quickly, right now, I don't really fancy getting a job. I fancy feeding chickens, pickling onions, stewing road-killed rabbits, splitting logs, writing tunes and busking to pay the council tax bill.

'OK,' I say, finally. 'We'll sell the car.'

* * *

Sometimes, in the night the silence wakes me. I lie in the shadows and listen to nothing, only the intermittent sigh and creak of the house, and Jay breathing. Occasionally he tenses and jolts like a captured animal. Sometimes he cries in his sleep, gasping like a dying fish as tears run into his hair and his pillow. I am too frightened to wake him: I don't know what horror he returns to in his dreams. Usually, I want to know everything about him. But this unnerves me, makes me stare into the darkness with my heart pounding in my ears; my breath held in and body rigid for fear of stirring him.

Lately I have been woken by tiny noises. Sometimes they sound like the cries of a child.

But last night I slept deeply; got embroiled in a dream, one of those dreams that somehow feel so real, where I knew where the key was for the locked door – it was on a nail in the wall behind the wardrobe – and saw someone wearing the purple velvet dress in that secret room with their wrists tied to the hooks in the wall while Jay was kissing them and mauling them and calling them Ruthie.

CHAPTER FOURTEEN

We celebrate Bonfire Night with a blazing mound of twigs that Jay has spent the last fortnight pruning and clearing.

Maria and Phil bring Lolly, who is underdressed in an inappropriate Playboy T-shirt.

Kevin turns up with a mahogany-haired man called Saaz and they huddle together, staring dreamily at the flames.

Of course, Rick is here.

We eat smoky baked potatoes out of the foil, slathered in real butter and salt, and Jay brings out bottles of homemade beer.

'Aren't we supposed to pour this around the apple trees to ward off evil spirits?' says Phil, nodding towards the orchard. 'That thing they do, you know, pagans?'

'I think you mean wassailing,' I say. 'And it's cider you pour on. I don't think Jay's dark ale would have the same powers.'

'Miss Know-it-all,' mutters Rick as he crushes up the foil from his third potato.

The bonfire is scorching my cheeks. I stare at the soporific flames until everyone around me disappears and all I can see is an orange glow. I think back to me and Nell – the last time I saw her alive – warming our hands over an autumn campfire, making plans for our year out where we would travel Europe. She was so pleased to get her new job, with surprisingly good wages. 'Just six months working away and then I'll be back,' she told me. 'A chance to earn big money for our trip.' I gave her my blessing for what it was worth, but she never returned. Best friend, boyfriend, all gone within a matter of weeks. A quiet melancholy wraps around me even though I know it's dangerous to dwell on these thoughts.

'I'm going in for a bath,' I say to Jay. 'I stink of smoke.'

'Don't be daft,' he says. 'We all stink of smoke. Surely you can wait till everyone's gone.'

'I fancy it now,' I reply. 'I'm getting cold.'

Inside, Lolly is sitting on the living room rug. She is chattering away in her soft, nasal tone to an invisible being who is trying to run past her towards the door.

'I've told you, Amos, about how dangerous cars can be. You need to stay here and not go out. Go on, sit down again. And all you others, pay attention.' She lunges her arms to the right of her body and pushes at nothing.

I watch in silence from the hallway. A wave of ice creeps over my skin.

'Stay there, Amos, don't make me have to...' Somehow, she senses my presence and slaps her hands over her face. She's back out of her unearthly world.

'Hi, Lolly,' I say. 'Who are you talking to?'

She shakes her head and pinches her eyes closed.

'Are you playing a game? Were you talking to your friends?' I remember our previous conversation about ghosts and feel the drag of a shiver lift the hairs on my scalp.

She hooks a toe into the top of her left sock and pulls it down, then repeats with the other one.

'I'm just going for a bath,' I tell her. 'Do you need the toilet before I go in?'

She huddles into a ball and ignores me.

'Don't miss the bonfire,' I say.

'Don't miss the bonfire,' a scoffing voice repeats behind me, and I turn to see the fat, jeering face of Rick. He's too close, in my space. I can feel the heat from his body yet smell the cold, smoky air around him.

'What?' I ask.

His eyes are taunting, full of hostility.

'You should go home,' he says. 'This place isn't for you.'

I don't know how to respond. I bite my lip. I look towards Lolly: a coil of limbs on the living room rug.

'What do you mean?' I ask in a small voice.

'You might think Jay loves you,' says Rick. 'Like you're the perfect girlfriend and all that. But *you're* not the right one. You're not even close. So, you'd be better off going back to wherever you came from. Sooner rather than later. I'm only telling you for your own good.'

He pushes past me and goes into the bathroom. I don't want to wait outside the door so I go into the living room and sit on the sofa. Lolly opens her eyes and gazes at me. I wonder if this freaky kid is the only proper friend I have.

I am on the edge of tearfulness as I lie in the bath. Two candle-nubs in old bottles stand on the toilet cistern: their flames duck and dive and ripple the darkness. I gulp the air and try to settle my thoughts. Think of the future, not the past, I tell myself. I need to be here, I really do.

I know I shouldn't get so hung up about Rick. But I really don't trust him: there's just something about him that gives me a bad vibe. He wants me out of the way and has taken against me for some weird reason. Perhaps he feels like I'm too much of an outsider, a 'southerner'. They don't seem to like southerners around here, just like they're not fond of immigrants. The district was heavily in favour of Brexit, Jay told me, with people turning out to vote Leave in droves. Wanting to get their country back.

Jay doesn't want me to go home. I know he doesn't. He likes that we are making a life together. He loves me. And – despite what Rick says – I can be the perfect girlfriend.

Anyway, I don't want to go home. I don't even know where that is any more.

My family are miles away. It's not that I have been particularly close to my parents: the last few years have been a nightmare of shame and embarrassment for them with me and Martin. And where to start with my sister, Lou, and all the mixed emotions I have with her. Sometimes I despise her for what she's become: how she always thinks she's better than me, wearing nicer clothes and having more money.

That last time I saw her: the day I got sacked, the day she gave me the white gold earrings, the day she felt she had to take me for coffee and advice. It was more than that. She had something to tell me, another thing to nag me about, something she had found out.

'You had an abortion,' she said. As if I didn't already know. 'Martin's baby.'

Well, yes.

Tears budged up in her eyes. 'Why didn't you tell me you were pregnant?'

How could I have told anyone? Nell would have been my first port of call but she was three weeks in the grave. I'd only told Martin thinking that it was my trump card, my way of freeing him from his dead marriage. How was I to know that he would go off the rails about it, seething as if it was entirely my fault?

It was only an eight-week foetus, but it was the fork in the road of our journey together. We sat in his car for hours, arguing in circles. Same thing the next evening. And the next. Eat, sleep, discuss inconvenient pregnancy.

In the end I knew that I couldn't keep the baby. It wasn't just Martin who convinced me. It would have stolen my life, I told myself. Given me sleepless nights and stretch marks. But I hadn't expected Martin to go home and tell his wife. I hadn't expected the ripples to run through his family, to his daughter, Maxine, who was Lou's best friend.

'I could have helped,' she said. A tear slipped onto her cheek. 'I would have been there for you...'

To hold my hand when I killed my baby? I thought.

The earrings were a sort of bribe. Some kind of deal agreed upon between her and Maxine to keep me away from Martin and stop disrupting their family. Stop going round kicking and screaming at their door in the early hours.

Martin had chosen. And his wife was the one that he had picked. Maxine had phoned Lou that morning to tell her.

I pretended that I already knew, pretended that it was me who had ended it.

'You need to sort yourself out now. Find someone else. Someone single, someone to have a proper relationship with. You're thirty years old, for goodness' sake and this has been going on for, what, fifteen years? It's like you've got that Stockholm Syndrome where victims fall in love with their abusers. OK, so he had a fling with you when you were young – and I thought at the time he really shouldn't have taken advantage of your vulnerability – but you've completely misinterpreted things all the way. He's never loved you, Lauren. He's just used you because you let him. And now you need to leave Martin and his family alone. Keep away from their house. One more incident and they will get an injunction; they've had enough.' Lou grasped her hands together and pressed the fist against her forehead. 'It really does need to be over this time. No pretending while you have a couple more one-night stands with other married men. It needs to stop, properly. People have done enough talking. And what Maxine and her mum have been through: I'm in the middle of it all. Think of me, too.'

I stared out of the café window. So. That was it. And to have to hear it from Lou. I curled my fingers round the phone in my pocket. There would need to be a text, at least. Surely it warranted that.

'They're going to redo their vows,' said Lou. 'So, it really is over. Martin has promised them.'

I shrugged, postponing my hopelessness for later when I was alone. Zoned out as she carried on with her recommendation about how I should see this period in my life as a chance to start again. Right from the beginning.

I realise I've made bad choices over the years. There have been shitty times and there have been fucking dark times. But I shouldn't resent Lou, not really. It wasn't her fault that I lost my boyfriend, my best friend, my job and home.

Nell though. She understood me completely. She was always there for me. Until she died.

So, here I am now where things are working well, things are being fixed. And aside from my small battles with Rick, I'm in a good position. It definitely feels like I am *meant* to be here. What I need to do is focus more on the words that Jay said: destiny and serendipity.

I'm certainly not in a hurry to go anywhere that I used to call home.

I slide into the steaming water up to my jawline and pull a hot flannel over my face. For some reason I remember the guy who wanted to take me for a coffee. Lou would have liked him.

Half an hour later, the door rattles.

'Come on, babe, we're missing you,' says Jay from the other side. 'Don't be antisocial.'

I sit up in the tepid water, reach over the side of the bath for the towel.

'You're missing all the fun,' Jay tries again. 'You're looking like a party pooper.'

'Give me five minutes.' I stand up and wrap the towel around myself. I hear Jay go through to the kitchen, get more wine from the fridge.

Perhaps I should go back outside. Pretend to enjoy their company. I ought to make more of an effort and not let Rick get to me because, really, that's what he wants. I pull the plug out: the water slops tamely from side to side and takes an age to go down.

'Game face on,' I tell myself, getting back into my smoky clothes. The road to fulfilment isn't always easy but I am on my way, and this is the point I'm at. Here. Just where I should be.

CHAPTER FIFTEEN

I prise the boards from the window frame in the studio, which is the name we have given to the room that used to be locked. Rick has borrowed some recording gear so that we can make a demo and Jay is excited for us to use the room for practising and recording.

The natural light changes the disposition of the room. A sense of déjà vu knocks me and I pick up the rope from the corner. I wind it around my wrist: there seems to be a memory lodged in my mind of its coarseness on my skin. I tug it, feel the bristly fibres, look underneath to see the type of welt it would make. I thread it through the hooks on the wall, yank my weight on it, feel how securely it holds. I let it go, and shake my head. Stupid dream.

I fiddle with the catch on the window so that it can be opened in order to air the room. It's already loose, and as I push it with the heel of my hand something inside the mechanism snaps. Shit. The window now opens but won't close properly. I pull it shut but it can't be secured. Will we be able to get a replacement catch for this type of window? Jay would be furious if any of Rick's recording equipment got stolen. I must remember to ask in B&Q if they have anything suitable.

I fetch the tins of paint that are left over from the living room. Time and economy dictate that it will be best to just paint over the woodchip wallpaper. I fold up the clothes horse and take it outside, along with the old electric fires. The velvet dress I leave in the bag, to later hang in the wardrobe. It's inexplicable, but I can't bring myself to throw it out. I unscrew some of the hooks from the walls and squirt the rest of the sealant in the dark gaps. The heavy-duty ones won't budge: I will ask Jay to tackle those later. I take some of the newspapers from the corner of the room – year-old copies of the local rags featuring stories about washing-line thieves, pothole anger and shop closures – and spread the pages around the edges of the room to protect the carpet from my enthusiastic roller. And I almost don't notice, because they are coloured black same as the newsprint, but there are rings of biro on some of the columns, and I pick up the pages and find that they are full of adverts for women seeking men. I didn't know that people still used newspapers. Surely it is all online dating nowadays? I put down the tin of paint and start to read through the ringed ones:

Stunning seductive dark haired twenty-five-year-old looking for discreet relationship.

Amy, brunette, nice figure, looking for someone to mend her broken heart.

Shy curvy thirty-year-old with long black hair looking for romantic nights in.

Sexy young divorcee, dark hair, blue eyes, looking for fun and frolics.

Samantha, attractive, brown eyes, black hair looking for adventurous male.

The date of the newspaper is back in early February. Months before we met. I am confused by my feelings and my heart is thudding again. There is an element of jealousy and some sort of perception that I have been deceived but it's hard to pinpoint how. If Jay contacted any of these women it was well before he got together with me. Has he stayed in touch? Is that where he goes with Rick? Or could it be that one of these women is the elusive Ruthie? I look again through the ringed adverts and notice that the shy curvy thirty-year-old has tempted Jay to score a line under 'long black hair'. The pen has ripped through to the page underneath. I unfold another of the newspapers and leaf through to the classified section. And there, again, another page of adverts, some ringed in red this time. I toss the pages to the floor and pick up another from mid-February. *Long black hair... Long black hair... Long black hair...* Every woman who has described herself with long black hair has her advert ringed. Each three-word phrase is heavily underlined. There are twelve on this page.

Frantically – obsessively – I go through every newspaper, checking the dates, counting the adverts, spreading out the pages around me. It takes almost an hour, and finally, with my fingers black and the carpet covered with sheets of newspaper, I have totalled a possible sixty-eight women with long black hair that Jay might have been involved with.

After I paint the walls of the studio, I screw up the newspapers and throw them into the stove. I vacuum the carpet and bring in all the musical gear. Jay comes in later, leaning on the door-frame wearing a smirk that says he's impressed.

'You're a real homemaker, aren't you?' He gazes around: the

winter light dribbles through the glass and into the clean new wall paint. His eyes rest on the hooks that are still there.

'Just shows what you can do with a tin of paint in a drugs den.' I won't mention the broken window catch, but I will ask him at some point later about the adverts: there are phrases coagulating in my mind that will come out wrong if I attempt an enquiry too soon.

Jay winks at me. He claps a dub rhythm onto his belly. Then comes up to me with that look on his face.

'Do you fancy a good night?' he says. 'Because I've got a special kiss for a special girl.'

Tongue probing, pushing, and I receive the special seed and swallow without being told.

* * *

Jay and Rick take my car to a dealer and come home with eighteen hundred pounds.

'I paid nearly four grand for that just over a year ago,' I say.

'It's not really been looked after, though, has it?' says Rick.

I ignore him.

'But just think,' says Jay, 'we don't have to find the money for tax and insurance now, or getting it through a test.'

I can't think of anything to say. I go into the studio and take my fiddle out of its case. I tighten and rosin the bow. I tuck the instrument under my chin, tweak the tuning, then play tune after tune after tune. Later, I hear the kitchen door slam and through the sparkling window I see Jay and Rick ride away on Jay's bike.

I return the fiddle to its case and go out to the kitchen where the pile of £20 notes is scattered next to the ashtray. Do I pay them into my account, the one that Jay knows nothing about, or do I pay them into Jay's account? I'm so new to all this cohabiting situation and don't know what the etiquette is. So I stack them into a tidy rectangle, then find myself washing my hands at the kitchen sink and staring into the garden.

Later, the money from my car sale is sorted. Jay takes half so that he can pay the electricity bill and a water rates final demand threatening court action, plus puts some aside for the campervan insurance. I pay the rest into my account with new thoughts of home improvements. The bathroom must be the next priority. I owe it to the house.

CHAPTER SIXTEEN

We meet my parents for a meal in Chesterfield. It's nothing fancy, they don't go in for that sort of thing. They like a place that does basic food that you pay for at the bar before you get it.

We sit at a sticky table in a pub near the Crooked Spire, and Dad's happy because they've got five different real ales on.

Then it's all polite conversation – I can tell they are both putting on a show. Dad and Jay talk about the best route from East Anglia to Derbyshire, and Mum interjects occasionally to tell me about the current best deals in Tesco: half-price chickens, double Gloucester cheese, jars of pasta sauce.

'We've got chickens,' I tell her. 'They're such characters.'

She says she doesn't know why we bother when you can get eggs so cheap anyway and doesn't really listen when I try to explain the difference between battery eggs and free-range organic.

'And how are you dealing with everything now?'

'What do you mean?' I should have just said 'fine' rather than open up a can of worms.

'You know, with Nell. I couldn't remember if you said you were going to go for the counselling?'

My face flushes. I sense that Jay has stopped talking to Dad and is listening in.

'Everything's fine, Mum. I didn't need it. I'm getting on with life and it's all great.'

'Who's Nell?' Jay asks. 'I've not heard you mention that name before.'

Mum jumps in. 'Lauren's best friend. It was so sad, wasn't it? They were so close, so alike…'

I pierce my fingernails into my thighs under the table. 'Not really,' I begin, my heart scrabbling under my ribs, as I am at risk of losing my shit in front of Jay, in front of everyone…

'…some people even used to think they were twins.'

My mother somehow decodes my glare and realises that I'm getting upset talking about Nell, just as the food arrives. It's cold and overcooked but I am so grateful for its entrance, and Dad comments on the efficiency of the staff. We return to small talk and safe subjects, and Mum brags about Lou's new car, a top-of-the-range BMW she bought last Thursday, and we all pretend that the food is nice. Dad gets another round in and Jay flashes me a look to let me know he's bored. He wanders off to find the toilets and I follow him a couple of minutes later. I wait outside the Gents until he emerges.

'We'll go soon,' I say, hemming my arms around his waist. 'They're doing my head in too.'

Jay kisses me, his mouth hoppy and warm. He pushes a hand up my T-shirt. 'We may as well be drinking at home.'

'Just give it another twenty minutes,' I say. 'I'll make it up to you later.'

Mum has a bag of Christmas presents in the car, and I tell her that I will send theirs with Lou.

We huddle and hug at the side of Dad's car boot as carrier

bags are shifted around and pleasantries exchanged. Then the wind gets up and rain starts to spit from a darkening sky.

'Thanks for all the pressies,' I say.

'And the meal,' says Jay.

'Have a safe journey back. See you soon,' I say.

'Merry Christmas,' says Jay, although it's weeks away and he's not even looking at them any more, and Mum's not looking at us either: she's rummaging through her bag for her umbrella.

* * *

Winter charges in and freezes everything. We take hot water bottles to bed, wear scarves and fingerless gloves around the house. The front room fire is stoked up as well as the Rayburn in the kitchen and we keep all the internal doors open to circulate heat into the icy loft bedroom. Our breath makes perpetual haloes around our heads. The water in the toilet freezes and I squat over the bowl because it is too unbearably cold to sit on the seat. Fronds of ice grow on the insides of all the windows. Central heating becomes an aspiration.

During the night I am jolted from my dreams as Jay jumps from the bed and lunges towards the window.

'What's wrong?' I climb out after him and hear the screeches as he pulls open the skylight.

'Fox,' he says.

It is there, drenched in milky moonbeams: a pitted, mangy animal. The cockerel squawks and flaps in its jaws. Another chicken gasps and flutters on the frosty grass, its feathers scattered like ripped love letters.

I can't move my body as Jay hurtles downstairs. The house rattles as he tugs the door open. I touch the cold glass and my breath chokes me as my heart booms and races. The fox sees Jay and lopes away into the forest with the cockerel between his jaws. The other chicken lies still. I feel my perfect way of life being stolen away.

'It's one of those things,' Jay says. 'It's a fact of nature, it's about survival of the fittest. The strongest and cleverest creatures kill the weakest ones. It's brutal, but that's just how life is.'

It's how love is, too. Martin was so much stronger and cleverer than me, able to take advantage of *my* weaknesses for years, all under the guise of love. He survived the endless gossip and judgement, keeping his job and home and family, while I ended up humiliated and broken, losing everything. He was the fox and I was the chicken. It was indeed brutal.

The chickens are all dead. It's the day after, and we bury them: Jay lays the mutilated bodies of the chickens into a grave and I go and look at the chicken house to see how the fox could have got in. A hole has been tunnelled under the coop. I collect two cold eggs from the nest box.

We go back inside to stare at the fire and open a bottle of wine, and I cry on Jay's shoulder.

'We'll build a better coop and get some more,' he says. He wipes at my tears with his rough thumb.

I sob and sob and realise that he's never seen me cry like this before. But he holds me and strokes my hair tenderly for a long, long time.

And later, he presses his face to mine.

'Special kiss,' is all he whispers, and I'm ready. I'm really needing my special kiss, because it always makes everything better.

* * *

A week has gone by and today it snows, the most we have had for decades. The main road is impassable; we hear nothing but silence and the creak of our feet in the deep white blanket as we go outside to get logs for the stove. We are isolated. We cannot contact anyone; for five days even the post doesn't come. The electricity goes off for seven hours on Wednesday and three hours on Thursday. We talk and drink and eat tinned food that has been in the cupboard for months: sardines, mushy peas, spaghetti hoops. We write new tunes and begin to record some tracks when the electricity is on. We watch the weather reports and the incessant coverage of gritting complaints, school closures and abandoned cars on the motorways. We see nothing of Rick. We are together, with no one else.

It's now that I mention the lonely-hearts adverts: it just feels like the right time. I'm careful with my words, though. The snow and solitude sharpen me.

'I went on a blind date once. It was quite surreal. A fellow musician vaguely knew this bloke through a brass band or something and set us up.' I laugh, brightly, and sip my coffee. Jay watches, smiling cautiously across the kitchen table. 'We went to a Mexican restaurant and the food was just so incredibly spicy. Eye-watering, mouth-on-fire kind of thing. Well, it set him off – I can't even remember his name – into some sort of fit. I don't mean epileptic, but like loads of tics and spasms. And all the time he was doing these jerky movements he was trying to tell me about the massive Action Man collection that he had, still in original boxes. I just sat there, sort of stunned, while he blinked and twitched and prattled on about grip-on hands and things. It was so uncomfortable. Never again.'

'You didn't go to bed with him then?' says Jay.

'Nooo,' I wince. I've exaggerated a bit about the twitching, but I needed to create the right atmosphere. 'What about you? Ever done a blind date?'

'Not really,' he replies, shrugging.

'What about dating websites, or ads in the paper? Ever done that sort of thing?'

He thinks, and he looks like he's going to confess something, but then it's as if he's seen how intensely I'm searching his face, or he's managed to read my mind because the mood just switches.

'What's all this about?' His eyes are icy and impenetrable like the lane outside.

'I just wondered...'

'You're trying to trick me into saying something, and then you're going to say that you've found something out and make it look like I'm hiding things.'

'Of course I'm not.' But obviously I am. I decide to do the right thing and come clean. 'I just spotted some lonely-hearts things that you'd marked in an old newspaper, that's all. I'm not accusing you of anything.'

'What are you trying to say? That I'm a perv or something?'

''Course I'm not saying that. I'm just curious, that's all. Let's not get into an argument.'

He stands up and walks over to the Rayburn. Crouches to riddle the ashes, then opens the door and tosses on another two logs.

'Lonely hearts,' he says, with his back to me. 'I was lonely at the time, been on my own for a while. I felt like I needed someone.'

I keep my mouth shut, but he knows I need more of an answer than that.

'I looked through quite a few. But I only replied to one. She sounded OK in her description and I arranged to meet her. She was already there waiting – in some pub out near Ashover – and I suppose I was a bit nervous. But when I saw her, well. I had a bit of a gander while I stood at the bar – made it look like I was with another group so she wouldn't know it was me – and then did a runner. She wasn't my type, I could tell straight away.'

'You just stood her up?'

'She wasn't what I expected. A bit on the big side. With the stupid fake duck lips. And her hair looked common. I prefer women with nice hair, but she'd got these sort of blonde streaky highlight things on top of black, and it was all straightened, just didn't look real. So I didn't bother.'

How do I believe him? All those pages of newspaper zealously ringed and underlined.

The logs rumble and settle into the stove.

'Well, you've got me now,' I say, 'you don't need to bother with blind dates.'

He turns and comes towards me, touches my face, then sinks his hands into my hair, lifting the locks and letting them run over his fingers like sand.

'Yep,' he says. 'You're all mine.'

CHAPTER SEVENTEEN

By Saturday lunchtime Jay is fractious. He tramps in and out, in and out for no reason, bringing cakes of snow on his boots that melt into pools on the kitchen floor.

'This house just won't warm up today,' he remarks, tucking his fingers under his armpits.

He's like a child that needs to burn off energy. For long periods he stands at the window and won't sit down. I offer to take him to bed but he ignores me. I wonder if he's missing Rick.

'Let's go for a walk,' I suggest. 'We could go up to the village and buy ourselves a treat from the Co-op. Whisky or rum or something to warm us up.'

'Nah. It'd take hours to get there in this weather. We'd die of hypothermia first.'

'Isn't there a different way?' I ask. 'You know, public foot-paths across fields? It looks to me like it would be much shorter going the other way round the pit tip rather than along the road.'

'You can't get round that way,' says Jay.

'But you know what I mean? If you took a path along the

side of our house, as if you were continuing the direction of the lane, I bet it would be less than a mile to the village.'

Jay doesn't answer. He's still looking out of the window.

I try again. 'You know, there's like a path towards that field...'

'For God's sake,' says Jay, 'why do you never believe me? Sometimes you just go on and on and I don't think you realise you're even doing it.'

He glares at me as I sit, stunned, on the rumpled sofa. Then goes into the kitchen, pulls on his coat and gloves, and with a stony face drags me up from my seat.

'Come on.'

'What?' I say.

'The path you're on about... I'll show you.'

And he's out in it, wading through the ridge of snow along the side of the house, with me struggling behind him, trying to keep my feet in his furrows, and we're into an expanse of bright whiteness, so dazzling and disorientating it makes you squint, it's like something out of a dream sequence in a film and we're heading further and further into nothing and my head and my eyes are hurting from the cold and the brilliance and my jeans are soaked up to my thighs and I can feel the skin of my legs red-raw underneath.

'Stop,' I shout to Jay, but my lips are numb; my face must be blue.

I stand and wait as he turns and strides back towards me. He grabs my hand and pulls.

'No,' I say. 'Let's go back, I'm freezing.'

He drags me with both hands, and I half-slide, half-stumble along his tracks.

'I can't,' I say. 'Please. It's too cold.'

His fingers are digging into my upper arm. His face is red with the effort.

'I want to show you something.' He holds on as if he thinks I might run away.

'What is it?'

He manoeuvres me so that I am in front of him. 'Keep going.'

'Where to?' I plough on into the arctic landscape.

He doesn't answer. There is no noise apart from the groan of our footsteps in the snow. It sounds like ropes on timber: a ship lost in fog. My feet are dead, beyond pain. I can't differentiate between the land and sky. Jay presses a hand into my back and I lurch forward.

'What?' My voice is high-pitched: it surprises and unnerves me as if someone else had made the sound.

But, being musical, my ears are trained and I hear the resonance of the word: the length and bounce of it as it lingers, almost an echo. And it is like a warning, so that I am uncannily aware before the next thing that happens which is either Jay saying 'stop' or me gasping at the sheer drop and cliff edge. And perhaps Jay's hand wasn't pushing my back, it was pulling me away, because here we are, on the lip of the quarry with its guts hollowed out and my frozen toes at the highest precipice of its deep, deep cavity.

It's not just the cold and the echo that does it. It's the shock of seeing the horrific drop, the actual deathly distance down to the bottom, because I suddenly find myself on my back, screaming, thrashing around in the snow with Jay trying to wrestle me to my feet. Icy tears are running down my cheeks and I am shivering uncontrollably as he pulls me up.

Jay laughs and squeezes his arms around me, rubs my nose with his.

'What are you like?' he says, his voice slurred from the frigid air. 'It's a great view from here.'

I can't look. I might have been down there, dead. He kisses my hair.

'See, I told you,' he says. 'You can't get round here to the village. There's the bloody great quarry in the way.'

He tucks me up in bed with a hot water bottle and a mug of sweetened Ovaltine. I press my face into the duvet. I can't find any words to say to him. He goes downstairs and I hear the buzz of the television and the click of his tobacco tin lid. Snow creaks on the roof above me. After my body finally stops trembling, I sleep for fourteen hours.

* * *

'Tell me about when you were a teenager,' says Jay.

I snort an indignant laugh. 'You tell me first.'

We sit cross-legged on the shaggy rug in front of the fire with a pack of cards abandoned between us. The snow still has us trapped: it has drifted above the living room windowsill now.

'What about you tell me three confessions, then I'll tell you?' he says.

'What sort of confessions?'

'Something you got up to when you were younger,' he says.

I don't know if I like the sound of this.

'OK,' I say, slowly, wondering what I will choose to tell him. I will start with Lou.

'Hmm. First one. Me and Lou, when we were kids, about nine or ten I think, we used to play in the graveyard quite often. It had some weird appeal. We used to steal flowers off the posh graves and put them on this really old, small grave that no one ever visited. All it had engraved on it was "Samuel, one day old".'

Jay has gone all pensive, as if his smile is trapped in his mouth.

'The vicar caught us one day and gave us a right telling.

Threatened to call our parents.' I pause and wait for Jay to say something but he doesn't. 'I thought you'd like that story. You know, with it being about wealth redistribution.'

He nods. 'Yeah.' But he's still thinking about something else. He tops up our glasses. It's homemade, from a red wine kit that makes thirty bottles in seven days.

'She sounds all right, your sister,' he says. 'What's she like?'

'She used to be nicer when we were younger. She's a bit of a snob now.'

'I mean, what does she look like? Does she look like you?'

'We looked more alike when we were children, really. Her hair is shorter than mine, not as dark. Her lips are thinner. She's slightly taller but probably a size smaller than me. She always envied my cheekbones though.' I touch my face, remember Lou's. 'You'll get to meet her soon. You can check out our similarities then.'

'OK,' says Jay. 'So... next confession.'

'Hmm... Once I stole a bottle of gin out of my parents' drinks cabinet and took it to school. Me and four others got off our tits in geography.'

'Nah,' he says. 'Everybody did that. That's not original enough.'

I wonder whether to tell him, whether to Confess My Sins. Perhaps I will just mention part of it, tone it down a bit.

'I got fingered by Lou's best friend's dad when I was fifteen?'

'Whoa,' he says. He shifts his legs, rippling the rug, and sits up straighter. 'What was it, abuse or something?' I can tell he's not sure whether to be disgusted or turned on.

'He was quite good-looking for an older man. Well, I suppose he would have only been about thirty-eight or so. But I went with Lou to a New Year's do at their house – I'd had a couple of ciders and came on to him a bit and he was pretty ratted too. I ended up snogging him and he managed to grope me in the utility room.'

That's all I will tell him about Martin. Jay doesn't need to know how I became obsessed with him after he took me out in his car and bought me gifts and told me that he was devoted to me more than anyone else in the world, more than his wife or daughter. How he made me feel so special that I thought sex with him was the physical embodiment of our love. How I was convinced that at some point he would leave his family home and be exclusively mine. But it was all a con. Lou was right. What I thought for years was a long-term relationship had actually been grooming that started when I was a child. It's something that I have only just come to realise now I have left it all behind and got a new start for myself.

'Wow,' says Jay. 'He sounds like a bit of a pervert.'

I shrug, wondering why I had not thought the same all those years ago, saving myself all the heartbreak.

Jay tells me that he almost got expelled from primary school for setting fire to kids' shoes with a magnifying glass. He tells me that he stole a television from the Mallet and Chisel pub: borrowed a TV repair boiler suit and just walked into the tap room one Sunday lunchtime while the dinners were being plated up, unscrewed the screen from the wall and carried it out. Funny thing is, he's even been in there for a beer a couple of times since.

'Tell me something rude,' I say. 'I told you about being fingered.'

'I didn't lose my virginity until I was eighteen,' he says self-consciously. 'I was skinny-dipping with a mate's sister in the pond at the bottom of the woods and things got a bit carried away. Didn't use johnnies or anything. And nearly got my knob bitten off by midges.'

I wish I hadn't asked. His confession unsettles me although I don't know why. He picks up the wine bottle and sees there's none left. Puts it on the hearth again. I look at the window. Snow is still coming down: big, dizzying, feathery clusters that fall and dodge unpredictably so you can't follow the path of any particular one.

'Anyway,' he says, 'you still haven't told me about... what's her name?'

'Who?' I ask.

'Your mum mentioned someone. Nell.'

I gulp down a lump in my throat. It doesn't feel right, talking about her here, in the place I have inhabited to cure her grief out of me.

'She was my best friend. It felt like she was all I had at the time.'

'Go on.'

I draw in a deep breath. 'She died quite unexpectedly. At a point when I needed her the most. That sounds selfish, doesn't it? She probably needed me too and I just didn't realise... I don't know.' A wave of emotion smothers me, the room tilts and my face is suddenly wet with tears.

'Babe.' Jay pulls me into his arms and kisses my hair, my ears, my neck.

I don't want to feel like this. My sorrow is out of place here. I want to be happy, to feel the joy that lies trapped in the little pills in his pocket.

'Please?' I ask, and he's ready, because he already knows what I want. He knows me, almost better than I know myself now.

* * *

The last day of November. Jay is twitchy, pacing in front of the window. He has been outside three or four times to see if the snow has melted on the road, or if the four-wheel drives from the posh houses have cleared a path that he could follow in.

'I might give it a go,' he says but he doesn't look at me. He knows I will say that we don't need anything, we are all right here with each other and there's food in the cupboard and in the garden.

He finds the motorbike keys and his helmet and stands there, feeling in all his jeans pockets for no reason. 'It's not too bad out there now. Seems like it's thawing. And there's loads of stuff we need. Cig papers, milk, butter, bread.'

'I was going to bake some bread today,' I say. 'We don't need butter, there's loads in the fridge if you move things and look properly, and we can manage without milk a bit longer if you use the coffee whitener.'

'Rizlas?' he says, as if I'm stupid.

'Well, why don't we take the camper and go and do a proper shop?' I ask. 'Surely that's safer than riding a bike in this?'

'It probably won't start,' Jay says. 'Battery's been dodgy for a while. And you don't realise how crap it is in snow. I'll just get a couple of things and come straight back.'

So off he goes. I stand on the drive and watch him taking it steady with feet stuck out like a child trying to balance on a first bicycle. He's siphoned away into the whiteness. I blow into my hands and totter gingerly towards the kitchen door. He's gone to Rick's, I'm sure he has.

I'm going to prove to him that we didn't need anything getting. That we could have survived another day or two, or three without going to the shop.

I get vegetables from the shed, and chop and fry them. I add herbs, lentils, stock cube, slosh of white wine and water. I leave everything to simmer to a thick, bubbling soup while I bake bread. The kitchen is warm and full of comforting winter smells. I consider making a cake while the bread is rising, but I can't bring myself to use the eggs that sit in the fridge. Jay says we will get more chickens, probably in the spring: he will put bolts on the henhouse, make the fencing fox-proof. I don't want to think about it yet.

Jay returns a couple of hours later. The bread is in the oven and I am stirring the soup.

'Mmm,' he says, kicking the bottom of the kitchen door into place so that the catch clicks shut. 'Smells good.'

I say nothing. I carry on stirring. I don't mention the fact that it doesn't take two hours to go to the village shop, even in the snow. He stands beside me and looks into the saucepan. Then kisses my cheek.

'You're so good at this self-sufficiency thing, you know,' he says. 'And gorgeous. And a good shag.'

Why am I always seduced by him? Tricked into smiling by a certain phrase, or a wink, or a touch? And then there's the special kiss. I ought to be stronger, I really ought to be.

*

'Keep still.' He holds her chin while he drags the lipstick around her lips. It's not easy to be precise in the sputtering candlelight.

'Scarlet looks good on you, Ruthie,' he says. 'You should wear it more often.'

He stands back a little to take in the effect, to see what more needs to be done. She dangles casually on the ropes, arms in a submissive position behind her head.

'Let's undo a few buttons.' The tiny silver fastenings are tricky, but he feeds them through the holes one by one, until the bodice is splayed and her breasts are exposed. 'Lovely. That looks perfect.'

Momentum and adrenaline are both building in him and he enjoys the thrill of the anticipation as much as everything else.

'Oh God, Ruthie, kiss me.' He moves in and swoops his mouth onto hers, hard and rough. She knows what he likes, and her tongue is there, searching, hungry, as he presses himself solidly against her. Their saliva mixes, wets their chins, and then he pulls away to drag his face down to her breasts, to gorge himself, the scarlet lipstick spreading like blood over her nipples.

'Tell me what I need to hear, Ruthie. Please, tell me.' He murmurs into her skin as he hoists the skirt of her dress.

'I love you.'

'I love you too, Ruthie. I'll love you until we die.' He spins her body round on the rope to face the wall and rips down her knickers.

CHAPTER EIGHTEEN

DECEMBER

A grey sky sags with the threat of rain. Mucky mounds of snow on the pavements have melted and exposed dog crap and litter. Pound shops are heaving with children being forced to buy Christmas presents for distant relatives. Down in the precinct, the Salvation Army band are playing carols. Plump ladies in their uniforms and tightly fastened bonnets rattle tins at the passers-by. Cornets and euphoniums and trombones parp and oomp seasonal spirit.

'Let's have some time apart,' I say to Jay as I lay my violin in the case and fold the velvet lining around it. He stuffs the heavy carrier bag of change into the pocket of his guitar case. I can tell he's satisfied by the way he has been weighing it in his hands, spanning the sphere it makes inside the plastic.

'What do you mean?' He's still thinking about the money, guessing the amount of it, wondering if we should have played more Christmas songs.

'I just mean let's go and do some shopping separately. So I can buy you a present.'

'All right,' he says. 'Back at the van in an hour then.'

He walks in the direction of the car park as I stride towards the shopping centre. I know he will sit in the camper and count the money; he won't be able to wait until we get home.

The good-looking bloke from the solicitors came again today: he must have heard us from his office while we were in our spot outside the empty frozen food shop. He stood in front of us in his suit and tie and expensive shoes; locked eyes with me as he took out his wallet and slowly pulled a fiver out. Dropped it in the fiddle case with a smile and a quick wink that was no more than the flick of an eyebrow. He didn't look at the note. It could have been a twenty for all he knew. He walked away. I carried on playing the tune and watched him. He turned and looked back. Jay bobbed and snatched the fiver up before any kids could come and steal it.

I walk through the precinct. I have no intention of buying Christmas presents. What I do is go into Wilko, upstairs to the home department. I buy a huge mirror, the largest that can fit under my arm. It has a black frame, mock art deco. I buy a black chenille rug, a green gingham roller blind, and another tin of cream paint. All these things are for the bathroom that needs doing before Lou comes.

* * *

Sometimes I say the wrong thing. It just comes out, usually when I've been drinking. Like last night. We were wasted again, not completely, but guards were down and we were at the point where the conversation was flowing. And in those times, I don't want him to stop. I want him to open up and tell me everything about himself. And he was doing just that. He was telling me about the day after he left school at the age of sixteen: how he'd

argued with his mother's new boyfriend, the one she went to
Spain with. Jay was livid. He'd been told to clear off, so he'd
packed all his stuff into two carriers, nicked twenty quid from
his mum's purse and walked it to Bolsover. He'd kipped down at
a mate's house for a few nights, then ended up squatting with a
couple of other lads in one of the derelict pit houses. Later, he
got a job in the local chippy five nights a week where the leftovers kept him fed. Life hadn't been too bad. He'd had a
mattress and a sleeping bag. There had been running water in
the house. And it was during that time he'd learned to play the
guitar, a cheap acoustic thing he'd picked up from Cash
Converters.

He'd paused at that point, like he was remembering a signif-
icant moment. I almost expected him to start talking about Ruth
again, but I was glad that he didn't. She takes up too much negative space in my head: I've never met her but I have the sense
that she's not a good person with all the secrecy around her.
And I'm pretty sure that she's still in the locality, still in contact
with Jay, and Rick too.

So, I don't know why I said it, or why I said it at that point.
It was just one of those completely random things and not even
anything to do with the conversation we'd been having. But
we'd had a bottle and a half of red wine and I just asked him if
he'd ever thought what it might be like to kill someone.

* * *

The walls glisten with moisture. I try to wipe away the damp
and condensation but every day it's back. It's running down the
windows, pooling on the ledges and growing triangles of blackness in the corners of the ceilings. Sometimes I long for the ease
and cleanliness of the flat that I shared with Rachel.

The bathroom is my task today. I have scoured the grubby

tile grout with a toothbrush and thick bleach. I have only just started painting the area above the toilet when there is a hammering on the door. I sneak into the hallway to peek through the living room window and see the campervan in the drive. The kitchen door shakes in its frame from Jay's kicks.

'Calm down,' I shout as I unbolt it.

Jay pushes in and strides through to the living room like he's looking for something. 'What are you locked in for?'

'I always lock the door when I'm on my own,' I say.

He looks at me. His eyebrows are lifted.

'What? I've been doing the bathroom.'

He strolls over and pokes his head around the door. 'Has anyone else called in?'

'Like who?' I begin to laugh. 'You're not thinking I'm having it away with the postman, are you?'

He grins and smacks my arse. 'Just checking.'

I go back into the bathroom. Jay comes and presses his body to the back of mine as I drag the paintbrush up and down the wall. He nibbles my neck. Then he gets another brush and makes a start on the wall above the bath. It feels good, working together. Knowing that there's an edge of jealousy to him: he's possessive about me. I like that.

By lunchtime we're done. Jay goes to wash the brushes in the kitchen sink and I clean out the bath, trying to get a gleam on the plastic. Foamy water laps around the sides and won't go down the plughole.

'Have we got a plunger?' I yell to Jay, and he returns with a misshapen bit of rubber on a stick and his sleeves rolled up.

He dunks it in and out a few times. It slurps and pulls up black gunky balls of hair. The water starts moving. He plunges again. Pulls out more detritus like a magician with a string of handkerchiefs up his sleeve.

'Hair,' he says when all the water has gone down. A handful

big enough to stuff a soft toy with. It's someone else's hair, not mine. Maybe it's *hers*. Ruth's.

Long black strands dangle from his hand. Wet and matted with old soap scum. It drips onto the clean lino, and my stomach flips.

CHAPTER NINETEEN

I asked Jay about the squat he lived in. The thought of it: it was something that unsettled yet excited me. But I reckoned that if I could get him to keep opening up to me then maybe it would ease some of my worries, take away some of my suspicions.

He said the other lads had squatted in places before. Budgie and Jonno. They were older than him by a few years, looked after him, showed him how you could get stuff out of skips to use or sell at car boot sales: old furniture, copper pipe, bath taps, half-decent carpet.

Jay said it had been a fun time, an adventure, an experience. But then Budgie and Jonno, they took it up a gear. Started thieving. Not just people's throwaway stuff, but proper break-ins.

Then things changed. There'd be people calling at the squat, different people, shady characters. There'd be furtive huddles with Budgie and kids off the estate, and Jonno being dead secretive about what was in the scruffy rucksack that he took everywhere. Their mobiles were ringing all the time. The squat lost its chilled-out vibe. Jay knew they were dealing.

'Dealing what?' I asked.

Es, crack, even heroin.

'I wasn't involved in all that business, though,' Jay said. 'But I was looking over my shoulder all the time. That's what it felt like. Guilty by association.'

'But you must have had a sense of that all the time. Living in a squat. Waiting to get kicked out.'

'This was different,' he said. 'This was waiting for another kid to die on drugs, or somebody's dad or brother or uncle to kick our door down and stab us while we slept, or set fire to the place, or get raided by the cops. This wasn't fun any more.'

* * *

The cold persists into a monotony of jumpers and scarves and gloves. I spend most days huddled over the fire, poking at damp wood. Sometimes in the afternoons I crawl into bed with my clothes on and stare at the greyness and sleet that throws itself at the roof window.

I remember Rachel's flat and how you could walk around in T-shirts and bare feet in the winter. I think about Lou's under-floor system on automatic timers. I think about the perfection of her carpets and curtains and the absence of mould around her windows. I remember that she will be coming here in five days.

In front of me is an incomplete shopping list: feta cheese, marinated roasted vegetables, artichoke hearts, smoked salmon, small granary rolls (part-baked). I sit on the rug with the duvet pulled around me. Flames jive on a gnarl of birch in the fire grate. *Come Dine with Me* is on the television and the first contestant has just forgotten to put sugar in her fruit crumble topping. I add 'strawberries' to the list and wonder where I can get decent-flavoured ones at this time of year.

There is a thumping at the door: it only opens with a good booting at the base now.

'What are you up to?' Jay is back, pulling his gloves off and tossing them onto the sofa.

'Shopping list,' I tell him. 'Just a few things for Lou coming next week.'

'Why don't we go into town now? I've nothing else to do this afternoon.'

But everything needs to be fresh, not five days old. I would rather go on my own: Jay doesn't need to know how much everything costs. And I have to get a new duvet set for the bedroom. Perhaps a matching lamp.

'Don't worry,' I say. 'I'll go next week. I know you only get bored shopping.'

I fold the list into a tight rectangle and push it into my pocket.

'Let's get a Christmas tree outside the front of the house,' I say to Jay.

'Why don't we have one inside?' he says. 'So *we* can see it.'

'Both,' I reply. 'But a huge one with lots of lights outside. It would make the place look so nice.'

It would block out the ugly fifties brickwork and flaking window frames, distract eyes from the crumbling concrete drive.

'We could get one with roots on it in a big pot, you know, one of those wooden barrel types to have as a permanent feature.'

Jay asks if I'm just trying to keep up with the houses further down the lane. I laugh at his remark. But of course I am. Lou will have to drive past half a dozen stunning properties before she reaches our house. There's no back way to take her.

'Are you wanting me to sort us out with something?' Jay asks. 'Off the estate?'

I don't normally condone that sort of thing, but the size of tree I want from the garden centre would cost over a hundred pounds.

'Don't get into trouble for it,' I say.

The estate has got acres and acres of woodland. The Duke of wherever won't miss a couple of Christmas trees.

I explain to Jay that ideally, for outside, I would like a tree at least seven or eight feet high, and the long-needled variety that have the upward flicking branches, rather than the prickly short-needled ones.

Jay smiles and scrabbles the top of my head. 'I'll get whatever's easiest to dig up and fit in the van without being seen.'

* * *

I drive the camper into town and park in the precinct car park. The shops are busy with dithering old people, and young mums pushing irritable kids in pushchairs, and unshaven men zipping about irresponsibly on mobility scooters. Windows display glitzy tat and the tinny whine of a cover version of 'Last Christmas' trickles into the shopping centre.

Outside the broad window of a shoe shop, I stand and envy a pair of jade stilettos that seduce me with their glamorous shine and sleek pointed toes. They are only twenty-five pounds, reduced from fifty. A few months ago, I would have bought them in a shot. But now... I have to make do with admiring them and remembering the parties and wine bars that used to be part of my life.

'They would look fantastic on you,' a low voice murmurs over my shoulder.

I turn and see the blond guy from the solicitors grinning at me.

'Go on,' he urges, 'treat yourself.'

'I was just looking. They're not really my sort of thing.'

I stand there, in well-worn walking boots and jeans, with an old grey parka that belongs to Jay hanging off my shoulders.

'You had longing in your eyes.' He shakes his finger at me. 'I saw it. You wanted them. And I bet they're just your size.'

'True.' I laugh. 'Good guess.' I can't tell him that I can't afford them.

He looks at his watch. 'Hey,' he says, 'what about a coffee? I've got a spare hour and nothing to do.'

I'm tempted. Then I wonder what Jay would think. Then I wonder what Lou would think. Then I remember that I've got two hours parking left on the camper.

'OK,' I say.

We go to Costa and sit on a slippery leather sofa with cappuccinos and blueberry muffins on the low table in front of us.

His name is Damien – a name you would have thought, he said, after *The Omen*, no mother would have wanted to call her child – and he works for a firm of solicitors, dealing with divorces, custody battles, conveyancing and neighbour disputes.

He asks about me, and I tell him my name and that I play the violin.

'What happened to your wrist?' he asks with a furrow between his eyebrows.

I pull my sleeve down over the imperious red welt.

'Oh, nothing. It's probably a gardening injury.' I notice a bruise fading to green on the back of my other hand and tuck it away under my thigh.

He watches me with a concerned face, which deepens the cleft in his chin. 'Are you OK?'

I give a plausible laugh. 'Yes, I'm fine. Everything's great. I do a lot of outdoor stuff and we've got chickens and the shed door can sometimes be a bit tricky to open...'

'I just wanted to check. I'm not prying or anything but... Oh God this is sounding wrong, I don't know but. Well, I just had this kind of sense and got worried about you. So if you ever want to talk... But, well you're obviously all right.' He's flustered, feeling in his jacket pocket, then looking quickly at his watch. 'Oh shit, I just remembered something.'

Suddenly he stands and puts his cup on the table. 'Could you just hang on here two minutes? Don't go. I'll be back pronto.'

I sip my coffee and stare out of the window. And, almost immediately, he is back, beaming, pushing a carrier bag onto my lap and saying, 'Happy Christmas.'

'I can't. Really, I can't.' I don't take the shoes out of the bag and look at them: I grip them awkwardly while making feeble protestations.

'Well, I can't return them now and they'd look ridiculous on me,' says Damien. 'Please. Just enjoy wearing them.'

'Thank you. You're really kind.' My face is flushed with embarrassment. I put the bag on the floor next to my other one that has fallen over letting the Toilet Duck slip out. I knock my elbow on the table as I fumble to push it back in, and as I rub my funny bone Damien says, 'I need to get going now,' and leans to kiss my cheek just as I turn at the wrong moment so that his kiss hits my lips. And it's then that I see Maria in the queue, six feet away, looking directly at me.

Perhaps I should have gone straight up to her, been honest, explained there and then. And although I replayed the scene in my head so many times afterwards, rewinding it and having me moving away from Damien's kiss, or giving back the shoes, or going straight up to her and saying, 'Look it was nothing, he's just a friend,' what I did was the stupidest thing. I made out that I hadn't seen her. I let Damien leave and sat for a minute or so pretending to drink the coffee that I had already finished. Then I gathered up the carrier bags and without looking in Maria's direction, manoeuvred through the tables and pushchairs – smiling at a slavering child – and strode back to the camper, where I took off my boots and socks, slid my feet into the cold new shoes and drove home.

CHAPTER TWENTY

There's nothing more to be done, really. But I keep busy. Picking fluff off the rug. Re-stacking the logs at the side of the fire. Tweaking the curtains.

'Leave it,' says Jay. 'It looks fine.'

Fine? I have transformed this place in fewer than four months on a very tight budget. Although there is still the bedroom to do properly. A new duvet set and co-ordinated runner can only go so far in such a grotty space.

He flops into a chair and takes out his tobacco tin.

'Can't you go outside?' I say. 'Please? Lou doesn't smoke and I don't want the place to smell.'

He huffs and puffs and gets up again. I smooth out the throw that he's ruffled. Check my wristwatch. Carefully poke the fire so that the flames flicker evenly across the wood.

There are two seven quid bottles of Chardonnay chilling in the fridge. There are cling-filmed dishes of deli items: things that are drizzled with olive oil and strewn with torn basil. A bag of beetroot and parsnip crisps that sits waiting to be tipped into a bowl. Roasted peppers from Delia's recipe. A rustic-looking goats' cheese and red onion quiche that I made myself but used

Sainsbury's ready-made shortcrust. Greek salad. Tray of small, seeded rolls waiting to be warmed through in the Rayburn. Jay, intrigued, observed me putting out all this fare, watched me moving the plates around on the new red-checked tablecloth until it looked like the front cover of *Good Food* magazine.

We have a Christmas tree in the living room, twinkling and decorated with purple and silver baubles and beads. We have an enormous spruce outside, some sort of medium-needled variety that snagged most of my hair as we tugged it out of the van. It sits in a planter that Jay has constructed out of old pallet wood and painted black. The lights flash gently in a subtle way, unlike some of the more gaudy, spasmodic ones I've seen on other trees.

'Don't let all the cold in,' I shout to Jay as he smokes on the kitchen doorstep.

Suddenly, there's the noise of an engine at the front of the house.

'They're here,' he calls.

I go through to meet them as they appear on the doorstep.

Lou comes in first.

'Oh,' she says, looking down at the kitchen floor. 'Is it shoes off or not?'

I know she's making a snide comment about the tiles, just because there are a few cracked ones. She doesn't realise how much I've scrubbed and polished them.

'Keep them on,' I reply. 'Don't worry about the floor.'

She gazes around the room with a condescending expression on her face, and Dom pushes past her to give me a hug.

'This is a bit out of the way,' he says. 'Probably knackered my suspension, bouncing along that lane.'

Jay comes in and closes the door. He touches Lou's shoulder and she turns to fasten her eyes on his. There is a sudden spill of pink through the foundation on her cheeks. She clasps her hands together and twiddles with her wedding ring.

Suddenly, Jay looks across at me, breaks the spell. 'Anyone want a drink?'

'There's wine in the fridge,' I say quickly, bustling to get the chilled bottle out before Jay starts offering home-brew. Dom takes his coat off and hands it to Jay and they go through to the living room. Lou is still by the door. I catch her eye. She blinks and glances away. Stoops down and takes off her shoes after all.

'That was a bit intense,' Jay says later. He pours the rest of the Chardonnay into his glass.

Lou and Dominic have just left. My nerves are frayed. The edges of me are chipped, splintered. My head thumps.

'I need a drink.' I pick up the wine bottle and squint at its emptiness. 'Get me some wine. Anything. Home-brew.'

Jay goes out to the shed. I begin to clear the table. Put the rest of the roasted peppers in the space where half the quiche has been. Cling-film the bowls again. Put the remaining rolls into the bread bin.

'What did you think?' I ask Jay when he returns with two bottles of elderberry that was harsh and earthy when we sampled it a fortnight ago.

'She seemed all right. Husband was a bit up himself though.'

'What do you mean?'

'Well, you know.' He sips and thinks. 'Using long words and things. I just thought he was a bit of a ponce. Beige jumper. Who wears beige jumpers?'

'He's normally OK,' I say. 'The jumper was probably an expensive designer one. Anyway, I thought it might be Lou who would offend you.'

'Well, to say you went to so much trouble with the food, she could have made an effort to eat some of it.'

'She's strange with her eating,' I explain. 'She can't do it in front of people.'

I wondered if she might have made the effort on this occasion. At one point she leaned over the dish of olives as if to take one, extending her forefinger and thumb quite elegantly to display her manicured nails. But she just picked out a hair – one of mine in fact – and made a great show of tottering to the sink to drop it in. Later though, after the rest of us had eaten and were sitting in the living room, Lou got up and said she was going to the bathroom. I watched her through the crack in the door: she had slipped into the kitchen and was cramming a slice of quiche into her mouth.

'Well, on the plus side, there are some nice leftovers for us tomorrow,' says Jay.

The Christmas tree twinkles in the corner. Lou's presents to us are underneath. They are wrapped in a quality gold-coloured paper, wound around with red velvet ribbon. They clash with my baubles and beads. I might put them away in the bedroom until we open them.

'You seemed awkward with her,' Jay says. 'Not as sisterly as I expected you to be.'

'Did I?' I can feel a flush on my cheeks. It's probably the alcohol. 'Well, I haven't seen her for ages. And we weren't on particularly good terms the last time I saw her. Maybe we need to clear the air properly rather than just gloss over things and pretend it's all sorted.'

'So, you had a fallout?' he says. 'What was that about?'

I really don't want to talk about her tonight. My head is full of her. I am sapped with the remembrance of the day: how she behaved with Jay, the comments she made, the expressions on her face as she looked around the house, each smirk and flinch and word. When I get to bed I will go over it all and work out what she meant by it.

'Some other time,' I say. I pour another glass.

Interesting, in a sort of quaint way. That's how Lou described the house. Her tone was sardonic when she said 'how tiny' at the bathroom, without mentioning the colour of the suite. She winced and giggled at the bedroom, describing the dark furniture as 'wartime'. And the living room: 'a hotchpotch of styles,' she said, as if she was Sarah Beeny or somebody. I wanted to show her the garden. Desperately. I wanted her to see the other side of where I live, the forest, the lush grass, the plants with their vivid hues that make your heart jump, the weeded rows of vegetables, the sitting areas, the secret corners and the winding paths. The real side. I wanted her to see it as I saw it for the first time: to take her back to that summer's day with its cyan sky and scents of roses and sounds of birdsong. The garden was twenty times bigger and twenty times better than her garden: even she would have to admit that. But everything was covered in snow. She wouldn't even walk halfway down the path to get an idea of it. Said she had the wrong shoes on.

She was impressed by Jay though. She never said, but I could tell by the way she blushed when he spoke to her, could tell by the way she kept sneaking looks at him, studying his profile. At one point I overheard her in the kitchen with Jay, with him saying that she would look fantastic with jet black hair, and her giggling and saying, 'Really, do you think so?' and I could just imagine the teasing, pouty looks she would be giving him. Oh, I know that she would never let herself go for that type. She always goes for the clean, smart, safe ones: boy band members and young sports presenters would be ideal. Or Damien. But I could tell that if she were to go in for a bit of rough she wouldn't kick Jay out of bed.

* * *

Lolly turned up the other day. Just came at twenty past eleven
one Thursday morning. I said I didn't know that the schools had
broken up yet, and she just gazed up at me through that bush of
orange hair, with a rascally look on her face, and I gathered from
her expression that she should have been at school but she just
hadn't gone. Her hands and legs were purple with cold. Her
socks weren't long enough and her skirt was too short. She
didn't even have a coat on.

She gave me a picture. She had drawn it herself. It was a
picture of a boy in a red jumper in our garden.

'Look,' she said, behind the protection of her hand, 'it's him.
He's there now.'

Puzzled, I looked through the window but there was no one
but Jay outside, splitting logs. I took Lolly out to him and he
slung his axe into a block of ash and offered to drive her home in
the camper. She climbed in and waved to me. Jay said later that
she didn't speak to him. Not a word.

I folded up the picture and fed it to the Rayburn.

*

It doesn't always go to plan. Sometimes she can be too playful, too feisty. Although he likes it rough and likes a struggle, he needs an element of submission. He's ended up with a scratched face and a split lip one too many times.

Tethering round the neck usually fixes it. With wrists secured behind the back and a loose noose threaded through the hooks she soon knows how to behave. He's as considerate as possible though, using a piece of towel over the rope so that it won't leave a mark around her throat.

Flickering candles, a couple of generous spliffs that they can share, and she will be ready for him to feast on the banquet of her body.

'Hey, Ruthie.' He holds the joint for her to inhale. 'You love all this, don't you? All our fun and games?'

She gives a subdued laugh. 'Yeah.'

'It feels good, doesn't it?' He knows that her mind will be buzzing, horny as fuck. 'You love me, too, don't you, Ruth?'

'Yeah.'

'Say it, Ruthie. Tell me you love me.'

'I love you.'
He flips her to the wall and hoists the dress to her waist.

CHAPTER TWENTY-ONE
CHRISTMAS EVE

It's charged at us while we had our backs turned. It's arrived in a blathering of snow and new weather warnings. Jay has brought in armfuls of mistletoe, cut from the forest. We are having something of an event tonight. All Jay's musician friends and their partners have been invited, and I have a recipe for mulled wine so that I can use up some of the elderberry that we have in copious quantities. The party was my idea. I thought that if Rick came round on Christmas Eve, then he might leave us alone on Christmas Day and Boxing Day.

Jay said, 'Make that roasted pepper thing again, it was gorgeous last time.'

So I have. The fruits flop their soft red bodies into each other, trickling their oily salty garlicky flavours into the bottom of the bowl. I have made a prawn salad. I have sliced baguettes into diagonal chunks and spread them with real butter. I have put out a huge wedge of Stilton that is produced on the estate farm. I have chopped our home-grown celery and carrots into crudités and arranged them around a dish of lemon hummus drizzled with chilli sauce.

Jay says I'm good at this sort of thing: putting on a classy spread. But he brought two packs of sausage rolls back from the Co-op when he went out earlier. Said that's what we missed when Lou came.

I paint my nails and wash my hair while Jay watches *Home Alone* on television.

'Aren't you going to get changed?' I shout to him as I plug in the hairdryer.

Macaulay Culkin's voice is cut off mid-sentence, and Jay appears in the bedroom.

'I'm ready for a session tonight,' he says. 'It should be good.'

'It's Christmas tomorrow though,' I say. 'We don't really want hangovers.'

He looks at me as if I'm mad and pulls off his T-shirt and jumper in one yogic movement.

We light candles and joss sticks to create ambience. I squirt bleach down the toilet. Cushions are plumped. Jay brings extra chairs through to the living room. In the kitchen I make a start on the mulled wine. Outside, the snow still falls.

Rick arrives first. He kisses my cheek under the mistletoe and presses a podgy hand on my bum for too long.

'Christmas greetings,' he says, but there's derision in his voice and mockery in his eyes.

He tells me it's bad outside, even the main road is covered: the car was sliding around everywhere and the windscreen wipers were next to useless.

'I'll be surprised if anyone else turns up,' he says.

And at this point I'm wondering if it was something of a ridiculous idea, this scheme of a party: I'm wondering if we might end up spending the evening with Rick and four litres of mulled wine.

At a quarter to eight Rick starts to fill his plate. Four sausage rolls, Stilton, bread, prawn salad. He turns his nose up at the peppers.

'Well, everyone was supposed to be here for seven,' I say. 'This is why we need a landline.'

'A landline won't get people here in the snow,' says Jay. He is pouring himself a beer: the mulled wine didn't do it for him.

'Well, at least they'd be able to let us know they're not coming,' I reply.

But five minutes later there's the sound of revving out on the drive. Then Maria, Phil and Lolly traipse in with snowy boots. They have brought twenty-four cans of lager and a big tin of chocolates.

'This is it,' says Maria. 'Kevin's just texted me to say that he set off, but he's turned round because of the snow, and Patryk rang about teatime to say that his road's not been gritted and he couldn't get out of the drive. So, it's just us.'

'Plenty more food for the rest of us then,' says Rick with his mouth full.

'Party time.' Jay turns up the music, rips open the box of lagers and hands them out.

Maria pulls me into the bathroom and closes the door. I know what's coming.

'I saw you in Costa,' she says. 'With a bloke, a couple of weeks ago.'

My heart is pumping in my throat. I toss my hair back.

'Oh,' I say lightly. 'It must have been when I met my cousin. Damien. I've not seen him for ages.'

'Cousin?'

'Mmm.' I nod.

She raises her eyebrows and gives just the tiniest shake of her head before turning and going back into the living room. I should have told her. Should have just joked about it. She would have understood. But now I'm fretful, tapping my thumbnail against my teeth, imagining, thinking, worrying will she tell Jay, won't she, and I have to stand there and take deep breaths to calm myself down.

We eat. We drink. We talk about the weather. Periodically I look through the window at the cars and the inches of snow gathering on them. By half past nine the tyre tracks have all been covered over and the drifts are halfway up the car wheels. But there is no urgency when I mention this to everyone. They are absorbed in drinking; music and conversation and a blazing fire have won them over. I settle on one of the kitchen chairs near the doorway: everyone else has claimed the comfortable seats, slumping into the cushions with their feet tucked under themselves. Maria has been giving me the dead eye all night. It's because of that cousin business, I know it is. Damien. The unintentional kiss. I think of the carrier bag with the jade shoes in, stuffed at the back of my T-shirt drawer.

Lolly is in our bedroom with her sketch pad and pencil case: Maria sent her up there so that we could tell dirty jokes in comfort, but I will be annoyed if she gets felt-tip pen on the new duvet cover.

At eleven o'clock I am troubled that people have had too much to drink to be able to drive home: there are four empty cans at the side of Rick and I know that he also had a pint of Jay's home-brew.

'Come away from the window,' says Jay. 'If it's snowing it's snowing.'

'It's really deep out there. I'm concerned about everyone driving home.'

I shouldn't have said it. I should have anticipated what Jay might say. I should have known what he was like by now.

Because he says that everyone is welcome to stay: in fact, everyone will be better off staying. They can kip over, get ratted, not worry about getting breathalysed or getting stuck in a blizzard. On Christmas Eve.

So then it's like everything just gets out of hand. The speed of drinking goes up a gear, Phil asks if Jay has any weed and Rick shouts, 'Food fight!' before starting to throw sticks of carrot at Maria. I crouch and pick them up, rubbing the smears of hummus out of the rug. Maria picks a prawn off her plate and wipes it across Jay's cheek.

'Right, you cow,' he laughs, and begins to tickle her so that she's shrieking like crazy and kicking her legs out, and next thing he's on top of her and her skirt's right up to her arse so that everyone can see the pink thong she mightn't as well be wearing, then they're on the floor, on the rug, wrestling, with Jay's hands up her top and her legs wrapped around him, and I look at Phil thinking that he ought to be annoyed or jealous or something, but he's just laughing, egging them on, and Rick's loving how they're rolling around so that he can catch flashes of Maria's knickers and the edges of her pubes, and Maria's giving it back, slapping Jay's backside, grabbing his balls, biting his neck.

I hold my breath and leave the room quietly.

At the top of the stairs there is an empty bedroom. Lolly's felt tips and colouring sheets are all over the floor but she is nowhere to be seen. Has she slipped outside into the snow? Surely not. A child could die of hypothermia in weather like this.

Suddenly, the wardrobe door swings open. I jump, slap my hand to my mouth and give a small shriek.

'Boo!'

The gawky frame, blotchy and bruised, topped with an orange bush of hair is crammed among the rail of garments.

'Lolly!' The relief comes in a rush of breath. I press a hand to my fluttering chest. 'You scared the life out of me! What are you doing in there?'

She steps out, in silent hysterics at her practical joke. There's a jangle on her wrist, a glint of gold.

'What's that?' I ask.

She darts her hand behind her back, looks furtive.

'What is it?' I say, going over to her. 'Show me.'

Reluctantly, slowly, she holds out her arm to display the bracelet. Heavy gold, a jewelled snake with a chained clasp from the head and tail. My blood runs cold. My legs tremble like a newborn foal.

'Where did you get this?' I ask. 'Where?'

Lolly closes her eyes and shakes her head.

'Tell me,' I urge. I grip the top of her arm far too hard, feeling skin and bone. 'This is important.'

She points her finger, mouths the word '*bed*'.

'My bed?'

She points her finger again, mouths the word '*under*'.

'Under the bed?' I'm baffled, breathless, as my heart thuds in my ears. The bed is a basic divan, no drawers. There is a narrow gap between the bottom of it and the carpet. 'Show me.'

Lolly kneels at Jay's side of the bed, reaches into the thin space with her scrawny arm, sweeps a semicircle and pulls back out again. She opens her hand to reveal a pound coin and two ten pences in a ball of fluff.

She giggles nervously, puts her other hand over her face. 'Can I have it?'

'You can keep the money,' I reply. 'But let me look at the bracelet.'

She slips it off her wrist – her bony hand wouldn't have held it on anyway – and passes it to me. I weigh it in my trembling palm and turn it over, feeling sick. The name *Eleanor* is engraved in swirly script on the underside just like I knew it would be.

'Don't tell anyone about this,' I say to Lolly. 'No one, ever. Bad things could happen to me if you do. This is a secret, OK?'

She nods earnestly and tucks the money in her shoe.

'Oh God.' I inhale deeply and pace the room, to try and hold back my tears.

Fearful of my emotions, Lolly stands with her back to the wall watching me carefully behind her fingers as if I am a horror film.

'Oh God.' I sit heavily on the end of the bed, gasping and faint as the shock takes full hold.

Finally, I uncurl my fingers to look at the bracelet again.

This sculpted gold band confirms everything I feared, every reason that I came to this place. Everything that I didn't want to be true.

Nell was here.

CHAPTER TWENTY-TWO

My head is a mess. I need to drink brandy or something to calm myself down. Evidence, this is the evidence in my hand that I have been searching for. This is the place – Jay's bedroom – that Nell was in before her body was found lifeless at the bottom of the quarry.

But what do I do now? I can't go downstairs with the bracelet and confront him. I still have no proof that her death was unlawful, apart from my own suspicions. Other things have niggled me, other doubts, since I arrived here in August. Rick, for example, is top of my list of suspects. And the elusive Ruthie: what involvement did she have with Jay or Rick or this house back in January, when Nell died? There's a lot more to know about *her*.

I need to bide my time for now. I must act normal. So, I'll pretend I don't know about it; that it's never been found. That's what I'll do. I take some deep breaths to steady my racing heart; I kneel on the floor at the side of the bed and skim the bracelet like a pebble back to the middle of the dark space.

'Here, put this on,' I say to Lolly, giving her one of my

jumpers. I'm feeling bad that I have frightened her with my behaviour and need to make amends. 'It's really cold up here.'

She puffs out a cloud of breath to demonstrate and smiles at me, before pulling the jumper over her head. She points downstairs and then puts her hands over her ears.

'I know,' I say, interpreting her sign language. 'They're very loud, aren't they? That's why I've come up here.'

I sit on the edge of the bed and pull the duvet around my shoulders. I've had four months now to get to know Jay and his mates, to integrate myself into his friendship group, and find out what happened to Nell. Tonight feels like the start of something. I know I'm finally on the right path.

'Do you like me?' I ask Lolly, and she nods, vigorously, and blows me a kiss.

'I like you,' I say. 'You're my favourite out of everyone.'

I hear the creak of the living room door and someone going into the bathroom to piss loudly and leave again without flushing the toilet.

'Do you want some more food, Lolly?' I ask. 'Another drink? I'll make you a hot chocolate if you want.'

She shakes her head and picks up a picture of a cat to colour in.

'I'd better go back down,' I say.

From the top of the stairs, I can see Jay who has gone into the kitchen to get another can. I can see Maria as she sidles through to him, pulling him under the canopy of mistletoe to press her breasts against him. I can hear what she says to him, as clear as an alarm bell.

'What about a special kiss for Christmas?' That's what she says. 'What about a special kiss?'

Her words conjure up surreal thoughts: they make me taste elation; smell the room that used to be locked; feel the purple dress that isn't mine, with tender wrists and aching thighs; hear the whiz of a rope being pulled through a metal hook. I must have drunk more wine than I thought tonight.

I go downstairs and shut myself in the bathroom for a while. My head is too crammed to think properly. In the mirror I check my make-up, apply extra lipstick, I don't know why. I rearrange the toiletries on the side of the bath. I flush the toilet and squirt more bleach down. Then I hear Jay calling me, an idle effort of a shout from someone on the verge of falling asleep or passing out.

I take a deep breath and open the bathroom door. Go into the living room to the stink of cannabis, the sight of roasted pepper crushed into the new goats-wool rug, a skid of Stilton on the laminate floor. Jay is sprawled on the sofa, arms and legs akimbo, with Maria's head resting against his shoulder. Her eyeliner has smudged, giving her a scary, emo look.

'Just skip the CD,' says Jay. 'It sounds like it's stuck. I can't move, I'm too wasted.'

'Good gear,' says Rick without opening his eyes. 'I'm getting the munchies though. Hope there're some sausage rolls left.'

I stop the CD and find a radio station playing Christmas music.

'I hate this,' says Maria.

Phil looks up and waves a hand at me. 'D'you think you could get me a drink of water, Ruth?' he asks.

In a story, in this sort of situation, everyone would freeze in panic. That's what would happen. But it doesn't in this instance. Everyone comes to life. It's like someone's just pressed a remote control and set them all back in action.

Rick's eyes pop open and he turns to Jay. Maria picks up Jay's tobacco tin and hurls it at Phil, who holds his palms out and makes a sudden humming noise. Jay sits up rigidly and pushes Maria away from his shoulder. He looks at me and smiles.

'Get him a drink of water, babe,' he says. 'He's losing his mind.'

I walk calmly into the kitchen.

Ruth. With her initial in the self-sufficiency book. Her name branding the wall under the aubergine paint.

So. *They* all knew her.

And Nell. With her snake bracelet under the bed. Did they know *her* too? Do they know what really happened to her? Are they all covering something up?

I pour myself a glass of wine and drink it in one pull. I watch the snowflakes tumble past the kitchen window until they make me feel woozy. I think about my new life and Jay and how being here has somehow saved me from myself and brought me away from all my grief and obsession; but now I know that Nell was definitely here I have work to do. I can't believe that she would have taken her own life: we had plans and dreams together that she would never have given up on. There is so much more I need to find out. I certainly can't let on that I suspect anyone.

Just carry on as before, I tell myself.

I take a pint glass and fill it with cold water for Phil.

'Merry Christmas,' says Lolly, from the foot of our bed. She has the neck of her T-shirt pulled up over her nose and mouth.

Jay is motionless beside me, his beery breaths deep and heavy. I don't want to wake up yet. The glare of snowy daylight through my eyelids is enough to make my head ache.

'Go back downstairs,' I tell her. 'Put the television on.'

'There are presents in here,' she says through her clothes. She must have seen the bags at the side of the wardrobe from Mum and Lou. 'You should open them now it's Christmas.'

'Later. Go downstairs and watch a film or something.'

Reluctant footsteps fade. I doze again.

They all stayed the night. Lolly and Phil in the armchairs, Maria on the sofa. The new cream throws had to be used as blankets. Rick took the bed cushions out of the campervan and put them on the floor of the studio, using the old duvet which was in a bin bag waiting to be thrown away.

'Spirit of the blitz,' said Jay. He was drunk, really wasted. Slurring his words and falling over things. Kicking a can of lager over the new rug. Making a cigarette burn on the laminate floor.

We got to bed at half past three. I stayed awake and stared into the dark for another hour, visualising the snake bracelet beneath me, under the bed.

Merry Christmas, Nell. But my silent wishes went unacknowledged.

It felt like everything had changed. Where once there had only been speculation, I now knew without a doubt that Nell had been here. In Jay's house. In his bedroom. But after all this period of healing for me, of becoming the perfect girlfriend for Jay, I didn't want to believe the evidence I had found. I was settled into my get-away-from-it-all life, and this new information could destroy everything if I handled it wrong. So, for now, things had to remain the same. My thoughts on the subject of Nell had to be locked away.

I contemplated the pending day: present opening, dressing up, cooking the lunch. All the rituals that needed to be done. What if everyone still couldn't get home? The roof window was layered with snow. I couldn't tell if it was still falling. Someone was snoring downstairs.

The sound of shrill laughing wakes me. I look at the clock. It is almost ten. Jay is still fast asleep.

'Jay.' I shake him. He groans.

'Come on. Everyone's up. It's Christmas.'

He rolls away from me. 'Leave me alone. My head aches.'

If he thinks that I'm going to go downstairs and entertain his friends while he recovers from his hangover he can think again.

'Get up, Jay. I'm not getting up first.'

'Just give me half an hour,' he pleads. 'Get me a drink of water. I'll be OK then.'

'It's ten o'clock.'

More laughing from downstairs seems to stir him. He forces himself to sit up and rub his fingers viciously into his temples.

'Why do you let me drink so much?' he asks as his picks yesterday's clothes off the floor.

'You're big enough to know better,' I say.

He stumbles downstairs holding his head. I look at the clock. Five minutes, then I'll get up.

Twenty minutes later I pull my clothes into the bed and put them on under the duvet. I hear Jay raking the ashes out of the Rayburn. The fire must have gone out in the night: we were too drunk to stoke it up with fuel before we went to bed.

I put on an extra jumper and comb my fingers through my hair as I go downstairs. Lolly is sprawled on the living room rug scouring a purple crayon into a notebook. Everyone else sits like zombies staring at a smouldering log in the grate.

Maria says, 'I made you a coffee but it's probably cold now. In the kitchen.'

'What's it like outside?' I ask.

'It's stopped snowing,' she says. 'Looks like it's thawing a bit. We're going to get off in a minute. Lolly wants to open her presents.'

I take the dining chairs back through to the kitchen. Jay is in there, squirting white spirit into the Rayburn to try and light the wet wood.

'Could be a while before we're eating turkey at this rate,' he says. He brought the bird home a couple of days ago: a small, cold creature wrapped in greaseproof paper, with pimply skin and black stubble, and legs and wings that dangled slackly like a tiny dead child. He said, 'Don't ask me where I got it,' so I didn't.

Phil, Maria and Lolly come through to the kitchen, wrapped and buttoned, ready for the outside.

'Might need a push off the drive, mate,' says Phil, so Jay puts his boots on.

'See you,' shouts Rick, from the living room. 'Have a good one.'

There are squeals outside; the thud of a snowball; the sound of the drive being scraped. Then the heavy thump of a snowy door closing; the rev and spin of a car and Jay stamps back in. He says it's not too bad out there but you probably need to set off in second gear. Things are melting a bit. There's an inkling of sun in the sky.

I flick the electric kettle on. It'll be an hour before I get a coffee if I wait for the Rayburn to get hot. The turkey reposes casually at the side of the sink. I wish I had made the stuffing yesterday.

Jay comes over and brushes an eyelash off my cheek.

'Merry Christmas, my special girl,' he says, kissing me gently with icy lips. I wrap around him and slip my tongue into his mouth. Close my eyes and put the gold bracelet out of my mind. Absorb him and his passion and his sooty, boozy scent.

Suddenly, Rick is there in the kitchen with us, and Jay breaks off, like he's doing something wrong.

'I'm gonna have to go,' says Rick. 'I can't hang around here all day. I've got a family to get back to. Three course dinner and all the trimmings.'

I can tell he's sneering at our small turkey, at the fact that the Rayburn won't be up to temperature to cook it until the evening.

'OK, mate,' says Jay, slapping him affectionately on the arm. 'Take it steady on the roads, all right? Give my regards and all that. Tell your mum I'll be over soon.'

He's such a creep around him. I know there's a hold over us with the house being almost rent free, but really, we're doing them a favour looking after the place.

'Bye,' I say to him, in the kindest voice I can muster. 'Have a good Christmas. See you soon.'

Jay follows him out onto the drive, and I begin to peel potatoes.

Jay drops an armful of gifts into my lap. They are wrapped in magazine pages from the *Big Issue* and *The Socialist*. None of them have tags on. This is Jay all over. I don't know what Lou would have thought if she had seen them under the tree.

'Ethical Christmas prezzies,' he says. 'Recycled.'

'I didn't know if you'd got me anything,' I say, unwrapping the biggest one. It's a book, obviously second-hand, on meditation. There is a fifty pence price sticker inside the cover.

'It was in the library withdrawn section,' says Jay. 'They sell them off cheap. I thought meditation would be good for you to get into: you worry too much and need to chill more.'

'I don't worry,' I say. 'What do I worry about?'

'You fuss over things, like cleaning and decorating and what people think of the place. Anyway, read it. Be a bit more laid back.'

The next gift is a CD, a bargain from a charity shop. *Folk Tunes from the British Isles.*

'It's pretty shite,' Jay says. 'I've had a listen already. But we might be able to use some of the tunes and rearrange them.'

There are two small packages left. The squashy one turns out to be a pair of kinky black knickers and when I ask how they are ethical he says he thinks they are made from something organic. The last one is a small box, the sort you might get a ring in. I open it carefully. Within it is a necklace: a leather thong with a circle of green stone on it.

'Thanks,' I say. 'Very ethnic.'

'It was from the Oxfam shop,' Jay says. 'But it's new. Why don't you put it on?'

I wind it round my neck until the smooth stone is touching my throat. The fire flickers and spits. Lights on the tree twinkle. Jay grins at me. This, a new Christmas.

I make a wish for Nell.

CHAPTER TWENTY-THREE

'What happens around here New Year's Eve?' I ask.

But Jay says that nothing happens, the two remaining village pubs are crap and there's more of an atmosphere up his left nostril. 'The village used to have loads of pubs. Before the pit closed, and before everybody started thinking that it was cheaper to get their booze from Tesco's and drink it at home. So now there's nowhere decent to go out to. You basically have to make your own entertainment.'

'So, what then?' I ask. 'We stay in and watch Jools Holland with a bottle of wine and a spliff?'

'Sounds fine to me. Or we get the crew round again like we did on Christmas Eve.'

I don't think so.

* * *

At night the house hums. A soft, murmuring low C: it crawls through the silence. Maybe it's the fridge. Sometimes I long to hear the bustle of the city: throaty Subarus, pumping stereos, shrieking hen parties out on the razz. And, although I keep telling myself that my life here has purpose and conviction and is recovering my sanity – I can't help having my occasional doubts.

I'm anxious. Not just about how Nell's bracelet ended up under Jay's bed, but about things like the neighbours a mile down the lane who stare disdainfully when I walk past. About thieves getting into the studio and stealing the music equipment because I broke the catch on the window and haven't replaced it or owned up to it yet. About having no telephone in an emergency. I don't trust Rick and his influence on Jay. I suspect that Ruth may have been involved in Nell's death even though I have no evidence yet. I have flashbacks of when the chickens were killed: their torn bodies fluttering death spasms on the grass. I remember fearfully the time in the snow at the edge of the cliff. I worry that too often I find myself in the room that used to be locked, bewildered by the sight of the hooks that are still in the wall.

Dreams intrude like thieves. I have periods where I dread sleep. Nightmares gatecrash my mind and vague scenes appear like unrecognisable classmates at school reunions. Ropes. Kinky sex. Unaccountable sores and bruises. The coarse feel of velvet being pushed up around my thighs.

Sometimes I don't recognise myself any more. Sometimes I wonder if I'm going mad out here in the wild.

* * *

On the morning of New Year's Eve, I go into Sainsbury's and buy an Indian meal for two. I get white wine, bottled lager, a lemon cheesecake and a copy of *Your Home* which has an article on designing cottage-style bedrooms and a free wall calendar. As I am taking my trolley back in the car park, I see Damien getting out of a shiny black sports car.

'Hi,' he shouts across, putting a hand up.

I smile and say hello.

'Where's your instrument?' he asks, as if I take it everywhere with me. 'Have you been playing in town today?'

'No, I've just been doing some shopping.' I want to walk away, but I don't want him to watch me. I'm embarrassed to be seen getting into the camper.

'Are you going anywhere tonight?' he asks. He's wearing sports clothes and clean trainers, as if he's on his way to a gym.

'I don't know,' I reply. I feel guilty that I am not wearing the jade shoes. I remember that my hair needs washing and I don't have any make-up on.

'There's a load of us starting a pub crawl from the Red Lion,' he says. 'About half eight. Come along if you want, I'll look after you.'

'Oh, I'm not sure,' I say. I remember the curry and lager in the back of the camper. I start to back away and jangle my keys.

'Is everything OK?' he asks. 'You know, just in general?'

'Yeah, fine. It's all good. You don't need to worry about me.'

'Well, if you change your mind we'll be in the Red Lion.'

I slink around the car park and wait until he's gone through Sainsbury's doors before getting in the van. Going out is tempting, something that Jay and I never do. The thought of hot, bustling pubs with loud music and atmosphere and fun. Getting dressed up. Wearing the jade shoes. Slapping make-up on. Doing my hair.

But it's not just the fear of Maria seeing me or Jay finding out that keeps me from being unfaithful. It's the new me, the one who isn't seduced by money and cars and suits any more, but takes delight in simple things like nature and home-cooking and creativity. The one who is now on a mission for the truth about her best friend's death.

New Year's Eve. It's an ending and a new beginning.

CHAPTER TWENTY-FOUR

JANUARY

So. Another year starts. A blur of bottle tops and corks and me and Jay sprawling on the sofa while Big Ben does its thing. There are no texts or phone calls or 'Auld Lang Syne'; just me and Jay kissing while the room waltzes around us. We stumble to bed within seconds of the last chime. We leave behind glasses and plates with the smearings of rogan josh and the crusty edges of a naan. And I leave behind the worst year of my life.

Finding Nell's bracelet sent me into a quandary. It's almost as if I would rather not have known about it. Because a big part of my life has started to feel good again. I have banished thoughts of Martin from my mind and now he means nothing to me. The house and garden have soothed my soul and boosted my positivity. I'm indebted to this sprawl of ground and shabby shell of a property: I want to tend and cherish it and bring it into glory. And Jay. There's a big part of him in my heart, too, despite my irrational suspicions. I can't help being attracted to him: we have great sex and many moments of pure bliss, and we generally get along together. How do I balance that with how I feel about Nell's death?

Changes are necessary. Small steps. I should make a plan and stop being distracted. Stop all this dossing around in bed with hangovers. I need to be motivated, organised, friendly enough to gain everyone's confidence. I am here to infiltrate this circle of people, to track down Ruth, and to find out what really happened to Nell.

* * *

Jay has three weeks of hard graft lined up on the estate: new hedging, wall and fencing repairs, clearing all the fallen trees. He needs it though: we are almost out of logs and the only money we have left apart from my secret stash is an ice-cream tub half full of busking change. I have thought about how I can earn some money to pay my way and so I sit at the kitchen table and write out an advert to put in the newsagent's window. *'Violin Tuition. Beginners to Grade Eight. All styles.'* I write my mobile number followed by *'please leave a message'*.

I pull my coat on and take cash from the busking tub to buy flour and milk that we have run out of. Jay has the van so that he can bring wood home with him, which means that I will have to walk to the Co-op but I can put the advert in the newsagent on the way.

On my way home I glance down a side street. Portland Crescent. It looks like a respectable area, with detached houses and Audis straddling the pavements and the skeletons of trees that will provide leafy dapple in the summer. It's just a quick look as I cross the road. But it's long enough to notice Jay's camper pulling out of one of the driveways. I stand on the corner and watch as he drives off in the opposite direction. My heart wallops the inside of my rib cage.

The wind brings a light drizzle in, and by the time I get home my hair is plastered to my head, stringy from the rain. My face and feet are freezing. My stomach rumbles in anticipation of lunch.

The campervan is in the driveway although Jay told me he wouldn't be home until dark. There is a new pile of logs by the kitchen step.

I kick the door open. The house is silent.

'Hey!' I call. 'What're you doing home?'

But there's no answer. I peer around the living room door.

Jay is sitting in the armchair with his head thrown back and his eyes closed; dark lashes smiling. His arms rest on the chair arms, palms upwards. He is not quite cross-legged: his limbs link in a gangly way and the soles of his bare feet are black with ash-dirt from the kitchen floor. I've come round to thinking that it's better to keep your shoes on in this house.

At first glance he looks as if he's meditating, but I can tell he's jittery. His thumbs flick at nothing; a shoulder jerks; parts of his face twitch like a rabbit.

I watch him soundlessly from the doorway. He's been on something, or he's coming down from something. I don't know what he takes or where he keeps it. There are no hiding places left for me to uncover. It feels like I must wait for the house to choose its own time to reveal Jay's secrets.

Later, when I ask who lives on Portland Crescent Jay is defensive. His face colours. There's the hint of a tic under his right eye.

'Why are you asking?'

'I saw you there. Coming out of a driveway.' I don't take my eyes away from his face. He blinks three times. Looks to the left.

'It's one of the vegetable box deliveries. That's all.'

I know it's not. But I've got an idea what it is, and I'm going to check it out.

* * *

It's a midweek morning, but as part of my new motivational routine, I decide to pamper myself. In the bathroom I light vanilla candles. A gratuitous slug of aromatic bath oil goes into the running water. I place my Christmas gift toiletries around the edges of the bath and step through fragrant steam into the hot water.

Afterwards, I daub myself with body lotion. But as I smear it, I notice bruises. I turn and look in the mirror, check my legs, my buttocks, my back. See the patches of purple and blue and yellow and green. I remember someone who bruised easily finding out that she had leukaemia. Perhaps I will go for a check-up.

I hang my head upside down and swish the hairdryer at my dangling hair. It feels thin and straggly and I realise that it hasn't been trimmed for almost six months.

Next thing, Jay is back from work. There I am at the sink in my bra and pants with my make-up everywhere and he's bouncing around, galvanised, rattling on about some festival or other.

'Our first festival gig,' he says. 'Out on a farm in the Peak District. Two thousand capacity. The farmer and one of the organisers came over to the estate today to ask about temporary housing for their sheep while the festival is on. I was in the office, mentioned the band, said you'd played with some big hitters and they were impressed. Want to book us.'

'That sounds great.' I pack my pencils and lipsticks and brushes into the make-up bag.

'It's an eclectic line-up. They've got trance, reggae, folk, poetry, all sorts.'

'Wow,' I say.

Jay stands there beaming. 'Get your best frock on. Go on. I'm taking you out to celebrate.'

I put on a dress that I have never worn before for Jay. A turquoise shift in silk: short and clinging. Lou gave it to me in a bin bag after one of her wardrobe declutters. It still had the label on. She said it wasn't her: she'd bought it on a whim and couldn't be bothered to take it back.

Then I remember the new shoes in the back of my drawer, feel a little pop of joy inside that I have the opportunity to wear them, to co-ordinate with the dress. I will tell Jay that Lou gave me the shoes too. I pull out the drawer and rummage under my T-shirts until my fingers are touching the plastic carrier. There's an eddy of excitement in my belly as I take it out. I tip them onto the bed and the delight of seeing the colour and pointiness and newness of the footwear turns into something else: fear, confusion, a jumble of things like a sudden storm interrupting a summer day. They lie there on the bed, all the bits of them. A new pair of shoes with the heels snapped off. I know exactly what this means. Maria told him.

It's a warning, I know it is. It tells me that Jay won't accept infidelity. I know where I stand. My mouth is dry, my heart is pumping so that I can hear it. But the sight of the shoes, such beautiful things, deliberately damaged: it makes me wonder what Jay is capable of. Pushing someone over a cliff edge? Covering for someone else who did it?

I return the shoes and heels into the bag and shove it back

into the drawer. I have a pair of black court shoes I can wear tonight.

'Don't be long,' Jay shouts from downstairs.

I'll act normal. I won't mention this: to bring it up would mean having to explain about going for coffee with Damien.

I take a deep breath. I will go out with Jay, have a great night, pretend that I don't know about the shoes.

I rummage through my small jewellery box. I pull out the jade-coloured necklace that Jay gave me for Christmas and tie it around my neck. I pick out the white gold earrings from Lou. The abortion earrings. I can't think of them any other way.

So, we go out together. A celebration meal. A posh restaurant pub with real ale awards and antique beams and middle-class diners. I don't mention the shoes. Jay orders our steak and a bottle of house red with pride.

Later, back home, we make love, but I am distracted, picturing the moment that Jay snapped the heels – quickly, forcefully, like an animal's neck – so I close my eyes and hang on to his hips. He licks my nipples and I feel nothing.

'Babe,' he whispers. 'My special girl. I adore you.'

I remember the moment at the edge of the quarry; remember the fear I felt. Something happened, but I'm still not sure what. I'm beginning to realise that there's more to him, a lot more, and I have only uncovered the top layer.

It is the first time I have had to fake an orgasm.

* * *

Jay takes the bike to work, so I drive the camper into the village and park outside the health centre.

Inside, there is a queue for the receptionist. I take a seat in a leatherette chair and old people hobble in and out with ulcers and zimmers and bags for life. I remember that I should be able to get a signal here so I take my phone out and switch it on.

There is a voicemail from a plummy-voiced woman about violin lessons for her fourteen-year-old, who is already Grade 6 standard, asking me to ring her back.

When the queue has disappeared, I go to the receptionist and fill in a registration form. She tells me that I can't see a doctor until I have had a check-up first with the practice nurse, which will be next Friday morning. If I have an urgent issue I will have to go to A&E.

'It's OK,' I say. 'I can wait until the check-up.'

When I go back out to the camper Jay is sitting on his motorbike at the side of the driver's door. His arms are folded over the helmet in his lap.

'What's going on?' he asks.

'I've just been to register. It's something I've been meaning to get round to.'

Why is he here? Why isn't he at work? Has he followed me? I fumble in my bag for the camper keys.

'Who have you registered with?'

'I don't know, they didn't say, I just filled a form in. They won't let me see a GP until I've had a check-up.'

'So, what's going on then? What do you need an appointment for?'

I don't want to talk about the spectrum of colours on my body out here in the car park. I pull the keys from my bag and turn to unlock the door. Then he's off the bike, a hand on my shoulder, pulling me to face him.

'What's going on? What are you checking up on?' His breath smells of coffee and tobacco.

What is he suspecting me of checking up on? I have no idea what I am being accused of. I push his hand away and try to open the camper door, and we jostle in the slim space between the vehicles. The bike is knocked and the helmet topples off the seat and onto the ground.

'Leave me alone,' I tell him, somewhat hysterically, and a man walking his dog stops to look at us.

'Hey,' says Jay softly, holding his hands up and backing away. 'Calm down.'

My chin quivers and I try to hold back tears. Jay looks at me like I'm a freak.

'I'm just stressed,' I say. I gulp in the chill air and close my eyes, and Nell's face drifts into my mind. I climb into the driving seat. A hot tear spills onto my cheek and I wipe it with my sleeve. I put the key in and start the engine. Jay taps on the window.

'Go home,' he says. 'I'll follow you. We need to sort this out.'

I pull out of the car park steadily. I see Jay through my rear-view mirror, putting on the helmet, zipping up his jacket. A moment of madness bursts into my brain and I consider driving off somewhere, away from Jay, just slamming my foot onto the accelerator and going to another place, without collecting my belongings or telling anyone. But where? Certainly not home to Mum and Dad. Or Lou. Not now I've finally managed to leave my old life behind. And there isn't the option of Rachel any more.

Then, the growl of a speeding motorbike and Jay is arching past me, holding his hand up, leading the way, and I follow him carefully up the frosty lane to the house.

Inside, Jay drops his keys and helmet onto the kitchen table. I follow him into the living room and stand in the doorway as he slides a Stone Roses CD into the player.

'I think there's something wrong,' I tell him. 'That's why I wanted an appointment.'

He wheels round and steps towards me. Maybe he thinks I'm going to announce that I'm pregnant.

'I just keep finding bruises all over me,' I say.

He reaches out to pull me towards him. 'My fragile love. My special girl. Perhaps I should be more gentle with you.' He wraps me in the warmth of him, holds his cheek against mine, strokes my hair.

'You don't need to worry,' he says. 'I'll be careful next time.'

Jay said, what's the point of going to the doctor's: they can't do anything about bruises. They're just the symptoms of rough sex, not a terminal illness. He said I had to stop worrying, stop being so suspicious of everything, chill out more.

And then, on that Friday morning of the appointment, when I woke up Jay had already gone out with the camper, a cruel torrent of sleet was lashing around the garden and it just seemed easier not to go.

CHAPTER TWENTY-FIVE

Hannah is a sullen, mousey-haired girl who is only at Grade 4 level despite the boasting of her mother. But her violin is an expensive one – at least twice the value of mine – and the house they live in is a dream.

It is like *Build a New Life in the Country*, with the Shaker-style kitchen and polished slate floor, and wood-burning stove in the beamed-ceiling living room. A rocking chair nestling in an alcove; a dining room with an oak refectory table and a piano in the corner; a tiny latched door into a wine cellar.

Hannah's father shows me round the ground floor after I remark on the loveliness of the place, and talks to me about his collection of jazz records and various musicians he has known in the past.

I conduct the lesson in the dining room: we play duets of varying difficulty so that I can assess the girl's capability. She isn't an ardent pupil: her intonation is sloppy, there is no passion or contrast in her playing, and twice when I am talking to her about timing and expression she takes out her phone to scan through Instagram.

Hannah's father sees me out, handing over crisp notes with the reminder, 'Same time next week?'

It feels like a positive step: sorting out my life, earning some regular money. Small beginnings are what I need. And although things aren't moving quickly, I'm getting there. It's all going to be good.

* * *

'Tell me about your past again,' I say to Jay. 'About when you lived in the squat. Where did you go after that? What was going on with Rick?'

We are on the elderberry wine again. It seems to have matured a little since Christmas.

'I didn't know Rick then,' Jay says.

His statement takes me by surprise. Completely. I'm sure he had told me before that Rick had been a lifelong friend, since infant days.

'You weren't at school with him?'

'Nah,' Jay replies. 'I got to know him through various pub folk nights. He saw me playing at a few of the local ones: bought me pints, lent me CDs and things.'

'Sounds like he fancied you or something.'

'Don't be daft. Anyway, he got me the job of doing his mum's garden. And then she let me have this place. So, it worked out well. It seemed like he sort of rescued me. Otherwise I'm not quite sure how I would have moved on from the squat.'

'Rick the saviour,' I say.

'I don't know why you're like that,' says Jay. He tops up our glasses. 'We do all right out of this place. The thing I worry about is what we do if his mother ever decides to sell it. It could be worth a fortune.'

'This? Worth a fortune? A cowboy-built fifties bungalow?'

'I would have thought you'd see beyond that, being a fan of all the *Grand Designs* stuff. Have you never heard of bungalow-crunching? Some builder would snap this up and put four quality properties on this plot.'

He's right. My heart plummets. I swig my wine and realise how much I am attached to this place. This living room with the aubergine wall and sleek floor that I created. The snug kitchen with all my design touches and accessories. Even the avocado bathroom in candlelight. It's mine; it's embedded in my soul.

* * *

I suggest to Jay that we ought to cut down on the drinking a bit, what with all the stuff in the news about liver disease.

'We don't drink that much,' he says.

But I have been keeping a personal tally of my units. Thirty-seven last week, forty-two the week before, already twenty this week and we're only three days in. And the special kisses seem to be getting more regular, too. The idea of having a routine didn't work: we're back to our lifestyle of mayhem. It's all sending me somewhere else, somewhere away from myself. Making me go mad. I need to refocus, keep myself on track, make some kind of progress. I promised Nell, didn't I?

* * *

My behaviour is getting more obsessive; my mind isn't my own. I thought I was improving since being here, but it's almost back to how I was with Martin. Finding Nell's bracelet hasn't helped: I have been turning over the house and its contents to try and gather more evidence. Every cupboard, drawer, shelf, every pocket or tiny cavity that is capable of hiding something as small as a bus ticket has been checked.

I can't stop thinking about her, can't stop thinking about

what she was doing here, with Jay, and then the moment she died. The actual instant from leaving the edge of the quarry to smashing all the way down to the bottom of the rock.

Did she take her own life?

Or was she pushed?

I remember that time when I asked Jay if he'd ever thought what it might be like to kill someone. He looked stung. Slapped.

'What's that supposed to mean?' His eyes accused me of something.

'Nothing,' I said quickly. 'I was just... I don't know.'

'Why, have *you* killed anyone?'

I remember the whiteness of the abortion clinic, the forms and the false sympathy. 'Of course I haven't.'

'Well, what makes you think that *I* have?'

His expression scared me. I thought of Nell again, at the bottom of the quarry. Would *Jay* have been capable of hurting her? Could he hurt *me*? I looked down at a purple bruise on my forearm. I didn't know where they kept coming from.

'It's not that I think you *have*. It was just a stupid thing I said. It was like that confession time we had. Remember? You said about stealing a TV?'

I watched as he exhaled. Swigged his wine. Shifted back into his old psyche.

* * *

I have no idea what time the primary school finishes so at half past one I put my coat on and set off for the village. The campervan is on the drive – Jay took the bike today – but the keys are nowhere to be found. My phone is also missing again. I take some change from the busking money tub so that I can buy some sweets for Lolly.

At three o'clock I am outside the school with a packet of Starburst in my pocket. A gathering of parents, grandparents and pushchairs are on the pavement. Cars double parked, yapping dogs on retractable leads, the scant sight of a lollipop lady behind a white van.

'What time do they come out?' I ask a woman beside me, who answers, 'Now,' while typing a text on her phone.

Then, out they swarm: a variety of children with PE kits and book bags and the rustle of letters to parents. Lolly is easy to spot with her orange hair. She skips into the playground, away in her own other world. I shout and wave to her. She is oblivious to my signals, is on the verge of walking right past me when I lunge and catch hold of her shoulder.

'Lolly,' I say. 'It's me. I've come to meet you.'

Her puzzled face looks up and a brightness spreads across it. I hand over the sweets and she takes them with a quick giggle.

'Show me where you live,' I say as I hurry along with my hands on her back, following her down the road towards the housing estate that I have just walked around.

She unwraps the sweets and offers me one but I decline.

'They're for you,' I say.

I don't know how to start the conversation. What if she won't talk to me? I look over my shoulder to see if there is anyone behind who might hear. 'The boy in my garden,' I say quietly. 'The one you drew a picture of.'

She looks up. She's interested.

'Who is he, Lolly? Is he something to do with Jay?'

She blinks hard and pushes a sweet into her mouth. Keeps a hand over her mouth and nose. Perhaps she's going to say something.

'Is he?' I prompt.

She nods quickly, just once. Takes her hand away and unwraps another sweet.

'And did you know someone called Ruth?' I dare to ask.

Lolly scrunches up her eyes and covers her face with her hands. She stumbles on the edge of the pavement and I catch her arm to stop her falling.

'Is Ruth something to do with the boy?'

She won't speak. She won't remove her hands. Won't open her eyes.

'Lolly,' I say gently, shaking her shoulder. 'Don't be silly, you need to look where you're going.'

She ignores me and staggers on, and I have to guide her as if she's blind.

'Can I have a sweet?' I ask, and she remembers them and opens her eyes, removes the hands from her face, offers me the sweets. 'Can you tell me about the boy?' I try again.

She looks up at me, does a hand gesture to indicate zipping up her mouth. She turns onto the estate, and we pass a house with a broken window and the curtain flapping out.

'Does it upset you to talk about him?'

Another brisk nod.

'Did something happen to him?'

She looks at me. Tears puddle in the corners of her eyes. We reach a gate and I follow her through it, to a concrete semi with a big metal butterfly on the front of the house, a dreamcatcher in the window and a string of leftover Christmas lights dangling from the guttering. Lolly goes to the back door which opens into a kitchen: a modern affair of beech-effect units and sparkly lino floor. Maria is sitting at a small table with someone: a hard-faced blonde woman with chunky black mascara around her eyes and two gold studs above the left side of her lip. They have coffee mugs and an Avon brochure in front of them.

'What's gone off?' Maria says when she sees me on the step.

Lolly looks towards me – with an expression of fear it seems – and holds a hand over her face as a tear spills down her cheek.

'Hi,' I say. 'I bumped into Lolly outside school. Thought I'd walk home with her.'

'What were you doing there?' she says. 'It's nowhere near the shops.'

'Oh, just out for a walk. Nothing else much to do.'

They look at me with suspicion until Maria tells the other woman, 'This is Jay's, er, new girlfriend.'

I see the rise of an eyebrow, a slight smirk on the pierced side of the woman's face as she flicks her eyes towards Maria. She doesn't speak to me: she licks her index finger and turns to the perfume section of the Avon book.

'What's wrong with *you?*' says Maria, rather harshly, to Lolly who is still standing there.

Lolly stares at me and shakes her head.

'Well, go and put your stuff away then,' says Maria, tapping the orange hair.

Lolly leaves the kitchen, scampers up a staircase.

'Weirdo,' says Maria. She fills the kettle and switches it on. I am still standing on the step with the door open.

'Did you want a coffee or something?' Maria says to me.

I don't really feel as if I am being offered one.

'No thanks,' I say. 'I need to get off really. I'll see you soon.'

I pull the door behind me and walk quietly down the path at the side of the house. A burst of laughter comes from the kitchen. I look at the butterfly as I close the gate. Lolly waves to me from an upstairs window.

CHAPTER TWENTY-SIX

Jay has arranged for Maria, Kevin and Patryk to come and do some recording with the equipment that Rick has borrowed. Maria is stretched out on the sofa. She is wearing thin stilettos that I'm sure have marked the new floor. They are glossy, turquoise, almost the same shade and style as the ones that Damien bought me: it's as if she wants to taunt me. She stretches her face into a gaudy yawn and tucks a thumb under the shoulder of her jumper to pull up her bra strap.

'What made you want to come and live here with Jay?' she says. 'Just out of interest. Because I mean, it was all a bit sudden, wasn't it? Like you spend a weekend with him at a festival and then two weeks later you're here, moved in.'

'Well, yes it was a bit of a whirlwind,' I reply. 'But it seemed like the right thing. And I like it here, the lifestyle and everything.'

'Hmm. You've no regrets then? Not thinking of going back to where it is you're from?'

'No. Everything's good. Why would I?'

'No reason. I just wondered, that's all.' She wraps her arms around herself and shudders. 'It's freezing in here.'

Kevin is still twiddling away in the other room. I go into the kitchen to make coffee for everyone and fetch more logs for the fire. Rick arrives as I'm filling the kettle.

'We don't need you,' I tell him. 'We're recording tonight.'

He casts a sarcastic grin onto his face. 'I've come to bring good news, though. Although you might not think so.'

I don't ask what it is, but he taps his nose. Tells me I will find out sooner or later.

It takes us four hours to record two tracks. Rick interferes with suggestions, saying where the bass needs to make an entrance, where the rhythm needs to change, where the fiddle should keep quiet. As if he knows anything. Jay, exhausted by the end, declares the tracks adequate.

I retire to claim the sofa and scan the channels for a property programme as everyone heads off home.

There's the guggle of car engines outside as Kevin and Patryk manoeuvre in the drive. There's the scraping of a chair in the kitchen as Rick shambles his body through, as Maria lugs her heavy djembe past the table.

'I haven't told you the good news yet,' I hear Rick say to Jay and Maria.

I don't want to know what it is. I stretch out a leg from the sofa and swing the door closed with my foot. I jab at the remote control, to turn up the volume of *Ugly House to Lovely House*, so that I can catch up with the bit where George Clarke is insisting a perfectly good conservatory needs to be demolished.

So, I don't properly get to hear the gossip in the kitchen, apart from snippets where Rick is saying something about new drugs and going somewhere to get them and how they will change everything. And I'm starting to prickle inside, partly because I'm apprehensive about my associations with Jay's involvement in illegal stuff, but also because the word 'drug' nowadays seems to trigger some kind of erotic reaction in me.

Then, suddenly, there's an explosion of noise: celebratory whooping, laughing, stomping and table-slapping, and Jay yelling, 'Really?' over and over and over. 'Really? Really?'

I mute the television; the din continues.

And because no one comes to tell me anything, I swing my legs off the sofa and go through to the kitchen to find out what is going on.

They stop. They slip the happiness off their faces.

Jay looks at me like I am nothing.

'When?' Maria asks Rick in a restrained voice.

He shrugs. 'Could be months away. We're waiting to find out. So, in the meantime we just carry on as usual.'

He looks at me with a false smile as he opens the door. 'Anyway. See you later.'

'What was all that about?' I ask Jay afterwards. 'I heard you talking about drugs.'

'Just... something to do with Rick's mum. Medical stuff.' He sits down heavily. His mind is somewhere else. I have a feeling that the news wasn't about Rick's mum. It was something to do with what goes on in Jay's other world: the dark place that I'd rather not know too much about. I return to my television programme in time to see them fitting the new patio doors.

Jay stays in the kitchen. Through the crack of the door I see him lean his head into his hands and stare at the table. Cigarette smoke filters through and I make a show of coughing but he doesn't comment. Something has changed him: maybe Rick's news about the drugs? I start to wonder if it is something that might change us, our relationship. He knows that I don't like him being involved in drug-dealing. I continue with the programme but Jay still doesn't return to join me, he just rolls another cigarette and stays apart with his thoughts, as if I have done something wrong.

This feels worrying. Is it something I *have* done without realising? I switch off the television and bustle around noisily, picking up cups and taking them through to the sink.

'Are you OK?' I ask as I run hot water into the bowl.

'Yeah.' He smiles but there is no real expression on his face. He scratches his head and stubs out his cigarette.

I go through to the studio to collect the rest of the mugs and ensure the equipment has been switched off. Patryk has left his heavy amplifier behind the door and I have to drag it into the corner because it's too heavy for me to pick up. The carpet ripples under its weight. I wedge the amplifier over my foot while I pull the carpet back into the corner, and it's only then that I notice a folded piece of grubby paper poking out from underneath.

I almost don't bother picking it up. But then I do. Then I almost don't bother unfolding it to see if it is anything of interest. But then I do. And I have to sit heavily on the amplifier because – oh fuck – just the sight of the handwriting and I'm suddenly faint. The quirky loops, the e's like back-to-front threes: I would know it anywhere.

It's Nell's writing.

There's a smudge over one of the words from what looks like spilled liquid, but the rest is completely legible:

If I don't make it out alive it is <unreadable> Ruth that is killing me

The scrape of a chair being pulled back over the kitchen floor makes me scrunch the note quickly and shove it into my pocket. I stamp the carpet back into the corner.

Jay sticks his head round the door. 'I'm knackered. See you up in bed?'

'OK, I'll just finish washing the pots and be right up.'

My head is banging and my cheeks are suddenly burning. What the actual fuck have I just discovered? Evidence that Nell was murdered, that's what. She didn't take her own life. I go to the kitchen and plunge my hands into the scorching water, listening to Jay moving about in the bedroom above.

So, Nell had been in the locked room. What happened to her in there? Why did she think she might not get out alive? Did Ruth lock her in, and is that why Jay didn't know where the key was, because Ruth had it? All these questions crowd me, but the timeline doesn't add up of when Jay and Ruth were in a relationship: something to do with a baby, Ruth being at university... Why can't I remember what Jay told me?

My mind is swirling. Because everything has just changed gear. I have indisputable information from Nell herself that Ruth was involved in her death. And that means one thing.

I have to find Ruth. And I have to get revenge.

* * *

It is morning, the day after, in bed, in a pocket of cosiness, with the sun spilling onto my eyelids, in one of those half-sleeps where there's an electrical buzz in your brain like a badly tuned radio and you can't quite remember who you are or where you are. Where you're partway through a dream but you can hear birds chortling on the roof, cups clattering downstairs, the kettle almost whistling. Where you don't want to open your eyes or be properly conscious and you hear voices in the kitchen and Rick saying to Jay, 'Ruth needs you. She needs to see you.'

Then I'm awake.

. . .

I pull my dressing gown on and stand at the top of the stairs in silence. Clattering. Murmuring. A jangle of keys. Then the kitchen door being hauled open and shut. I run down the stairs and watch from behind the living room door as Rick and Jay get into Rick's car and reverse out of the drive. I go into the kitchen, trembling, to find a cup with instant coffee and sugar in the bottom, ready for me to put milk and water in. I sit at the table. My head tingles.

So. Ruthie. She is still involved with Jay. She has Rick as a go-between. The three of them are hiding something from me, covering something up. I know this is all linked to Nell.

But none of them know the intensity of my feelings for Nell. They don't know the strength of my character. They don't know that I will do anything to find the truth. Anything.

I try to ask Jay about Ruthie when Rick drops him off in the afternoon.

'Where have you been?' I am unable to keep the nagging wife tone out of my voice.

'Nowhere,' he replies. He shifts his eyes from side to side.

'Nowhere?' I say sardonically. 'So, you leave me in bed and just disappear for' – I check my watch – 'six hours, but you haven't been anywhere?'

'Calm down,' he says, holding his hands up. 'I always go out on a Saturday morning to deliver the veg boxes. You know that.'

'But you haven't even delivered any!'

'What are you accusing me of?' He starts rolling a cigarette.

'You've been with *her*, haven't you?'

He stops – a pinch of tobacco dangling from his fingers – and looks at me. 'Who?'

I don't want to say the name. Don't want to taste the bitter syllables in my mouth. 'I heard Rick this morning, telling you in the kitchen. I was awake.'

He makes a face like he is thinking back to then. 'He said his mum wanted me. That's all. One of the trees in her garden: a branch had bent over with the snow, nearly snapped it, so she wanted me to take it off. I've brought it back to saw into logs. It's on the drive.' He drops the tobacco into a paper's waiting 'V' and saunters through to the living room to smoke it.

CHAPTER TWENTY-SEVEN

FEBRUARY

Snow returns. For a few days at the beginning of the month we are conned by cobalt skies, pregnant buds on trees, cordial breezes from the west. Then it's back, overnight: a virgin shroud up to our ankles that hides the daffodil shoots and flattens the shrubs. Makes the roads impassable again. Takes us back to square one: the rug in front of the fire where it's only us and our selective histories that we weave together with the patchy bits that we keep returning to. I have to get to Ruth. And I have to get to Nell. But I cannot take the direct path of questioning so I have to travel the cul-de-sacs and rings around the subject of them both in the vain hope that something will give me a lead.

So I ask Jay about his mother. The woman who sent him a Christmas card with 'Mum and Gerald' scrawled inside it – no other message – like she was in a rush.

Her name is Kath. Jay says she was all right as far as mothers went. She cooked meat and two veg dinners and had her hair done at Clive's in the high street every six weeks. She had a couple of boyfriends after his dad left, but nothing serious until Gerald came onto the scene when Jay was sixteen. Gerald: fat, with dandruff in his eyebrows and a hankering for quiz nights, wore moccasin slippers to drive in and always talked of taking Kath away from it all.

'So, when did they go to Spain?' I ask. 'Have you ever been to visit them?'

Jay says they've been there about fourteen years now. They might even be married for all he knows. He's never been over; never had a passport, can't be arsed with queuing in airports. He's seen his mum a few times since: she's been back to visit friends and met up with him for the day in Mansfield, even came to the house a couple of years ago and kipped on the sofa after a night of gin and orange. I imagine her with leathery skin and false eyelashes and inappropriately short skirts: the type of person who thinks it's acceptable to sit on the toilet with the door wide open and talk to people.

'Do you have any pictures?' I say. 'I love looking at family photographs.'

He shrugs. Somewhere around the house, he supposes.

But I've looked over every inch of the house, in every cupboard. I've never found any photos of anyone.

He puts another CD on. Nick Cave and the Bad Seeds. I can tell he doesn't want to talk about his mum. He wants to talk about the band, let his ideas flow out. Next thing he'll be urging me to get my fiddle, try a tune. It needs a measured approach to get every piece of information out of him. He might not want to talk about Ruth or Nell just yet, but I can wait. I can wait for as long as it takes.

* * *

There is a spy thriller on television. Jay is sprawled out on the rug propping up his chin with his hands. I sit on the sofa with my thoughts. Ruth. Ruthie. With the long black hair and the purple dress and her name under the paint and the kisses in the self-sufficiency book. I think about her and who she is and what she might be capable of. Then I think about Nell. With her long black hair and her gold bracelet under the bed and warning note under the carpet. One of them is still alive and the other is dead.

I look at the picture on the screen. A man and woman are running.

'Whoa,' says Jay suddenly.

There is the sound of gunfire. There is espionage and double-crossing. The plot is baffling. I see the film for two hours. I don't know who is on whose side. And I wonder how I can find Ruth, and what she did to Nell, and all I can think about is Ruth and Nell and the fact that they both had long black hair and the fact that I have long black hair, and I don't know if *my* life is in danger from Ruth or if Jay loves me as much as he loves Ruth, and there is still so much that I need to do to the house while I hold my life together.

* * *

Jay put on his boots and gloves and old wax jacket and walked to the estate. The lane is still thick with ice and snow: some of the neighbours had made feeble attempts at getting out in their Range Rovers but have slid around and returned quickly to their warm kitchens and coffee machines.

I take a tape measure upstairs and lay it along the boundary of the carpet before hauling the bed two feet away from the wall. Nell's bracelet is still underneath, but I don't want to look at it again. Moving the bed drags the carpet away from the skirting board and exposes a layer of lino: thin, wood-effect spattered with beads of yellow emulsion. I go down to the kitchen, get a vegetable knife and bring it back to pare at the sticky covering: peel it away like avocado shell.

And there it is: my nails scrape the splintery grain before I see it. There it is: wood. Floorboards. Real planks with nails and tongues and grooves. Timber that can be sanded and varnished. Amidst all the stress and anxiety, this has made my day.

So I take the camper and go into town to buy sanding sheets and bin bags and varnish for the bedroom floor.

When I return to the car park, I see from afar something tucked under the windscreen wiper of the campervan. Parking ticket. I begin to curse myself, but then remember that I *did* put a ticket on. Perhaps it's a flyer. But I can't see flyers on any of the other vehicles. As I get closer, I see that it is an A5 envelope, blank, sealed. I pull the wiper blade up and remove it. My breath is trapped like a bubble in my throat. I look around the car park anxiously as I open the flap. Is it a letter for me, or is it intended for Jay? Could it be from Ruth?

I take out the piece of paper that's within, unfolding it to find a photocopied newspaper article. The photograph that looks up at me is Nell.

My eyes are swimming. I can't focus on the words: all I can see is the picture, with the headline:

WOMAN FOUND DEAD IN QUARRY

I unlock the van and climb in. Run my fingers through my hair. What is going on? Although I obviously know everything about this incident, I have never seen this particular article before. So, what the fuck is going on? Who has put this here? Who *knows*?

I sit there for fifteen, twenty minutes even though my ticket has expired. I read the photocopied article for the umpteenth time.

The body of Eleanor Moran was discovered on Friday evening by workmen in a local quarry. Eleanor, 30, had been employed locally as a live-in carer. Her family have said they are devastated and shocked by her death and reported that Eleanor had been suffering from depression and mental health problems. Police are continuing their investigations.

I don't understand. Why has someone put this on the van? Is it a warning? Some kind of threat? And who has put it there? Is it someone who knows why I'm here? But surely no one knows. I haven't told anyone, not Lou or Rachel. What if someone has figured it out, made the connection between me and Nell? Maybe it was Rick. Or Maria. Or maybe…

Ruth.

The house on Portland Crescent is where Rick lives. I'm sure of it. I saw Rick's car pull out of the same drive when I walked past the end of the road on my way to the Co-op. His flat face looked in my direction but he didn't acknowledge me. I pulled my hood around my cheeks and strolled on.

I don't know why Jay didn't tell me that when I asked him. Why wouldn't he? Why wouldn't he want me to know?

And why would Lou drive for over three hours to meet up with Jay? I ask myself the same question over and over, ponder the possible reasons.

This is because of an incident last week.

Jay came home from work – early evening, on the Thursday, I think – and dropped a roadkill pheasant into the sink before shrugging his jacket onto the back of one of the kitchen chairs.

'I'm ready for a smoke,' he said, going through to the living room.

And there's me, hands in a baking bowl trying to make shortcrust pastry, waiting for the chance to ask him if he'd taken my phone, because I'd been looking for it all day after wanting to use the calculator on it.

And since I didn't get chance to ask him because he'd gone into the living room for a smoke, I wiped the flour off my hands and had a feel in the pocket of the coat that he'd just put onto the chair.

And bingo, there was my phone. I looked at the last text, which was from Lou earlier that day, and which Jay had already opened.

Is the Queen's Head in the town centre? she had put. *I don't know which car park to use. Ring me.*

And, puzzled by the text, not knowing if it was intended for me, I felt in the other pocket of Jay's coat to find a receipt. *The Queen's Head*, it said on it. *Lunchtime special: 1 x Steak and Ale Pie, 1 x Caesar Salad.* Eighteen quid.

So. Jay had secretly taken my sister out for lunch. What was I to make of that? Had they met up previously? Why would Lou betray me?

I really didn't know what to think any more.

CHAPTER TWENTY-EIGHT

What I know is that there are times when it's safe to ask questions and times when it's not. And I'm starting to recognise these different occasions.

This morning he looks pliable.

I'm polishing the draining board. Unnecessarily, Jay might say. I can see through the window into the garden where he has been splitting wood. He's sitting on the chopping stump with his head in his hands. His left leg shakes. He rubs at his face.

He's been different lately. Quieter, pensive, away in his other world.

I edge carefully into the corner of the kitchen and watch him from the side of the window. The unanswered questions have been mounting up into a surfeit: maybe today I could make some progress.

I go out there. Stand in front of him while he sits on the stump.

'Why don't we go for a walk?' I suggest. 'You look like you have things on your mind. And I'm here for you.' I reach out and touch his face.

He looks up at me. For a long time. He's going to go for it, I'm sure he is.

'OK,' he says. He takes my hand and leads me past the door – he doesn't bother to lock it – and onto the path around the front of the house, through a snicket, into the fields that lead to the quarry.

It's not snowy this time, but it's cold, muddy: my boots are heavier with each footstep, gathering a platform of clay. I stomp along beside him. His hand warms mine.

'This is good,' he says. 'Being out here, fields and woods and birds, with no one else around.'

'It's fantastic,' I say.

'I don't know how you used to live in a town. All that noise, everybody with their eyes on you.'

I remember well. The feeling of being watched, talked about. *Her with the married man. Slag. Whore. Home-breaker. Who does she think she is?* Even my mother got snubbed in the Spar shop. I couldn't go back to it. Not now.

'What do you think about me?' I ask him. 'Really? Be honest.'

He turns, a pained expression on his face. Crushes me into his arms. 'I adore you,' he says. 'You've been the perfect thing. I really don't know...'

'I didn't know if you were still seeing other people. Rick said...'

He pinches my lips between his forefinger and thumb.

'Rick is wrong. You've been so good for me and he knows it.'

He releases me, takes my hand again and we continue over the field.

'I heard that someone was found in the quarry,' I begin carefully. 'A woman's body. Down at the bottom...'

His hand slackens around mine. The pitch of his voice shifts up a semi-tone. 'Yeah. Someone daft enough to go out walking around the edge. She was suicidal, apparently.'

I don't know if I ought to say anything else. I stop walking. Look at him. Hesitate. He seems to see behind my eyes and into my mind.

'What?' he says.

'Did you know her?' I ask casually.

Jay shakes his head. 'Why would I? Anyway, how did you know about it?'

I think of the envelope on the van. 'Someone had left an old newspaper in the library.'

I don't know if he believes me. We start walking again. He swings my arm.

'Is that what you wanted to come out for? To ask me about that?'

I take a deep breath.

'Have you been talking to my sister?' I say quickly. 'Or seeing her?'

He pauses, thinks hard, as if trying to recall something that happened years ago instead of three days ago. 'Yes,' he says. 'Your sister. I don't want to hurt you by being negative about her. But she can be a nasty piece of work.'

I know that already. She's dropped me in it on plenty of occasions.

'I'll be completely honest with you,' he says. 'I've used your phone a couple of times. You know that. Just work stuff, really. I knew you wouldn't mind me taking it, you're cool like that. But I ended up pressing the wrong button and dialling her by mistake, one time. I said to her I'd only rung up by accident, but she sort of came on to me and even ended up being suggestive, saying some right dirty stuff.'

'You went to meet her though,' I say. 'It wasn't just a phone call.'

'She said she had something important to tell me about you. She said she needed to warn me. About your past.'

Anger is burning like white heat in my core.

'She said you had a thing about married men; you caused loads of trouble in her mate's family. She said you were always trying it on with her husband too... what's his name? Dominic.'

'That's not true!' I react wildly.

'She told me you murdered your kid.'

'No, it wasn't like that...' I am enraged. How dare the devious bitch try and wreck my relationship: I moved away, not just for myself and Nell, but for *her*. And now she drives to meet Jay behind my back so that she can spill the secrets I have run away from. I clench my jaw, my fists, feeling the loathing for her surge through me.

'I had an abortion,' I try to explain to Jay. 'It was very early on, only a tiny foetus. But I couldn't possibly keep a baby at the time...'

Jay shrugs.

'I'm not a murderer. I know some people are totally against abortions' – please, please don't let Jay be a hardcore pro-lifer – 'but the father didn't want it and everything was so difficult... My best friend had just died...'

He does a sort-of forced smile at me and takes a deep breath.

'I'm sorry,' I say. 'I should have told you myself. I should...'

He touches my lips to silence them. 'It's done with. You don't need to explain any more.'

I quiver and exhale, as my doubts about Jay and hatred for Lou whisk around together like liquid.

We have reached the edge of the quarry. I hang back a few feet, remembering the panic of the last visit. Remembering Nell.

'Come here,' says Jay, tugging at my hand on an outstretched arm.

'I don't like it,' I say.

'Please,' he says. 'Trust me.'

I edge forward. Glance down into the stony ravine. Wonder how tiny Nell's body looked at the bottom of it.

'It's a long way down,' he says. He takes a finger to turn my face towards his, to scrutinise it, to fasten his eyes on mine. That greenness, that mystique.

'Abortions aside, d'you think you could ever be capable of killing someone?' he asks.

I realise that while I have been looking into his eyes we have moved around. I am on the edge of the quarry with my back to it. Jay has a hand on my shoulder.

'Like, just push them over the edge?'

I laugh in a slightly hysterical way, because surely he doesn't mean it and I don't really know how to respond; but then his face hardens; there's pressure on my shoulder.

'What?' My heart is scrabbling around in my ribcage.

'Could you do it? If you had a good reason?'

'I don't know.' He's being preposterous. I laugh timidly, but he's not smiling yet: he's starting to really scare me.

'If you really hated someone? Or wanted to get revenge for something?'

I stare blankly at him. Is this hypothetical? Does he know about Nell and my desire to avenge her death? Does he think that I might kill Ruth? Or is he implying that I *should* murder someone? Is he suggesting I push *Lou* over the edge? He takes his eyes away, takes his hand from my shoulder. Holds out two fists in front of him, like a conjuror.

'Which hand?' he asks.

'I don't know,' I say. I don't know what we are doing here; I don't know what we are discussing. All I know is that there is a killer drop right behind me.

'Which hand?' he asks again.

I tap the right knuckle. He turns it over.

'Good choice,' he says.

He opens his hand. There is a tiny pill in it. It's ready for a special kiss. My heart is on the point of bursting: my body is aroused at the sight of it. He places it on the end of his tongue and I surge forward with longing, close my eyes and press my lips onto his.

*

Candlelight is good, she looks perfect in candlelight. A sort of virtual reality. Yeah, he likes that phrase. Virtual reality. But without all the computer shit.

He tried a different method last time, just for a laugh. Tethering by conjoined ankles and hanging upside down. But it didn't work with the dress, didn't work with her hair and obviously didn't give great access to the succulent places that he wanted to devour. And he'd possibly left her in the position too long that it had made her violently sick, so that vomit had run into her eyes, her hair, up her nose. She'd choked for a while and he'd started to get worried that she might asphyxiate. So no, it wasn't a success. Maybe just ten minutes would be better, and maybe if he'd knotted the rope around each ankle separately...

It's an idea he can try another time.

He returns to the traditional tried-and-tested method. Through the hooks, rope tied around each wrist individually. It gives her a bit of freedom, a bit of animation.

But she doesn't want to share the cigarette he's rolled, turning her face to the side when he tries to place it between her lips.

'OK, it's like that, is it? You're being defiant, Ruthie, tonight, are you?'

He lifts her dress and runs the lit end of his cigarette lightly up the inside of her left thigh, smiling as she moans. He knows that if people were being judgy they'd see it as a sick, offensive thing, but she isn't like that. She's away, in some indescribable euphoria that she never wants to wake up from.

'I love you, Ruth. Don't ever forget it.'

CHAPTER TWENTY-NINE

It is half past eight on a sparkling blue morning. The sun is warm enough to make the roof tiles creak and crack above me. It is the day when I will banish the horrible bedroom carpet and bring the old floorboards to life.

Jay has left with Rick. They have two thousand hedging whips to plant on the estate: hawthorn, blackthorn and dogwood. He tells me that it's back-breaking work and he will be out until at least five. I tell him that I will have a hot bath and a bottle of wine ready for him when he gets home. I don't mention the floor.

I empty the contents of the drawers and wardrobe into bin bags. I drag the mattress and bed base onto their sides. On the floor is a dark square of dust and hair, a sprinkling of coins, three black socks and Nell's gold bracelet. I pick up the bracelet and put it in my pocket. I will need to find another hiding place.

Suddenly, there is a tap on the door: a soft, flat sound. I hold my breath and tiptoe down to the hallway to peek through the living room window. There is no car in the driveway. Another knock, three more taps.

Is it *her*? I wonder. Has she come to see Jay? I stand still and listen carefully.

Then, childish steps skipping around the side of the house. A tangle of orange hair and an innocent face pressing up to the living room window. Disc of gauzy breath on the thin glass.

Lolly.

I go and pull the door open and she runs back down the path to me. She stands and smiles, in a Disney T-shirt, with bare, bruised legs.

'Is it half-term?' I ask, and she follows me into the kitchen without replying.

'Does Maria know where you are?' I ask, and she nods. She sees the roll of bin bags on the table and reaches out to touch the black edge. And I realise that Lolly could be useful.

'Do you want to help me? I'm clearing out the bedroom.'

She nods again vigorously.

So I take her upstairs and she heaves the mattress down with me onto the studio floor. We brace ourselves to drag the heavy wardrobe away from the wall but find, surprisingly, that it glides away in a semicircle on casters. Behind it, on a nail in the wall, is a key. I look at it with a start, knowing immediately that it is the key to the dining room. Did Jay really not know where it was?

And there, underneath the nail, cut into the woodchip, with a yellowing coat of gloss and small chrome handle, is a square door giving access to the loft space.

'A secret door,' Lolly says, behind her left hand.

The room suddenly seems stifling and I have to pull off my cardigan. There are answers behind that door. I know there are.

'Are you going to look inside?' says Lolly, peering from behind her fingers.

I don't know what to do. Part of me wants to wrench it open and pull out all the evidence. But Lolly is here. I don't want her to see me finding these things and getting emotional.

'*I* would,' she says.

I have to decide.

'Come on,' I say to her. 'Do I look like the sort of person who wants to go into a place where I've heard mice running about? We need to dismantle the wardrobe and get this carpet up now and it would be great if you could help me.'

The door is forgotten. Lolly is on her knees tugging at the flimsy turquoise covering. I will look behind the door later, when she has gone.

Lolly works hard. She is a good help. I seem to have a connection with her, a way of bringing her out of her silent world.

We pull up the carpet and lino; we dismantle the bed frame and smash up the drawer carcass; we drag everything down-stairs and put it out on the drive.

'What next?' says Lolly.

'Do you want to strip the wallpaper? And I'll start the sanding?'

She nods enthusiastically.

So, we work together with the music blaring and it feels good; it calms me, keeps me from thinking too much about what might be behind the door. And by three o'clock the walls are bare: there are no declarations of love behind the paper; and the floor is smooth but dusty.

'Well done,' I say to her as we scoop up the swathes of soggy paper. 'It's looking good.'

'I like doing it,' she says. 'I'd do it again if I could.'

Suddenly, the rain starts. An outburst of fat droplets hitting the roof window that makes Lolly gasp and point her finger to the sky. It pelts so loudly on the roof tiles that we can no longer hear the music.

'I'll get wet if I go home now,' she says. 'I haven't got a coat. Or an umbrella.'

'Don't worry,' I say kindly. 'I'll take you.' But I remember

that Jay has the camper and I will have to wait until he gets back
with it, which means that I will get no time alone to look behind
the secret door.

I need to look in the loft space before Jay returns. And it
wouldn't be right to send Lolly home in the awful weather.

'Why don't I run you a nice bath?' I suggest. 'You've worked
really hard today and deserve to relax. You could have a long
soak and I'll light the smelly candles and put some more music
on for you. You'd like that, wouldn't you?'

She nods.

'Then I'll take you home when Jay gets back. OK?'

She nods again. 'Or I could stay the night.'

'Well,' I say carefully, 'we haven't really got room, especially
now we can't use the bedroom.'

'I could sleep in the living room. I did at Christmas.'

'Well, anyway,' I say, 'let's sort out a lovely bath for you.'

I fill the tub almost to the top, and pop in a bath bomb. I
light the vanilla candle which flickers and hisses in the steamy
room. I put on a relaxation CD and drag a speaker to the bathroom door which I leave a finger ajar.

'Have a nice long time in there,' I say to her. 'Doze off if you
want. I sometimes do.'

I listen and wait until I hear her step into the water, then I
go upstairs.

I open the door to a draught of cold air and the scent of musty
wood. Just inside is a saucer of blue rat poison and a large
plastic storage box. Maybe the box contains more bait. I unclip
the lid and the sweet, distinctive smell of cannabis rises out.
Inside are old jam jars all crammed with weed. I shuffle them
around and underneath find bags of the small white pills. The
special ones. My heart starts to race as I try to count them:
maybe fifty in each bag, and ten bags in the box. What are they?

Ecstasy? LSD? Some kind of cocaine? I'm still not sure. It isn't completely dark in the roof space: some light from the bedroom is seeping into the doorway but it looks like the area is empty. I close the door. Open it again to just have another look and make sure. But no, I'm fairly certain there's nothing else in there.

And then I remember the bracelet in my pocket. I go downstairs, take a plastic bag from a drawer in the kitchen and slip the gold band inside. I go out to the garden, into the narrow gap between the hedge and the back of the shed, and dig a hole with a spoon. Eight inches, nine inches deep, then I press the wrapped bracelet down into the soil, scoop the soft earth back over and grind it hard with my heel.

Jay's face is hard to read when I take him upstairs. Pinched, with a tremor below his left eye, he presses his fingers to his lips. But he must have suspected the current spate of DIY: the hotch-potch of furniture panels and bags of carpet outside the kitchen door had him bursting in, flummoxed to find Lolly with a towel turbaned around her hair.

'This will look fantastic when it's done,' I say to him. 'Like a proper cottage bedroom. These floorboards are great: you can just imagine them varnished, with the grain brought out.'

'Won't it be freezing in winter, though?' says Jay. 'It already feels colder up here.'

'It'll be lovely with rugs down. And we should put insulation in the loft cavity. That would make a big difference. I've ordered some new furniture which is coming next Monday. Bed, wardrobe, drawers, bedside cabinets. All self-assembly, so there's a job for you.'

'Great,' he says. But his voice is dead. He mauls his face, seems embarrassed. Perhaps he feels awkward about me paying for all the stuff.

He doesn't even look at the door into the roof cavity.

* * *

Hannah's dad says a funny thing to me when I go to their house for the second time to teach violin to their disinclined daughter.

'Do you live on Portland Crescent?'

The words jolt me. 'No, why?'

'I saw your campervan down there yesterday. A man with longish hair was driving.'

Jay. Going to Rick's. When he was supposed to be working on the estate all day.

'We have a friend who lives down there. My partner gives him a lift to work sometimes,' I reply.

'Well, I waved but I don't think you saw me.'

'Me?'

'You were in the passenger seat,' he says.

There's a sour taste in the back of my mouth. I can feel myself sweating. I didn't go out yesterday. I was painting the bedroom.

'Are you sure it was me?' My voice sounds small and dry.

'Well, if it wasn't it must have been your double,' he laughs. 'Same hair and everything.'

I touch my hair and a strand comes away in my fingers.

The lesson is difficult. I can't think properly and end up playing tunes in the wrong key. Hannah stops halfway through one of the melodies and stares at me as if I'm stupid.

'Sorry, I'm not with it today,' I say. 'Let's try another piece. You choose something.'

She stares again. Shrugs. Gazes out of the window at a boy walking past.

I shuffle the pages on the music stand. My eyes don't see the titles. My hand picks up my bow and slides it across a cube of rosin, but my arms, my fingers, my whole body, they don't seem to belong to me; my mind has detached itself from them.

The door opens; Hannah walks in swigging from a can of Coke. I didn't even realise that she had left the room.

'So, what am I doing then?' she says in a voice as flat as her fiddle playing.

'Let's do some of the jigs again that we played last time,' I say. 'They're good for developing speed and intonation.'

We play, but I don't hear her mistakes, her bow scraping the wrong string, her crochets that should be quavers. I am wondering who lives on Portland Crescent if it's not Rick.

CHAPTER THIRTY

I drive down Portland Crescent before I go home. At the house I thought was Rick's there is a big, black Renault parked in the driveway, a people-carrier type. No sign of Rick's car.

Maybe Rick doesn't live there. Maybe Ruth does. I can't get my head round all this.

I drive out of the village and then I'm back home without realising how I've got there. Rick's car is parked in front of our house.

Steadying my breathing, I hear music blasting out as I walk down the path. I kick the kitchen door open. There are dirty pots all over the place. Muddy carrots sitting in a colander. Noodles trailing over the edge of the sink. Teabags on the drainer. Coat thrown over the table. Lumps of coal and a smattering of white ash around the base of the Rayburn.

Rick's maddening laugh ruptures from behind the living room door. I turn on the hot tap and squirt washing-up liquid into the bowl. Then Jay cracks up and cries, 'Whaaat?'

I go into the living room. The stodgy aroma of cannabis combined with patchouli hangs in the air as I stand in the doorway and look at them.

'Hey, babe,' says Jay. 'How'd it go?'

The television is on. I don't know what they're laughing at. It looks like a police drama and the sound is muted while the CD plays. Rick sits there with a smirk and filthy trainers on, scuffing the floor.

'Kitchen's a mess.'

'Sit yourself down and chill,' says Jay. 'I'll do it later.'

Rick sniggers for no reason and it sets Jay off again. I close the door on them and go and switch off the tap. I collect and stack the plates into the foamy bowl and leave them to soak.

I go upstairs to the empty bedroom. Clean, unsullied, with blank walls and glossy pine floor that bounces your shadows. It cheers me, the sight of it all, the promise of the new furniture, the sense of achievement.

Weighty footsteps on the stairs turn me round. Rick pokes his head up.

'Just wondering what you're doing,' he says. 'It looks like you're getting rid of a lot of our stuff without asking.'

'I'm just putting value on your inheritance,' I say placidly. 'And the furniture was old and crap. You could have taken it ages ago if you were bothered.'

He gawps around the room but can't think of anything else to say.

'Do you live on Portland Crescent?' I ask.

'Yeah, why, what's it to you?' he replies, but he's looking behind him as if it's a trick question, as if he should have consulted Jay first.

'I just wondered,' I say. 'Couldn't remember the name of the road. It's posh down there, isn't it?'

'It's all right, yeah.'

I've confused him. He's standing there with a furrow between his eyebrows. 'Anyway,' he says. He turns. This is the longest I've ever spoken to him. A thought pops into my head.

'Another thing,' I say. He looks back. 'I heard that someone called Eleanor Moran died in the quarry...'

'Yes, she did indeed,' he interjects. 'But that subject is now closed. OK?' He gives me a frosty stare. Then wrings his lips into a withering smile. He bares his teeth and makes an intimidating hissing noise before going back down the stairs.

* * *

Jay's explanation about the woman in the van is simple. Hannah's dad is doolally: can't remember what day it is or what street he's on.

'It was you in the van,' he insists. 'That's obviously why he thought it was you. Durr.' He taps the side of his temple. 'But it wasn't yesterday, it was the day before.'

I remember being with him in the van the day before. We had been making some veg box deliveries.

'But not on Portland Crescent,' I say. 'I've never been down there with you in the van.'

'He's thinking of Portland Avenue,' says Jay. 'We have to drive down Portland Avenue to get onto Mill Street, which is where we took that box to: you know, the woman who's always baking muffins? We've delivered there about three times now.'

He's right. But something still isn't clicking into place and I can't think what it is.

* * *

We go into town to do some shopping. It's one of those rare occasions when we are together: usually I go alone to stock up on basics, browse around the charity shops, use the computers at the library. But Jay wanted to come and buy a home-brew kit from the herbal shop and get some onion sets from the market.

'We could have done some busking,' I say. 'It's not too cold today.'

'Mmm.' He turns his nose up. 'Chesterfield's better. We make more money there. Perhaps we should start going to other places. Doncaster. Nottingham. See what they're like.'

He stops suddenly at the smoking paraphernalia stall to buy some cheap disposable lighters and cigarette papers. I wander on without him and find a bazaar of ethnic clothes and jewellery tucked away in the middle of the market. A purple velvet dress hangs on a high rail and immediately I am drawn to it. I run my knuckles down the rough texture of the fabric; finger the beaded bodice, the deep lace cuffs. The vendor sidles towards me.

'Only one left in that colour,' he says. He twizzles the ring in his lower lip.

'How much?' I ask.

'Forty-five quid to you, darling,' he replies. He tucks his hands into his money pouch and shuffles the notes.

Next thing, Jay is beside me. I turn and smile, hold the skirt of the dress out for him to see.

'What do you think? I really like this. And it's my size.'

He moves behind me, rests his chin on my shoulder, circles his arms around my waist. The carrier bag in his hand swings against a bruise on my thigh. We look together at the dress.

'Yep,' he says. 'It's you all over.'

He nibbles my neck, my earlobe. 'But why do you want it when you've got one almost the same at home?'

I turn in his arms. 'But...' I begin. And it dawns on me that yes, I have: I remember seeing it in the wardrobe; I remember it clinging and falling from my buttocks, embracing my breasts; the lace cuffs caressing the backs of my hands. It's odd though, because I cannot remember ever consciously taking it off the hanger and putting it on to wear.

'You're losing your marbles,' he laughs, and we walk away from the stall, hand-in-hand.

But I can't quite recall if the dress really is mine, or if it belonged to *her*, and if it did, does this mean that Jay has forgotten that it used to be hers because he only thinks of it on me now?

And as we go back to the car park Jay asks me if I fancy a special evening, and of course I do: the S-word alone sets my pulse racing and starts to turn me on. I squeeze his left arse-cheek and he sinks his teeth into my neck and we giggle in anticipation.

Then we stop. We've seen it. The front windscreen of the campervan plastered with paper: some sort of flyers or pictures or newspaper. There's not an inch of glass left.

'What the fuck?' says Jay, letting go of me and running towards it.

My heart hammers. I feel faint.

The window of the van is a monochrome collage. Photocopied pictures of Eleanor in varying sizes stare at us. The short, accompanying article about her death is repeated and dotted around the glass. Some copies have been enlarged so that the type is eighty point, ninety point, visible from metres away.

'Who's done this?' says Jay, scanning his eyes around the car park, and I follow the direction of his glances but there's no one around, no one obvious.

He pulls at the corner of one of the sheets of paper: a strip of it peels and disintegrates into a point. It's all been stuck down with some sort of glue. I go to the passenger side and run my thumbnail under a photograph. A thin sliver lifts unwillingly.

'Fuck's sake,' rants Jay, slapping his palm down on the front of the van. He looks behind him. 'I'll rip their bastard head off if they're watching.'

I stand and shrug helplessly.

Jay drops his jaw and shakes his head at me. 'I'll sort whoever's done this, I really will. It's like somebody's trying to accuse me of something.'

'What is it about?' I dare to ask. 'Did you know her?'

'A couple of fucking dates, that's all. She was nothing to me. But everyone puts two and two together and makes fucking thirty-nine.'

He unlocks the door and gets in the van. Switches on the engine. Squirts the washers, puts the wipers on a couple of times. He gets out again and hands me a CD case.

'Get scraping,' he says.

I work neatly, balling the accusatory fragments in my left hand.

'You'd best not think I'm involved in any of this shit,' says Jay. He scrapes aggressively at the driver's side.

'I don't. You know I don't think that,' I reply meekly. But I think of Nell's note and how she said that Ruth was killing her, and I wonder what Jay knew about it all and if he could have colluded with her and covered it up.

Jay goes back into the van and squirts more water. We get funny looks from a mum strapping her toddler into the car beside us.

'We should stop coming here,' he says. 'We should shop somewhere else. I was only saying earlier about going to Chesterfield. We don't get this crap over there.'

I rub at the last fragments. There are smears all over the screen.

'I'll give it a proper clean with soapy water when we get back,' I say.

We chuck the handfuls of mushy paper into the sink of the camper and drive home in a weighty silence.

I look at Jay's face. I knew he'd had a relationship with Nell. I knew a year ago when she sent me a video of the pair of them larking about with glasses of wine in a pub garden, with the subject line 'new boyfriend'.

I knew from her messages that – long before I joined them – he was a big fan of Cuckoo Spit and often went to gigs and festivals.

It wasn't much information to go on, to be able to track someone down and get into their life.

But it was enough.

CHAPTER THIRTY-ONE

MARCH

The Argos lorry has to reverse down the lane through all the potholes. I had hoped that Jay would be here to help with the unpacking and assembly, but he has already gone out on the bike.

The delivery man brings all the boxes in and stacks them in the living room. I am excited by the cardboard smell, the potential of the unbuilt items that will transform the bedroom.

The man returns with the new plastic-covered mattress and a form to sign.

'Somebody's going to be busy,' he says.

It takes me less than an hour to bolt the bed together with the Allen keys. I iron the new white bedding, and bring up the scatter cushions I bought last week. My heart bursts with delight knowing that by the end of the day the room will be finished.

But before I start assembling the furniture something niggles me. I don't know why, but I get a torch and open the cavity door again. The saucer of rat poison and the plastic box are still there. I open the lid but the contents appear unchanged. I bang the torch onto a joist and listen for the sound of scurrying vermin. But there is silence, apart from an occasional breeze whistling through the roof tiles.

Should I? I ask myself as I climb into the loft space with the torch. I crawl along splintery joists towards the edge of the roof, shining my light in all the gaps. At the end of the row I scramble over the dirty beams to check the next section. Dust fills my nose; coats my face and hands. I can feel it thickening my hair and eyebrows.

Something glints in the beam, like glass, or cellophane or shiny plastic. I shuffle along the joist and scan my light towards the thing: the laminated pastel blue cover of a photograph album. It lies there, face up, between the rough wooden struts. The cottage has come to my aid again; it has revealed another secret.

It's not just any old photograph album, though. I pick it up, squatting in the grimy triangle of the roof space. It's not an item that has been hidden deliberately. It's something that has been lost, forgotten about. 'My Baby Album', it says on the front, in a fancy font decorated with teddies and rabbits. It creaks as I open it. On the inside page it says simply: *Amos, 4th April, 2014*.

Amos. What sort of name is Amos? Why couldn't it have been Jack or Liam or Daniel? Something of its time that you see in a newspaper or hear on TV; the kind of thing that everyone calls their kids.

But Amos? It's a name that's been thought about, pondered over, carefully considered. Evoked certain characteristics, set out its intentions for the child.

I find it hard to imagine a young person called Amos. I remember laughing in the playground at children with funny names. It wasn't just me: everyone did it. Miles. Joss. Caleb. All the names you never heard on telly.

But I don't need to imagine Amos. I have an album stuck with photographs here in my lap. I sit on the new bed, turning each laminated leaf.

Amos: a baby, newborn, with black hair and closed eyes and a half-yawn on rosy lips, held in the weary arms of a mother whose head is out of the photograph, but whose dark hair trails over a gowned breast.

Amos: a few months old, beaming a wet, open-mouthed grin as he's held in a sitting position by Jay's hands (I recognise the thin worms of muck under the nails).

Amos: sitting at the kitchen table, reaching out for a birthday cake oozing buttercream, topped with chocolate buttons and a single candle.

Amos: a toddler with dirty dungarees and teary cheeks standing next to the shed, chubby fingers clasped around a hoe-handle; a row of cloth nappies hanging on a line behind him.

They are all there: photographs only of Amos with occasional adult limbs in the scene to proffer a toy or hold the child into position. A pictorial timeline from birth to whenever. Whenever. I study the final snapshot in the album: it is not on the last page – half the album is yet to be filled. Amos: possibly three, four years old – it's not easy to guess the age of a child when you've never been a mother – proudly holding up a coffee jar of tadpoles to the camera; smear of snot across his cheek; circle of wetness darkening the front of his red jumper.

With shaky hands I cut the straps around the packaging of the pine wardrobe. I spread out the instructions and kneel over them, taking in the differences between the pre-drilled holes on the top and bottom sections, while I worry about how I will cautiously raise the topic of Amos later.

The photograph album is downstairs, on the kitchen table, waiting for Jay's explanation.

. . .

It is almost seven when I hear the chug of his motorbike outside, and I hurry through to the kitchen to stand beside the baby album on the table so that he can see the juxtaposition as he comes through the door.

He is already drained: sweaty, sagging, with a sigh on his lips and the damp night air shadowing him. And as he pushes the door to, he sees me and my silence and the lost book, and his body just slumps into a chair as he pulls the album to his chest.

'Where?' he asks. 'Where was it?'

'In the loft cavity.'

'You're going to ask me questions now.' He looks at me. His eyes are brimming.

'Too right I am.'

'Sit down,' he says. He opens the dusty cover. 'I guess it's time to tell you some stuff.'

CHAPTER THIRTY-TWO

He places the album carefully to one side of the table. He gets an ashtray from under the sink and puts it between us. He rolls two thin cigarettes and passes one to me.

'Tell me,' I say.

He gets glasses and a bottle of red wine, sets them on the table, unscrews the lid.

'You lied to me, didn't you?' I say.

He lights his cigarette and holds the flame for me. He flicks the end of his roll-up into the ashtray even though there's no ash on it yet. All these rituals, while I wait.

Then he looks at me. Pulls a deep breath into his lungs.

'Remember one night you asked me something and I reacted? I snapped and got angry.'

'Remember what?'

'You asked me if I'd ever thought what it would be like to kill someone.'

My mouth is dry, so full of tongue and teeth that I can't speak. Heat rises to my chest, my neck, my nose and cheeks. I reach over my wine glass to pick up his lighter and put a flame to the stubby candle at the other side of the table.

I look at him but he doesn't continue. Time seeps between us and drifts around with the smoke. I sip my wine. It's too cold, too bitter.

'So, have you?' I say finally. I don't know if this is going to be a confession about Nell, or about Amos, but this act of politeness and waiting and pushing things around the table feels like it is leading up to something earth-shattering.

He strokes the lit end of his cigarette across the back of his hand and I smell the burning of his hair, his skin. He doesn't flinch.

'I killed Amos.' He taps the photograph album. Manages a pursed smile. 'Snotty bugger. Always had a runny nose.' He stubs his cigarette into the gingham tablecloth, crushes it like a beetle with his forefinger. Then he swigs his wine, and I pick up the cigarette end and put it in the ashtray. There is a hole in the cloth and the Formica underneath is scarred black.

The night is difficult, like a long and painful labour. We open three bottles of wine. Smoke countless cigarettes.

They had a son, Jay and Ruth. And when he had told me before that they had lost the kid, what he really meant was that he had died when he was nearly five years old.

They lived here, a young family, with Jay doing gardening jobs and work on the estate, and Ruth taking on small eco-consultancy projects for private clients.

But one night, around two years ago, the three of them had travelled to a place up past Barnsley, to a patch of land where a group of hippies wanted to develop a green commune to live sustainably with wind turbines, solar panels, compost toilets, the lot. Ruth was happy to help with plans for a low fee and in return she could take photographs and write articles about the development's progress. The location was fantastic: woods and fields with no near neighbours. Goats, chickens, ducks, a polytunnel made from flattened plastic bottles and a huge, enviable log pile. A harmonious, chilled-out vibe, where they didn't need supermarkets or technology. Jay even considered taking Ruth and Amos to be part of the group.

They had driven home down the motorway, excited about the project. Ruth reminded Jay that they needed petrol but Jay said not to worry, there would be enough to get them home. Amos was asleep in the back seat, his lips slack around his wrinkled thumb – Jay had threatened to rub chillies onto it to break the habit, but had never had the heart. The motorway wasn't too busy. It was only nine-ish, and the weather was reasonable: a couple of pathetic showers had splashed down, but hardly anything worth putting the windscreen wipers on for.

Then the car – an old Micra – had started sputtering and gasping. Ruth thought it was the lack of petrol and started on an 'I told you so'. Jay insisted it was something else because the needle wasn't off the red yet, and they bickered as the car juddered and gradually lost power and Jay had to use the last bit of momentum to freewheel onto the hard shoulder.

'It *has* run out of petrol,' Ruth had said, and then Jay had realised that she was right.

'You'll have to walk somewhere and get some,' she had said to Jay, who was pushing at the button for the hazard warning lights.

'I can't get this to switch on,' he'd said.

Then the rain started tipping down: a sudden rush of weather front that they could see moving towards them in the headlights. And it seemed so cosy in the little car with Amos sleeping behind them and the thought of the services being miles away in the rain, that Jay told them to stay in the car, he would climb up the embankment and run over the fields to find a nearby petrol station instead.

I watch and wait for more as Jay shivers and covers his face with his hands. I need the toilet but don't want to move. It's as though I can't leave him alone at the table. He cries. He pulls at his hair. He picks up his lighter and flicks it on and off, on and off. He holds his thumb over the flame until I smell his skin again, see the blister start to puff. He doesn't look at me.

I slide my hand across the table towards his, to remind him that I am here, and he covers it with his own, sighing, with a sob trapped at the back of his throat.

'I should have made them get out and wait up the embankment,' he says. 'Everyone knows you shouldn't sit in a car on the hard shoulder.'

I turn my hand under his and squeeze his rough palm.

'If it hadn't been raining I would have made them get out. Or if Amos had been awake, I would have...' His voice falters, cracks into a different key.

He had stumbled through what seemed like miles of muddy fields, towards the lights of houses and pubs in villages that he didn't know existed. There had been cars and small shops and cottages and churches and everything but a petrol station. He had finally gone into a pub, soaked cold so that steam oozed from his clothes as he waited in the tap room. The barman had laughed, asked him where he had swum from, then told him the nearest petrol station was on the motorway, up the service road about two miles away.

By the time he got the petrol and set off along the hard shoulder over an hour had passed. And he could see flashing lights in the distance, hear the sirens, feel the uneasy rush of a police car, then a fire engine across the northbound lanes. The sick realisation that no traffic was driving southbound tormented him, made him run like a madman, with a stitch in his side and his heart ready to burst. It wasn't just worry; it was as if he already knew. Two ambulances and another police car screamed past him before he reached the scene.

He shouted their names with the breath he had left. He remembered seeing cars – at least three – mangled across the motorway. One was on its side. He couldn't tell which one was the Micra. There were firemen with cutting equipment. There were more ambulances and a paramedic car. There were police everywhere. They caught hold of him as he roared out for Ruth and Amos, and bundled him into a cop car that smelt of salt and vinegar crisps. Took the green plastic petrol can off him that he'd had to buy from the services.

It was a major situation and the police were trying to establish what had happened. They thought that a car had hit the back of the Micra while it was parked on the hard shoulder. Other cars had been involved. Caught up. They couldn't say anything about the casualties until they had all the facts. They were on their radios talking in codes, and in and out of the front seats and back seats asking him questions: what time had he left, how many people had been in the car, what were their names and ages, where had they travelled from, where were they going. On and on, who, what, why, as vehicles strobed their blue stripes around them and the screech of metal being cut tore at his brain.

Finally, he was driven to a hospital and given sweet tea and a blanket in the waiting room. Ruth's family came and they waited some more, saw doctors and nurses rushing around as if there was some hope of everything being all right. But it wasn't all right. They were eventually taken into a small room for the inevitable news. Jay couldn't even remember if it was the police or Ruth's mum who brought him home.

'You didn't kill them,' I say.

Jay shrugs. 'As good as. My negligence did. I should have had enough petrol. The hazards should have been working. I should have insisted they get out of the car.'

I have another thought. 'Lolly. Did she know Amos?'

'Yeah, she knew him. She used to come and play – she was a bit weird even then. Ruth used to feel sorry for her, well – you've probably noticed – Maria's not an ideal stepmother.'

'She's not very kind to her,' I agree. 'She says some awful things sometimes. And she doesn't dress her properly.'

'Well, anyway, Maria told Lolly what happened but she wouldn't stop coming round. Day after it happened, I look through the window and there's her, sitting outside on the grass, calling for Amos.' He shivers.

'So, she used to speak properly before?'

'Yeah.' He puts a hand behind his head, kneads his neck. 'Then she just went into her own little world. All this ghost talk, imaginary friends, hanging round the graveyard...'

'Maria just seems to let her roam around everywhere. It's not safe.'

'They're just trying to deal with her as best they can. It can't be easy for them.'

He has salty stains on his face, like a child who's been in the sea. The ashtray between us is full and there are burns on the tablecloth. He links both hands behind his head and stretches back against the chair.

'What a night,' he says. 'It's not what I had in mind.'

'I'm glad you told me. I wish you'd said about it sooner.'

'The guilt messes your mind up.' He points his index fingers to his temples. 'All you want to do is lock your thoughts in. Never let them out.'

'Sometimes you should talk about stuff.' I reach up to the side of his head to take his hands. Pull them down to the table. 'I knew you were hiding something. I never thought it could be something so sad.'

'Sad?' His voice is raised. He pulls a hand away from mine and knocks over his empty wine glass. 'It fucked my life up. You wouldn't know, you've never had kids.'

I think suddenly of the one I almost had. I imagine the weight and warmth of it in my arms and I'm unexpectedly over-come by an intense feeling of loss. A silent tear slips down my cheek. My baby. Would it have been a boy or a girl? Would it have looked like me? I never gave it the chance to gaze into my eyes or feel my kiss on its soft head. My chest hurts and my chin wobbles uncontrollably. I have never thought this way before, never properly dealt with what the abortion did to me emotionally.

'Let's go to bed.' My voice cracks into a sob. I'm messed up by the evening's reflections and revelations, and he's drunk and distressed and I don't want things to turn nasty. I stand and pick up the wine bottles, move them to the side of the sink.

He follows me up to the new bedroom in silence and flops onto the bed. He still has his dirty work clothes on.

'I'm so ready for this.'

'Do you like it?'

He pushes himself into a sitting position and starts to take his clothes off. 'You've done a great job. I'm sure I'll appreciate it tomorrow.' His voice is splintered, spent.

The night is full of owls and aeroplanes. My head throbs. It must be the combination of paint fumes and red wine. I fidget around on the new mattress. It has no hip-holes, no give in the springs like the old one. I have pushed the baby thoughts to the back of my mind. They are for another time, when I can be alone and settled, prepared to deal with my emotions with composure. Jay is flat out, motionless, beside me. One of his nostrils whistles gently when he inhales. It's like he has shed all his feelings so there's nothing left to agitate him: his energy has poured away with his tears and memories.

He has handed the images over to me. Slow-motion car crashes. Dead bodies. Ambulances in the rain. I toss them around in my head. Sometimes I remember what the new bedroom looks like and try to hold the thought. But ultimately it comes back to his confession in the kitchen.

How do I deal with this tragic information? Am I supposed

to layer this new grief on top of my own? I think about everything and track its butterfly effect, realising that if Jay had
remembered to put petrol in his car then I wouldn't be here in
this house and Nell would still be alive.

I go round in circles in my head with conversations and
dates. Jay's revelation tonight has exposed a flaw in my suspicions. The note that Nell left under the carpet couldn't be true,
and Ruth couldn't have killed Nell, because she was already
dead herself.

CHAPTER THIRTY-THREE

On a dismal afternoon, four days after finding the baby album, I stand outside the primary school at twenty past three.

'It's pigging freezing today,' says an old man at the side of me. 'You wouldn't think it was nearly spring.'

'I know,' I agree, pulling my hood up and stamping my feet.

I wave to Lolly and she bounds up to me like a puppy. Stands smiling and shivering in front of me.

'She needs a coat on in this weather,' the man says, as if he thinks I'm her mother.

'Come on,' I say to Lolly, giving her a big pack of Haribos. 'D'you fancy going for a walk?'

She nods and takes the sweets.

'Should we go the long way round? So we can have a good long chat?' I ask.

She nods and shivers, biting the packet to open it.

I take my coat off and make her put it on over the thin greying polo shirt and skirt that she's grown out of.

'I know about your friend, Amos,' I say. 'Jay told me about him. That's the boy in the garden, isn't it?'

She nods and pops a fried egg into her mouth.

'You know, just because he's not here it's OK to talk. You know that, Lolly, it's OK to talk?' I say.

She shrugs and starts to look tearful.

'Just like the way you talk to me. You say lots of things to me.'

She nods again. Bites the head of a red worm.

'Why's that? Why do you talk to me? Is it because I didn't know Amos?'

She pulls a corner of my coat around her face, like a yashmak. Then she puts the sweets into the pocket of my coat and pulls at my hand, skipping up the road towards the village, and I have to half run, half walk to keep up with her.

'Where are you taking me?' I laugh.

But she keeps quiet, says nothing, only pants now and then at the effort of skipping with my thick coat flapping around her. She takes me down roads and streets that I didn't know existed. Past stone cottages, bungalows, rows of tiny terraces and a boarded-up cobbler's shop. Until there in front of us is the church: an impressive, imposing, angular building a thousand years old.

'Are you taking me to church?' I say, and as we walk up the wide flagstones I realise where we are going: through the mossy gravestones, stepping between mounds that lie like bodies, around scrubbed plinths and gaudy plastic tulips stabbed into patches of soil.

We go through a gate that springs back like the snap of a terrier, into a mowed area full of tiny headstones in the shape of angels and Bibles and teddy bears. Lolly tiptoes respectfully in front of me, towards a simple grey stone. *Amos*, it says. *Died tragically. Four years, ten months.* The pot that sits in the base of the headstone is empty. I look at it for a while in silence. Lolly scratches at a patch of lichen on the front of the stone.

'Shall we do something,' I suggest to Lolly, 'that's good but a bit naughty?'

Her eyes light up. She bobs her head up and down.

'Come on,' I say.

We go back through the gate and weave through the graves until I spot the right one. *Dorothy Lloyd, ninety years old*, with three huge floral displays around a polished memorial.

'Quick,' I say to Lolly, 'come here, open the coat.'

I crouch, looking nervously around as I pull red carnations, white lilies and clusters of fizzy gypsophila from the first display. I pass them to Lolly who sweeps my coat around them, and move on to the next, to take variegated greenery, feathery ferns and a couple of blousy chrysanthemums.

'That'll do,' I say, and we go back to Amos's grave, to remove the pot and take it to the tap to swill out and fill with water, and arrange the stolen flowers through the waiting holes.

Lolly stands back, giggles and claps her hands.

'What do you think?' I say.

'Good idea!' She is still clapping. She hasn't covered her mouth, but I don't mention it.

There is a bursting feeling in my chest. Joy, goodness, something like that: not quite the bliss that comes with a special kiss, but a moment of pure happiness, nevertheless.

* * *

Perhaps I am just overthinking everything. Perhaps the people I trusted weren't completely truthful, and perhaps the people I suspected were innocent.

Because I know now that Ruth couldn't have killed Nell. The timeline makes it impossible.

Rick is definitely a suspect. I know from experience that he can be quite possessive and jealous of people around Jay. But would he really kill someone just to have exclusivity to his friend? I have examined the note over and over, thinking that maybe I had read it wrong, maybe Nell had written Rick instead of Ruth. But no. There is no mistaking the letters, the way Nell would always put a little squiggly circle for the dot of the 'i'. It isn't there. And the 't' is clearly crossed.

So, perhaps Nell wasn't telling the truth when she wrote the note. Maybe, despite my initial disbelief, she *was* having mental health issues: how else can I explain the fact that she has accused someone who was dead of killing her. Nell *must* have been depressed – psychotic even – and took her own life.

The thing is, I really don't think it can be Jay. Maybe once or twice I've had a flash of suspicion because of his odd behaviour, but now I know about his past, about his *loss*, I feel like it explains everything. And he has been so incredibly lovely over the past few days since he opened up to me. Gentle, caring, telling me how grateful he is for what I've done with the house, about how I have been his soul mate over the last six months, about how he only ever wants the best for me. I think I need to alter my mindset. I need to be done with the grief and revenge and get on with my new life.

* * *

The next time I go to the library there is an email from Lou asking why I have blocked her on my phone and suggesting that we meet up somewhere. She wants to clear the air, explain what's happened. She doesn't want bad feeling between us.

I think about things rationally. Even though she has tried to betray me she is still my sister and I ought to get her side of the story. So, I will meet her for one last time. I will tell her that my new life is here and I don't want her interfering in it, like she did with Martin. I will insist that she apologises for telling Jay my secrets. Perhaps that was what Jay meant when he asked if I could kill someone. Perhaps I need to cut Lou out of my life completely, disown her. Metaphorically kill her off.

After a lot of consideration, I finally reply.

How about Nottingham? The Malt Cross? Remember we
went there together while we were on a shopping trip once. I
could get the train. Meet up say one o'clock.

And almost immediately, there's an email back from her. I
click on the bold type.

Ring me urgently.

That's all it says.

The three words unnerve me. Perhaps it's bad news.
Perhaps it's something to do with Mum or Dad. I take out my
phone, stab at the buttons and huddle into the computer
monitor so that no one will hear me.

'It's me,' I say quietly, when she answers. 'What's wrong?'

'Let's meet somewhere else,' she says. She gives me the
name of an Italian restaurant near the Theatre Royal, a place
recommended by someone she knows. She always has to have it
her way. We may as well meet in the library. She won't eat
anything. But we arrange a time and date a week away.

'So, what's urgent?' I say.

But nothing is. It's just her being melodramatic.

'Jay might look through your emails. He might come after
you. This way there's no record of where you're going. He can't
follow a trail.'

'You're being ridiculous. He's got no idea what my email
address is anyway.'

'Just be careful,' she says. 'And don't tell him anything.'

I hang up and the absurdity of it makes me roll my eyes. As
if Jay would hack into a library computer to find out where I
would be meeting my sister for lunch.

There are twenty minutes remaining on the computer and a
couple of things bob into my mind that I may as well check out.

I go onto Google. I have always been a bit naïve with my

knowledge of illegal substances, and so I start to type. I get as far as *special k* before autocomplete starts making suggestions. *Special k drug*. It's weird, but my heart starts to race. A list brings up websites about ketamine. I click on one and find out that Special K is a street name for the drug which induces a dream-like state, euphoria and out-of-body experiences. There's a picture too, of powder, a syringe, two pills. The sight of them makes my face flush, makes me want the feeling, remembering Jay's lips on mine and the fantastic sex it leads to. I take a deep breath and notice the woman on the computer next to mine looking at the page. Quickly, I click it away. So that's what it is: all the little pills in the bags behind the door in the loft. Ketamine. Bliss, dissociative sedation and amnesia. Bags full of special kisses.

CHAPTER THIRTY-FOUR

When Lou arrives everyone's heads turn. They didn't ten minutes ago when I got here. But she looks fantastic. Skinny jeans with knee-high stiletto boots. Black military-style jacket. Expensive handbag. She's thinner than I remember her being before Christmas. Her hair is longer than it's ever been, glossy black – reflective even – with a big fringe, and sways as she totters in. I can't tell if her eyelashes are false or just heavily layered with mascara. Her face is different in places: deeper hollows under her cheekbones, poutier lips, rigid skin where the furrow of her brow should be. She's had some kind of Botox, or collagen. I won't mention it though. I try to slip back into the shadow of the alcove, away from the lamps and candles.

'This looks a bit quirky,' she says as she pulls out a chair and sits opposite me. 'I wasn't sure if it was the right place or not.'

'I think they need brighter light bulbs,' I say. Small talk before the attack.

A waiter appears next to us and smiles admiringly at Lou as he hands over our menus.

'I'm not really that hungry,' says Lou, as if I would have expected her to be. 'Although it smells quite nice.'

'I wouldn't mind a bolognaise, or carbonara,' I say, scanning the prices.

'Let's get a pizza to share,' says Lou. 'Something with prawns on.'

She always gets her own way. She won't even eat any of it. She catches the waiter's eye and orders a large marinara and two glasses of white wine. I check my watch.

'So,' I say, 'we've got stuff to talk about.'

She tilts her glass, lets the wine nudge her lips. Puts it down again. Wipes her thumb over the condensation on the side. Looks at me.

'It's not what you think,' she says. 'I was trying to do something for you. We were worried.'

'You tried to seduce Jay because you were worried about me? And then you come and tell him about my previous relationships. And even my abortion. How does that work then?'

'We got a bad feeling about him. You know, when we came over at Christmas? Dom thought he was a bit creepy too, and he's a good judge of character. He's got an instinct for that sort of thing.'

'Don't be stupid,' I say. 'Nothing happened at the Christmas meet-up anyway. We had food and swapped presents. How does that give you a bad feeling?'

'Well anyway. It just felt a bit, I don't know. And then there was the phone thing.'

'What, that he rung you by accident?'

'He probably told you it was an accident,' she says. 'He asked me what I was wearing. He suggested I try dyeing my hair black, which was strange because he'd said the same at Christmas. He just seemed like some sort of pervert.'

'So you did dye your hair. And then arranged to meet him in a pub,' I remind her. 'What the fuck is that about?'

The waiter arrives with our pizza. It has a wavy edge, like a chantarelle, and is an abstract work of pink and lemon and green.

'It's... oh I don't know how to explain.' She takes a prawn and nibbles delicately on it without letting it touch her lips. 'I wanted to find out more about him. And it was probably a mistake – I realise now – but I thought I could gain his confidence by telling him stuff about you—'

'You wanted to get off with him,' I interrupt. 'You fancied him at Christmas: it was so obvious. So you dye your hair and start making out that I'm some evil bitch and you need to warn him so that you can set up a meeting.'

'Just listen to what I've got to tell you. Something happened while I was there...'

'You're pissed off that you drove all the way over there and he wasn't interested after all.'

'Have you heard of the term "honey trap"?' she says. 'It was just like that.'

I give an empty laugh. 'Who do you think you are: Miss fucking Marple?'

'You've got to leave him, Lauren, he's dangerous. He's weird. He could be the next Fred West.'

'You're just jealous. You're blowing things up out of all proportion.' I shrug away her suggestion.

'He's not what you think...' Lou pulls out a triangle of pizza and twirls the tangle of mozzarella string around the point. She reaches over and puts the slice on my plate.

'You're just trying to split us up like you did with Martin. You can't keep your nose out of my relationships.'

'But you make the wrong choices,' she says, exasperated. 'You pick the wrong type every time. The relationship with Martin should never have happened.'

'Yeah, you keep saying it was abuse, grooming, whatever, but it lasted nearly fifteen years! He was going to leave his wife!'

'He was never going to leave his wife. You were just his bit on the side, his much younger bit on the side. If anything I should have got involved sooner. I should have taken your side rather than his. I have had so many regrets about that, about thinking that it was your fault because you kept coming on to him – a nice family man – and you were wrecking his marriage. But he should never have done what he did in the first place. You were fifteen, immature, still a child. He had you conned, just like Jay has now. You've always been too trusting of abusive men. You need to learn to be more assertive.'

'What? You don't know either of them like I do. I know I was young, but Martin loved me, at least for a while. I do believe that. But we had everyone against us, everyone judging, giving their opinion, thinking I was the guilty party. And then after you split us up I end up taking your advice and go to live with Jay – who I *know* loves me – and now you're trying to do it all over again. It's like you want to see me get hurt every time.'

'Lauren.' Her rational tone punctuates my emotional outburst. 'Let me tell you what happened. Just listen to what I say. Jay has killed someone before. He's drugged and raped someone.'

We look at each other in silence for five, six seconds. I rub my wrist. 'Where've you got that sort of information from?'

'While we were in the pub I went to the toilet and a woman followed me in.' She picks up her glass and lets the cold liquid touch her lips again. 'She said Jay had met her in a nightclub last year and spiked her drink...'

'But Jay hates nightclubs,' I begin to say, as doubt prowls into my head once more.

'...then he took her in his van to his house, tied her to some hooks in a wall and raped her. And the frightening thing is, I'm sure he put something in my drink, too. I only had two sips – you know what I'm like for leaving things – but I felt strange after, really woozy.'

My belly lurches. My mind is a shambles. I look at my sister with her half prawn between immaculate fingernails and wonder how much I can trust her.

She puts the morsel of pink flesh down on her plate, reaches into her handbag and takes out a folded piece of paper.

'You need to read this,' she says, unfolding it. 'This is a massive coincidence that will probably freak you out, and I know it's going to be upsetting for you but...' She turns the article so that I can see Nell's face. 'Have you looked on Google Maps? The quarry where they found *your best friend* is at the back of his house.'

I decide to come clean despite our differences, despite her being such an untrustworthy, interfering bitch. Because I have no one else to confide in but her. 'I know. I've been and seen it.'

'What? So you knew about Nell and him?'

'Of course I knew. Why do you think I'm here? I want answers. I want the truth about what happened to Nell. But the more I got to know Jay, the more I kept thinking he didn't have anything to do with her death. Obviously I didn't know anything about this woman from the nightclub.'

'She was totally believable. Describing Jay and the house and his campervan. She thought the drugs must have worn off sooner than he expected because she was sick. He was actually raping her when she woke up. He'd made her wear an old velvet dress which he took off her before she left.'

'What, she escaped from the house?'

'No, she pretended to still be drugged. She thought it was too dangerous to challenge him. So he put her in the van, took her back into town and dumped her in a car park near the night-club thinking that she was still unconscious. Then months later, when she heard about Nell dying in the quarry she worked out what had happened.'

'But Nell wasn't a one-night stand who had her drink spiked. She was knowingly dating him.'

'Something went wrong though, didn't it?' Lou twiddles

with a strand of her hair that has come out of place. 'Very badly wrong, and it got her killed. And you could end up in the same position. Have you talked to him yet about Nell?'

'Just a few careful questions so far. He doesn't know that I knew Nell.' A terrifying thought floods my brain. 'Oh, fuck, you didn't tell him that she was my friend, did you?'

Lou grabs my shaking hand. 'No, of course I haven't. Do you think I would do something so stupid that might get you killed?'

'I need to trust you completely with this. No one else knows why I'm here. No one at all. I've been pacing myself with things.'

'Oh God, please be careful.' Lou's face is porcelain, even through her heavy make-up. 'You're stuck out in his cottage with no phone or anything, with someone as creepy as that. The black hair fixation. It's just not normal. The woman who told me about him: she was another one with long black hair.'

'Well, he always seems to go for a certain type.' I remember all the ringed adverts in the newspapers.

'What do you think he would do though, if you dyed your hair, if you just turned up one day with it *blonde*?' She gives me a sly side-eye as she slips another piece of pizza off her knife and onto my plate.

'I don't know.' It would certainly test him. I would be able to find out if he really does love me for who I am.

'Do it then,' she says. 'Go blonde and see what happens.'

CHAPTER THIRTY-FIVE

I spend the whole return journey going over our conversation. Should I really have trusted her? Would she let me down? My life is completely on the line if she goes behind my back again. The edge of the quarry appears in my head: the memory of Jay's hand on my shoulder, his inference that I kill my sister; the anticipation of a ketamine trip. How would anyone prove if someone had jumped or been pushed? I think and think but cannot answer.

When the train reaches town, I make my way through to the station car park where I have left the camper. It's late afternoon, and although a slate sky promises rain it's not dark yet, and that may be why it is easy to notice Jay's motorbike. It's there: the black beast of a thing slanted jauntily at the passenger side of the van. I stop. Cautiously I look around, but can't see Jay. Should I go and search for him? Or should I get in the camper and drive home? The uncertainties start to make me nervous. I go back through the station to the platform, to see if he is there. I stick my head round the door of the café and the pub too, but he is nowhere to be seen. I finally decide to go and sit in the camper, wait there for a while. Pulling the keys out of my pocket, I walk round the back of the van towards the driver's door. Then almost trip over...

'Shit, you scared me,' I say breathlessly.

Jay is sitting on the floor, his head against the driver's door. He doesn't look up: he just talks to my feet.

'Where have you been?' A low flat voice. He taps his tobacco tin on his knee.

'I... well I went and met Lou for lunch,' I say. I try to hide the tremor in my voice. 'I hadn't seen her for ages.'

'Why didn't you tell me you were going?'

I shrug. Roll tiny bits of gravel around under my feet. How do I answer? 'It was just lunch. A spur of the moment thing. I haven't been out long.'

He stands up, puts his face close to mine. 'There's something going on.'

'There's nothing going on,' I protest. 'Like what?'

His eyes burn into mine. 'She's a devious cow. I don't trust her. You two getting together, her telling you stuff, poisoning your mind.'

'I fell out with her,' I exclaim. 'I'm on your side. I don't know why you seem to think I'm being disloyal.'

Jay blinks. Looks down at his dirty fingernails. 'You're going behind my back. Not just seeing her. But we said – I said – the other week that we shouldn't be coming into town any more after what happened to the van.'

I look at him. I can't answer that one. He takes my arm just above the elbow, grips it hard, pulls me to look at the front of the van where the paintwork has been scratched – carved – with the word SCUM. The letters are two inches high and have probably been done by a screwdriver: each stroke has taken the paint off down to the metal.

'Oh no,' I say. 'I'm so sorry. I never thought...'

Jay lets go of my arm, curls his hand into a fist and punches the word.

'Don't,' I say, but he swings back, does it again. And again. Until there is a dent in the panel and his hand is bleeding.

'We could report it...' I say, but Jay isn't listening, he's round the other side, kicking at the hubcap of the front wheel.

'You're making things worse,' I say, trying to reach for him.

But he stumbles, falls back into the motorbike, and over it goes with a crash, snapping the mirror off. He sprawls on the floor. I stand, watching, holding my breath. He puts his hands over his face like he is going to cry. There is blood all over his knuckles.

'Why is life so fucking crap?' he says.

I squat and stroke his hair, help him get up, get the bike back up.

'Let's go home,' I say. 'We need a drink or something.'

But later, at home, he doesn't speak to me. He sits in the kitchen and smokes; looks through the self-sufficiency book for a while; makes a cheese sandwich for himself.

I stand in the doorway and tell him there's a good film on but he doesn't look at me, doesn't reply. At half past ten I go to bed, propping myself up with pillows to read an old copy of *Your Home* magazine in the cosy enclave of my new bedroom. But I can't concentrate on the words: I'm distracted by Jay's silence below; I'm waiting for the sound of his feet on the stairs. I'm thinking of black hair and blonde hair. I'm thinking of the woman with the spiked drink who wore the velvet dress; I'm thinking of Nell dead in the quarry.

An hour later I switch the lamp off but Jay is still downstairs. He stays there all night.

* * *

'I've been thinking,' says Jay the next morning. 'The band. The music stuff. I'm just gonna go solo. I don't need anyone else.'

The aubergine wall moves towards me. Is my time here coming to an end? I swallow back the sick that has risen into my mouth.

'Is this to do with Rick?' I ask. 'Has he been advising you?'

'No. I just need some space with it all. There's a lot to think about at the moment.'

I'm being pushed out. Rejected. But how will he get rid of me? In the same way he did with Nell?

'Why are you being like this?' I ask. I need to bide my time. 'I haven't done anything wrong. You're just punishing me for yesterday.'

Jay purses his lips. Looks away. Stands up and goes to the window. His breath makes a silver cloud on the glass.

'Your sister told you about Eleanor, didn't she? You know, all that shit that got pasted on the van windscreen?' he says. 'She thinks I killed her.'

'You *were* seeing Eleanor, though,' I say carefully. I can't give any indication that I knew her, that she was my best friend. 'Yet when we were by the side of the quarry and I first asked if you knew her, you said you didn't. Remember? Why didn't you tell me about her then?'

'Why are you so jealous of everyone?' he says. 'Ruth, Eleanor, the one-night stand that I didn't even have before I met you. You even seem like you're jealous of Maria, watching us all the time. All you ever do is go on about who I used to go out with, wanting to know what they looked like, how I knew them. There's no wonder I don't bother telling you stuff. It's just not worth all the questioning.'

The mood between us is overwhelming. I don't know which way it's going to go. My resolve slackens; tremors take over my hands and I start to cry.

He comes over, sits down next to me. I feel the bristliness of his body but at the same time I'm hoping he's going to hold out his hands and say 'choose one' so that I can inhabit the happy me, the one that doesn't have to deal with shit like this.

His hands are empty though.

I take some deep breaths. Stare at the floor. Control my wobbling chin that nearly sets me off again. Think about how much I have changed.

And the thing is, it's not just the thought that my time here is nearly over which scares me. You see, I realise that I'm different now. I don't want the internet and phones and the sustaining flow of communication that used to hold me together. This little house is what drives me now, with its rotting window frames and tasteless bathroom suite and saggy furniture and fires that need constantly feeding. It's my baby, to nurture and care for and dress up to look nice. And in the garden signs of spring are everywhere: shoots and buds and tufts of green digging themselves out of the soil, the leeks fattening up after winter.

'Do you love me?' Jay asks.

'Of course I do,' I reply quietly. 'I love you, I love being here. It's everything to me.'

I reach out and touch his face. He moves towards me and I can't help but wrap around him – *cling* to him like we are wrecked in an ocean – and we kiss and kiss like it is the last time we will ever see each other.

'You don't realise how much I've needed you,' he says. 'I never intended to hurt you.'

I look up at him desperately.

'Please?' It's all I say, but he knows exactly what I need.

CHAPTER THIRTY-SIX

'That's right. Blonde.' I smile at the girl behind the desk in the college hairdressing department. 'I need it doing today.'

'The thing is,' she says awkwardly, 'although we have level three students who could do it today, you'd need to have a strand test done first. It needs leaving for twenty-four hours to make sure you don't have a reaction.'

I can't wait twenty-four hours. The idea is embedded: it needs acting upon immediately.

'It's OK,' I say. 'I don't have reactions, I'm not allergic to anything.'

'I'm sorry, we're not allowed.' She looks behind her, through the glass door into the beauty department. 'It's probably because it's a college. We can't take risks with people. You might be able to get it done at a normal salon.'

She nibbles the edge of her thumbnail. I look at her shiny, worn trousers with their fraying seams.

'I'll give you twenty quid,' I say, reaching into my bag. 'I won't tell anyone. You can pretend I had the strand test yesterday. I just really need my hair doing today.'

She glances over her shoulder again as I slide the note over the desk.

'OK,' she says, creasing it quickly into her palm.

I lean my head backwards: my neck slots into the cold cut-out edge of sink. A young girl – sixteen or seventeen – massages firm hands through my wet hair. She is involved in a banal conversation with another girl who is doing a perm on someone beside me.

'So I said to Libby it's not fair you always taking advantage...'

'She's been like it since Year Ten...'

'Even her mum said she should have given her the petrol money, you can't expect people to run you round all the time...'

'And she's always got something new from Primark. Did you see that blue coat she had on last Friday?'

I try to shift my position to make my neck more comfortable. The conversation stops.

'Are you sure you want to go blonde?' The girl is talking to me now.

'I'm certain,' I say to the ceiling. 'I fancy a change.'

'It's a lovely colour already,' says the girl. 'You don't often get people with hair this naturally black. It's going to take a lot of lightening to get it blonde.'

'I don't mind. Just do whatever you need to do.' I feel like I'm bubbling inside. Lou had better have my back with this.

I spend the best part of the day in the college hair and beauty department. Lightening applications, waiting, rinsing, conditioning, rinsing, tubes and bottles of this and that being mixed and spread on, more waiting, more rinsing, being moved around from sink to mirror to sink to armchair: it's almost exhausting. But at five past three the girl gets the hairdryer and a huge, tubular brush, and I watch in the mirror as my new hair takes shape. Eventually, I sit and stare at the girl in the mirror: soft blonde waves falling over her shoulders, tapered fringe, uncertain eyes.

My stomach churns as I drive home. The camper smells of peroxide and conditioner and hairspray. My hands tremble on the steering wheel. Why am I in such a state? For goodness' sake, it's only a colour: what difference can a colour make?

I pull into the drive and check my hair again in the rear-view mirror. The sound of the camper must have alerted Jay: he strides down the path mouthing the words *where have you been?* and it's only when he's right up to the side of the van that he sees what I've done.

His demeanour is transformed. He is enraged, fired up: a scowl shoved onto his face. He tugs at the door of the van; I hang on to the handle inside. I try to press the button to lock the door, but he's too quick, too strong: the door is flung open and he drags me out onto the drive.

'Please,' I say, 'don't hurt me.'

He grabs a fistful of my hair and pushes me so that I fall to my knees.

'I can't believe you have done this,' he spits. 'Are you trying to take the piss or what?'

I put my hands out onto the cold, damp concrete, afraid that he might smash my head into the ground.

'What were you thinking?' he bawls. 'What the fuck were you thinking?'

'I'm sorry. It's only a colour. It doesn't matter.'

He wrenches me to my feet with my hair and pushes me down the path towards the kitchen door. I stumble over the step and he pins his left arm around me. Inside, he wedges me against the sink while he yanks the drawer out to rummage for the scissors.

'Please,' I beg him. My voice is starting to crack. He holds me from behind, pinning my arms to my sides. I am wedged between him and the sink and I can feel his fury and his breath on my neck. He gathers a skein of my hair around his fist.

'Don't. Please. I can dye it back again.'

He chops the first tress close to the scalp: the cold metal brushes my skin as the blades close. I wince and bite my lip as the new blonde locks drop to the floor. I focus my gaze into the sink and the two small pieces of potato peel trapped in the plug-hole. He cuts again, a rough, untrained action that snags some of the hair into the scissors and jerks my head. I wriggle an arm free, grip the edge of the sink, press my fingers into the cold steel. Close my eyes.

He lifts clumps from the top of my head and hacks at them, pressing his body against my back and I shrink down, shivering as more of my head and ears are exposed.

Steadily he works around my head cutting and dropping. He exhales slowly and I feel his breath quiver through my remaining wisps.

'I'm sorry,' I say pathetically as a warm tear trickles down my cheek.

He drops the scissors into the sink – they spin for a second – then I twist my head round to see him: the last threads of my hair hang off his stubble, and his face is lifeless.

'Go to bed,' he tells me. 'I don't want to see your horrible hair.'

I sleep for hours. At some point Jay comes up with coffee and toast, and I wait until he has gone back downstairs before I devour it. Later he brings me a glass of orange juice and tells me that it's Tuesday when I ask him what day it is. Soon after, I hear the back door being opened and I look out of the loft window to see him in the garden forking over last year's potato patch. I dress quickly and creep down to use the toilet. While he's outside I sneak into the kitchen to see if the campervan keys are on the hook or the table or the windowsill, but they are in none of those places. I will have to make a run for it instead. Carefully, I push down the handle and pull at the door, bracing myself for the noise it will make that Jay could hear from the garden. But it doesn't shift. The door is locked and I am trapped.

I return to the bedroom to think what to do.

* * *

Later, I go downstairs. Jay is cross-legged on the floor, smoking, staring into a meagre fire.

'What are you doing?' His voice has no expression.

'I need the van keys. I have a violin lesson to do at Hannah's house.' I wind a beaded tie-dye scarf around my head. It makes me look like I have cancer. My body aches all over.

'You're not going.' He rotates the end of his joint delicately on the hearth until it is perfectly conical.

'Please. I'll only be an hour.' He thinks I'm going to do a runner, going to take off into the sunset with his campervan.

'You're staying here,' he says. He's not behind his eyes, he's in skunk-land.

'They will wonder where I am. I need to go.'

'I'll take you. I'll wait for you and bring you back.'

'You can't drive,' I say. 'You're wasted.'

He takes the keys from his pocket, dangles them in front of me. '*I'm* taking you.'

I pick up my handbag and my fiddle case.

'What's in the bag?' he asks, pulling it from me.

'Just stuff.' Phone, purse, tissues, pen, old receipts, make-up.

'It can stay here,' he says. He throws it onto a chair.

We go out to the van, getting in without speaking. I clip the seatbelt on. Jay drives slowly, waveringly, to Hannah's house.

'We're nearly out of petrol,' he says, peering at the gauge. 'I might go and fill up while you're in there.'

I get out and adjust the scarf around my head.

'Five o'clock finish?' he says. 'I'll be right here.' He switches off the engine and watches me walk down the path. Watches me knock on the door, go into the hallway and slip my shoes off.

Hannah looks at me like I'm abnormal when she sees the headscarf. We go into the dining room and she switches the light on, goes to close the curtains.

'Could we keep them open?' I say. 'It's not dark yet and I'm waiting for someone to give me a lift.' Jay is out there in the campervan, watching me, as I fold out the music stand, tighten my bow, tuck the fiddle under my chin.

'Whatever.' Hannah slouches to the music stand and makes a meal of putting rosin on her bow.

And while she's doing that I think about Ruth, I think about Lou, and something just hits me, smacks me round the head. It's one of those useless bits of information that gets published in the sort of magazines that Lou reads. It's to do with sibling names: the fact that parents pick them to go together well; they need that special ring about them. Lou told me about it. They have to have enough of the same sound within them to appear poetic, but not too much or you get an unpleasant jarring. And our names together: Lauren and Louise, Louise and Lauren. There's a pattern to it. And people like to think in patterns; they like that sense of orderliness.

And I think to myself: has a pattern been there all along and I have failed to spot it? Sibling names with that special ring. Richard and Ruthie. Ruthie and Richard.

And it dawns on me that Ruth was Rick's sister.

. . .

Outside, I hear a turn of an engine, and see smoke pumping out of the campervan exhaust. He's going.

'Which tune?' says Hannah.

The campervan moves away. I hear it drive down the street. I slam my violin and bow into the case.

'I've got to go,' I say. 'It's an emergency. I'll come back for my fiddle later.'

I scramble my feet back into my boots and dash out onto the pavement. My headscarf catches on the door and drags off as I close it behind me, but I leave it on the mat. I have no money, no phone, nothing. I will need help. I pull up my hood and cross the road. Portland Crescent, the sign says.

CHAPTER THIRTY-SEVEN

This is the second time I have seen Rick's house. The first time I walked past, carefully, one early afternoon, with a hemp shoulder bag of groceries that I'd bought from the village shop. The house was a lovely detached place, late Victorian, brick-built with a large bay window of leaded glass. The front door was glossy black with an ornate brass knocker, and set into a pillared porch. Tall, leafless trees guarded each side of the house, and a wide driveway at the front was empty. I could just make out a mirror on the chimney breast and a flamboyant chandelier hanging in the front room. There were no lights on. I strolled past as if I didn't know that it was Rick's. I certainly wouldn't have wanted him to see me looking.

Now it's getting dusky: it's quarter past four but the clocks haven't gone forward yet. As I approach, I can see the lights shining out through the leaded windows, see the twinkle of the chandelier. The swags of the expensive curtains that hang like ones out of *Period Homes* frame the window seat in the recess of the bay.

I can see everything in the room.

I can see the girl that sits on the window seat with her back to the glass.

I can see the long black hair that tumbles down her back.

And then I know it's her. Ruth.

She didn't die.

Oh God. I feel sick. Distraught, I think about the note from Nell, about my assumptions of her not telling the truth. And here is Ruth, sitting in a window. Jay lied about her death. He lied about everything. He made it seem like he had a terrible childhood, he played on the tragedy of his family getting killed in an accident and the subsequent grief, when all this time he was visiting Ruth and covering up the crime she committed.

I stand on the pavement with my legs shaking, knowing that I have to confront her: I must do it because surely things can't get any worse than they already are. I need answers. I need help. Resolutely, I march down the drive to Rick's house.

I ring the bell and wait in the porch until I hear the click of heels on a parquet floor behind the door.

'Hello?' says the woman who opens it: she is elegantly dressed in a wool skirt with a white linen blouse and a gold locket in the dimple of her throat. Her silver-grey hair is fixed in a loose bun.

'Hi, I wondered if I could see Ruth, please? Jason sent me to bring something for her.' I stand and smile, with my hood up.

'Jason sent you?' she asks, somewhat bewildered.

'Yes, I've got something for her.' Why can't the woman just shout her to the door, for goodness' sake: she's only in the next room.

'What is it?' she asks.

'Oh, it's a surprise. I need to see her personally.'

She backs cautiously into the hallway. 'You'd better come in. I don't know what...'

I follow her in, to a blast of heat, closing the heavy door. She gestures into a room on the right and stands at the doorway as I enter.

'She's in there,' she says.

Ruth sits in the bay window and stares at me. Even with no make-up, she is beautiful: olive skin, brown eyes and heart-shaped mouth in a natural pout are perfectly framed by the spill of black hair.

Nell's killer right in front of me.

I step towards her as confidently as I can.

'I've come about Eleanor. Remember her? The girl who died in the quarry?' I say. And then I realise – it suddenly, sick-eningly dawns on me – and I see what I didn't see seconds ago.

It's not a window seat she's sitting in: it's a wheelchair.

'Ruth?'

She blinks and judders sharply. Her mouth drops open and a glob of saliva runs onto her chin. Her left hand jerks out at nothing.

I turn to her mother, my hood falling to expose my blonde, tufty hair.

'What do you want?' she says, staring at my head. 'She can't understand you; she has a brain injury.'

I put my hands over my burning face. Ruth emits a low, animal noise and threads of dribble swing onto her chest.

'Jason didn't tell me, he never said she was like this...' I have to squeeze back through the doorframe, brush the wool of Ruth's mother's skirt, smell her thick, cloying perfume.

I pull my hood up. 'I'm sorry, I didn't mean...' I scrabble at the latch on the door until she comes up behind me.

'Did you say you came about Eleanor?'

I turn back to the woman. 'Yes, she was my best friend.'

Ruth's mother reaches to put a hand on my arm. 'I'm so sorry about what happened. She came to work for me; well, she was Ruth's carer for a few months. The police did investigate you know, so I'm sure there was nothing sinister about it all.'

'She looked after Ruth?' It's all getting too bizarre: Nell was in Jay's bedroom, she left a note in the locked room, she was here caring for Ruth.

'Yes, she lived in one of the rooms upstairs. We did treat her well, you know. We never realised she had mental health issues or we could have helped...'

I can't bear to hear any more. Ruth's mum is staring at my head again. The obstinate latch won't open even though I'm clicking the little knob and yanking the handle as hard as I can.

'Here, let me do it.' Reaching across to the lock, Ruth's mother opens the door with a nimble hand.

Outside, I guzzle cold air into my lungs and stumble back up the drive. How can Ruth, in her condition, have killed Nell? It isn't possible: she couldn't have got anywhere near the quarry. Rick, on the other hand, who is living here in the same house: he had more opportunity...

Fuck, I just don't know what to think about it all.

I walk back towards Hannah's house, to go and collect my fiddle, but as I turn the corner I see that Jay is back with the campervan, waiting outside the house for me to finish my lesson. His face is lit through the window by the streetlight: a hard, spaced look giving nothing away. And I know immediately – there's a sudden molten instinct in my gut – that I can't go back. It wasn't Ruth or Rick that killed Nell, it was him.

Jay.

And I have to get away from him before he kills me too.

I can't let him see me. Turning abruptly, I stride back the way I came, pulling up my hood. But only seconds later there's the growl of an engine behind me, the blinding full beams of the campervan lighting up the pavement. I break into a run, looking for an alley or a footpath. There's nothing, and I can't risk trapping myself in a garden at the back of one of the terraces.

'Get in the van!' Jay shouts through the open van window, crawling along beside me.

But I ignore him and continue blundering to where the houses run out into fields, where I can get off the road and away from him.

Suddenly, there's an opportunity. I scramble through harsh thorns guarding a gap in the hedge, sliding, stumbling along the perimeter of the field which circles back towards the village. The camper stops and I hear the distance between me and its engine as I leave it behind. Staggering on, I reach a block of allotments, a pony paddock, a deserted recreation ground where all the swing seats have been stolen. I check my watch – twenty minutes have passed – and try to gauge my bearings.

I think I can get to Maria's house without using any main roads. She is my only hope now. My boots are covered in mud and so are my hands. I find a snicket at the end of a cul-de-sac that takes me to a row of tatty garages, then a pub with a car park and a path to a cricket field, a copse littered with Strongbow cans and condom packets, a broken fence and then the school field. I climb over a railing, into the garden of a house in darkness, and onto the housing estate where Maria lives.

And then I run as fast as I can – with dirt flinching from my boots, my filthy coat flapping, the speed and breeze pulling my hood off – until I see the butterfly, the dreamcatcher, the shifting colours and lights of a TV behind the curtains. I rush through the gate, and bolt up the path to hammer on the kitchen door.

But I can't wait for someone to answer it: I push down the handle and burst in, to see Lolly at the kitchen table, swinging her bare legs under a chair as she sits with a plate of fish fingers and oven chips in front of her. Maria is on her way through: her jaw drops at the sight of me and my hair and the mud and my sudden quiver of tears that has come from the relief of getting here.

'Bloody hell,' she says. 'What's happened to you?'

'Can I wash my hands?' I sob. I move towards the sink, realising that I am leaving mud all over the floor.

'What's with the hair?' she asks as I turn and run my hands under the tap.

'Jay did it,' I say. I muster up the discipline to stop myself crying; pull a long breath of sweet, vinegary air into my lungs. 'I don't know what's going on with him but I'm leaving him. He's really lost it. He scares me.'

She comes to the draining board, scrutinises my face. 'Has he hit you?'

I think of the purple teeth mark on the inside of my thigh; the scratch at the base of my belly; the bruise on my right breast, my ribs, my upper arms; the new sores around my wrist.

'Not punched, exactly,' I reply. 'But everything else... all the weird stuff.'

'Fuck,' she says.

'I know about Ruth,' I say. 'I went and saw her.'

Maria gawps at me. Reaches for the dishcloth and wipes crumbs off the stainless steel. Then she starts to talk. 'It was so terrible, what happened, you know, the accident. It really hit everyone hard. We're all still trying to get over it. He's not really what you think – he's just basically a good bloke who's lost a lot.'

'He's not good though. He's done this, and not just to me. He's done it to others. He's drugged and raped people. And I think it was him who killed Eleanor.'

Maria freezes, dropping the dishcloth into the sink. 'Eleanor took her own life. It was nothing to do with Jay. We just made sick jokes about bodies in the quarry because... well, you know, sense of humour and all that.'

'Your jokes weren't really that funny though.'

'Well Jay didn't kill her. It was just a fling and then she turned into a nasty piece of work, really horrible. She wouldn't leave him alone, she got so obsessive.'

'What else do you know about their relationship?'

Maria stares at me and closes her face suddenly. 'What is all this? Some kind of investigation? Because I don't grass my mates up.'

I know I'm not going to get any information about Nell out of Maria. 'Look, I need to get away. I need some money. Jay's got all my stuff.'

'Well, it wouldn't be right for me to get involved. Why don't you just go back until Ruth...'

'Please,' I beg. 'I just need to borrow some money. I'll give it you back. I need to get a train to Norwich. Or at least find somewhere to stay until I can get one in the morning.'

Maria turns and taps Lolly's hair.

'Off upstairs, you,' she says. 'Earwigging every word, you mute little freak.'

Lolly slides off the chair and creeps out of the kitchen.

'I can't help you do this,' says Maria. She's hard-faced. The sculpted spikes of her hair, the lines of black kohl, the scornful eyebrows: they're all impeccable and they tell me she won't budge. 'Jay would never forgive me.'

'Just a fiver? Please?' I take the dishcloth and rub at a patch of mud on my coat. My sleeve is ripped from the thorny hedge. 'Look at me. How can you protect him after this?' I tweak at the blonde stubble on my head. 'All this black hair thing. It's not normal.'

'He's grieving. And grief makes you do strange things.' She holds her hands out as if that explanation covers it all.

I look down at the muck all over her sparkly lino. 'Looks like I'm walking to the station then.' I step outside, stamp some more mud off my boots. Move dejectedly down the path. There's a commotion starting inside the house: she's having a go at Lolly again, shouting, slamming a door, then suddenly Lolly is beside me, out on the concrete in bare feet, pushing a handful of pound coins, fifty pences, twenties, into mine.

'You can have my money,' she says. 'It's from my piggy bank.'

I press my face into her orange hair and begin to cry again.

'You are so lovely,' I say.

'Hurry up,' she urges, and I set off running, hurtling through the gate as Maria comes outside to drag Lolly back into the house.

It's almost dark now and I can make my stealthy way through shadows to the main road, to the damp cavern of a stone bus shelter that keeps me hidden. I get on the bus ten minutes later, buying a single ticket to trundle into town and plan my next move.

The office lights are just getting switched off as I arrive, breathless, outside the heavy glass door. Along the road, metal shop fronts are being pulled down, displays brought in, *open* signs flipped to *closed*.

'Hey,' I say as the door opens to let him out. 'Damien.'

He looks up, a little startled, and then – I detect – a little embarrassed. I know my boots and my coat are dirty, but my hood is up and the state of my hair isn't too obvious.

'Hi,' he says, coming out onto the street. 'Er, Lauren.'

'I really need your help. I couldn't think of anyone else.'

He inches back, wary. 'What's wrong?'

I breathe deeply. 'I need your help,' I say again. I'm not sure how much to tell him. 'I've had to leave everything behind. I've got no money or phone or car.' It's almost the truth: I only have five pounds twenty pence of Lolly's money in my pocket.

'This is a bit awkward,' he says. He's not looking at me, he's looking over my shoulder. I turn to see a smartly dressed woman clip-clopping along the pavement towards us. 'I'm actually meeting someone.'

So, this is the woman I could have been, with shining eyes and pearly teeth and quality clothes. She comes and kisses his cheek and stands beside him and looks down on me like I am a *Big Issue* seller. My chin trembles. I struggle to control it.

'Could I just borrow some money? I'll pay it back. Next week.'

He turns to the woman and she gives him a quizzical look. 'How much?' he asks.

'As much as you can,' I dare. 'Hundred? I promise I'll pay it back. I'll give you my parents' address and phone number.'

'Wait here a minute,' Damien says to the woman. He takes out his wallet, removes his bank card and walks across the precinct to a cash machine. I follow him, hang back a bit while he taps in his pin number and waits for the cash to eject.

He turns and hands me a thin wad of twenties.

'There's two hundred,' he says. 'It doesn't have to be next week. It can be whenever. I just want you to be OK.'

'Thank you, I really appreciate it. I will pay it back; I'm not trying to con you or anything.'

'I can see you're not.' He walks away, to the woman, to discuss meals and wines and a trip to the theatre.

I go into a mini-market and buy a packet of baby wipes, a bottle of water and a twin pack of egg and cress sandwiches, before walking all the way up to the station to find out that my route to Norwich will take three changes and the next available train will be tomorrow morning at nine fifty.

'Could you tell me where the nearest bed and breakfast is?' I ask a man on the platform, and he directs me to a place on Carlton Road which he describes as pretty basic.

I find the grim Victorian semi on a busy road, next door to a grotty pub. I swab my coat and boots with a few of the baby wipes and go inside to rent a room.

CHAPTER THIRTY-EIGHT

I sit in silence, still in my coat, on a candlewick bedspread in a room that smells of damp dogs and curry. I eat the egg sandwiches. There is no television, no tea-making equipment, no complimentary biscuits, shower cap or sewing kit. A thin crumb of plaster from the corner of the high ceiling suddenly drifts down like a snowflake into a cracked sink in the corner. I hear the creak of footsteps in the bedroom above me. Outside, there is the thunder and squeal of traffic; the scuffle of teenagers and a shout of 'come here, you fat twat'; the constant open and slam, open and slam, open and slam of the pub door as people go out to smoke.

I crumple my sandwich packet, pull up my hood and go downstairs to ask if there is a payphone but there isn't: I have to go out onto the street, past a bunch of smokers who give me dirty looks, to a phone box with a side missing and a handset that looks like it has been set on fire.

I feed in a pound coin, reluctantly pressing the buttons that have probably been spat on, and listen to Lou's phone ring and ring. Eventually I replace the receiver and pick up the coin that drops down into the well. Where is she when I most need her help?

The pub sells me a bottle of red wine, giving me an empty glass with it as if I'm going to sit and drink in there, that rough-arsed room with ripped seats and riff-raff clientele. Instead, I take it away, outside, up to my room in the B&B. I need a drink to sort my head out and the wine is good: room temperature, smooth, a change from the months of harsh home-brew.

I remove my coat and get in bed – clothed – and try to think logically about what has happened. I have to start at the beginning.

Jay. The complexity of his grief. He's had relationships, looked for the right person to fill the void that has been left by Ruth. He prefers women with long dark hair. He likes rough, kinky sex while we are stoned. He can be angry and unpredictable sometimes; at other times he is kind and caring and fun. He got involved with Nell – maybe she didn't actually move in like I did – but they were together for a time.

I pour another glass of wine. Gulp at it. Let it ease me. Put the glass down on the bedside cabinet that has a ring of something dark and sticky on it.

A dog starts barking downstairs, yap yap yap, on and on. It won't shut up. A door opens and shuts, allowing the blare from a television to briefly ooze out. The dog still barks.

I think about the edge of the quarry, the long drop down. How easy it would be to just push a shoulder, not leave any sign of a struggle. Is that what he would have done to me eventually?

'Will somebody shut that bloody animal up?' a voice yells from the room next to mine. I swig the wine. Top the glass up.

And the blind dates. Spiked drinks, the hooks in the wall, the blue rope. Surely the police would have investigated a claim of date-rape, wouldn't they? Did anyone actually report it?

I finish off the glass of wine, see there's only an inch left in the bottle now.

I get out of bed, put my shoes back on to go down the long passageway to the toilet because there is no en suite. The dog barks again at the sound of the bolt going across. Inside the bathroom the sash window is halfway up, letting in smells of cigarette smoke and greasy kebabs from somewhere outside. I sit on the cold, black toilet seat and massage my head. Close my eyes, try to flex my brain muscle to think what to do. I flush the toilet and wash my hands. Splash cold water onto my face. Go back along the creaky corridor to my room.

I sit on the edge of the bed and drink the rest of the wine straight from the bottle. Someone in the room above me puts music on: some sort of reggae or dub. It disrupts my train of thought, my loosening of recollections.

I need to do more thinking, a lot more. About Nell. About Ruth. But my head is fuggy and I need to sleep for a while. I get back in bed. Close my eyes. Let the thoughts of Jay fade from my mind.

I wake later, disorientated by my dingy surroundings, wondering why Jay is not beside me. The bedside lamp is still on, its dusty bulb smelling hot. The place is quiet: no music, no dog, no commotion from the street or the pub next door. My eyes are bleary and my dry mouth craves cold water. I take the wine glass and go to the sink in the corner. A pipe hammers through the silence as I turn the tap on and I wait for the dog to start again. But it doesn't. I drink the freezing, limey water and refill the glass. Take it back to bed, to think some more, turn over my ruminations like fresh soil.

The death of Nell. I need to look at the facts.

She went away and was employed by Rick's mum as a carer

for his sister, Ruth. That was how she met Jay. And then he killed her.

But the note. Why did Nell write that Ruth was killing her? Why?

I shiver. Then tremors take hold of my body, my hands. I get back in bed and pull the covers tightly round myself. I shake so much that the headboard rattles against the wall. I tuck my head under the layers of sheets, scratchy blankets and bedcover. My own hot breath on my face seems to sedate me a little. More than anything, I wish that I could be back in my new bed, in my recently decorated room, with all this turmoil gone from my mind. To have the light-headed exuberance and detachment you get from a special kiss. Is it addictive? I don't even know: all I'm aware of is that I'm craving it now, I'm so desperate for it...

It's the dog that wakes me this time. Yap yap yap. Yap yap yap again. A sound that I'm not used to in the suffocating darkness. I tug the covers away from my head, expose myself to the brightness of the lightbulbs and the damp air in the room.

It must be the stress of everything – or maybe the wine, or lack of illicit substances – but I'm suddenly sitting up in bed sobbing into my hands, making nearly as much noise as the dog downstairs.

Someone in the room above bangs on a wall, or it might be the floor. I take deep breaths and drink the rest of the water in the wine glass. I wipe my face on the thin sheet. Get out of bed and switch off the central light. Refill the glass with water and put it on the table beside me. The dog is restrained again. I really need to get some sleep. Recharge my brain so that I will be able to think properly tomorrow, make some sensible decisions, get myself on a train to Norwich, where I will have to beg Lou to let me stay with her for a while. Already I can see the scorn on her face. *Lauren has failed again.* It's the pattern that my life seems to be based on and I despise myself for it. But what else can I do now? I am at the point near the finishing line where the runner in second place has just passed me and I have no energy left to catch up. I was supposed to put things right for Nell, but I have failed. After all this, Jay is going to win; he's going to get it all. And I'm going to be left with nothing all over again.

I switch off the bedside lamp. The glow from a streetlight spills through a gap in the curtains, settles in a triangle on the carpet. I recline despondently, pull the lumpy pillow into the camber of my neck and close my eyes.

I topple into a dream where Lolly is running beside me, pulling my hand, her hair bouncing like an orange beach ball as we chase something out of view. But my feet won't move, they are tangled, and although I realise it's the candlewick bedspread that is stopping me, and I know that this is only a dream, I can't break back into consciousness: something is holding me just under the surface of it. My head buzzes. I try to shout, to speak, but all I can emit is the sound 'nnn'.

Suddenly, I'm out of it, snapped back into reality. My senses are fully alert and there's no way I will get back to sleep. I sit up and pull the blankets around my shoulders like a cloak. Thoughts are pestering to get in – or out – of my head.

Ruth. All the months of secrets, of trying to suss out Ruthie: that elusive woman with long black hair. I picture the purple dress. Remember what it feels like to wear it: the hang of it, the swing of it, the drag of the raspy fabric over my skin.

Ruth.

Now I have seen her, found out who she is, I can see her as being something abstract rather than an evil ex-partner. And anyone can go into that room – the one that used to be locked – anyone with long black hair who's had a special kiss: they can put on the purple dress, they can take it off, they can reach a state of rapture that they want to keep returning to, over and over.

Anyone can be Ruth. Nell would have been. I certainly was.

* * *

I wake just before nine, dejectedly opening my eyes to the grim surroundings. My head throbs from the red wine and I can't remember if I'm supposed to be somewhere downstairs for breakfast. Unfortunately, there is no smell of bacon cooking.

I rinse my face in cold water and try to remember my middle-of-the-night thoughts, because maybe they made sense, maybe something of all this shit got solved while I spent the night here.

Ruth.

I did a lot of thinking about Ruth. And about Nell. And the locked room. I think back again to the note I found in the room that used to be locked, picturing that chilling sentence in my mind: *If I don't make it out alive it is...Ruth that is killing me.*

And then it hits me. The unreadable word.

Being.

It makes all the difference to the meaning: *If I don't make it out alive it is being Ruth that is killing me.*

All of us with the long black hair who went into that room were *being Ruth.*

We were her tribute, her substitute, her replacement.

CHAPTER THIRTY-NINE

There is no breakfast. I stick my head round the door that has a *Dining Room* sign on it, but the room looks like a storage area for car boot sale stock with bags and boxes everywhere. The woman who checked me in last night appears in the hallway and says that she could make me some toast and coffee to take away. I decline the offer.

'It's OK,' I say. 'I have a train to catch.'

'Get yourself to the café up at the station,' she tells me, taking out her phone and scrolling to a photograph. 'There. That's their mega-breakfast.' A plate the size of a toddler contains enough sausages, bacon and eggs to feed a family of six.

It's only a few minutes before I'm in the car park, looking for signs to where I can purchase a ticket. And because I'm engrossed in my task and stressing over the fact that I will be relying on Lou to welcome me back with open arms, I don't notice what I should have noticed when I first arrived.

The campervan. It is parked on the edge of the spaces next

to the trees. But it's empty. I look around in horror, wondering where Jay is, thinking: *shall I just run towards the platform and hope that there will be people who might help me, or run back down to the bed and breakfast?*

And my dithering is not the best course of action, because suddenly Jay is there on the pavement, running towards me, and I try and sidestep him but he catches my arm.

'Lauren! I've been everywhere trying to find you. Maria said you were going back to your sister's.'

'Leave me alone.' I try to tug my arm away, but he wraps himself round me and kisses my face, my tufty hair, my neck.

'Lauren, come on. Please don't be like this with me.'

'Get off me, I'm leaving. I have to catch a train.' Again, I attempt to pull away, to free myself from him but he clings on.

'I need to explain everything. Please. Let me tell you about Ruth.' Tears are running down his face. 'Please? Let's just get in the van and talk. I'm not going to hurt you.'

'You don't need to tell me about Ruth. I already know about her, even though you told me she was dead.'

'*You* assumed she was dead. I never told you that.'

I don't notice that he has been dragging me to the camper at the edge of the trees.

'Why didn't you tell me the truth?' I ask. 'Why all the secrets?'

'She still needs me. It helps her when I call in. You've seen how she is: she can't speak properly, she's virtually lost the use of her legs, can't feed herself. I wouldn't be able to look after her. So the least I can do is visit. That's all it is.'

'You just want me to *be* her, don't you? I'm just her replacement. Just like Eleanor was.'

'Babe, please. We don't need all this. I would never hurt you. Let's just get in and talk.'

I point to my head. 'Look at my hair. How can you say you'd never hurt me?'

'I'm sorry. So sorry. Please, you have to believe me.' He takes my head in his hands and kisses me again. Then unlocks the camper and opens the passenger door. Guides me in with a gentle push. 'Come on. I'm taking you home.'

Too easily pliant, I sit in the passenger seat conned by his show of emotion.

He gets in the other side and starts the engine. Takes my hand in his and looks at me with a sob bursting behind his lips. 'I can't lose you. I'm so sorry. We can sort it all out, can't we? There's still a chance for us, isn't there?'

And at that point I'm even thinking that maybe there is, and perhaps with a lot of discussion and some compromises it's possible that we could return to all those times of bliss and happiness and my lovely little cottage in the forest with the divine garden that it would break my heart to leave behind...

He's driving away, out of the car park, through the town and I've just let him take me. I haven't screamed and yelled and hammered on the window or tried to open the door and jump out when we had to stop for the traffic lights. My demeanour is calm, resigned. I'm not on the train to Lou's house – and there is an element of relief in that itself – instead I'm here again with Jay, absorbing his grief and asking myself if I'm doing the right thing just like all those times I relented and went back to Martin. I'm such a sucker for a crying bloke.

'We'll be OK, we'll get through this,' Jay says, rubbing a gentle hand on my leg. He wipes the tears from his face with his shoulder.

And it's funny because I'm pacified, almost accepting that we're going back to resume our relationship and I'm on the point of turning my head to Jay to give him a little smile of agreement when we drive past the sign for the quarry.

Something activates inside me. An armoured device sounding all the sirens and alarms to pull me out of my compliance and question what the hell I am doing sitting here letting him take me back to the place where he killed my best friend.

There is only one reason that I should be going back there.

And that is to get revenge.

I won't waver any longer. It's time.

* * *

He kicks open the kitchen door and ushers me through. I scan the place with different eyes. Mentally locate the accessible knives, the heavy objects, the sharp corners. A lock of my blonde hair is still in the sink. Behind me, Jay locks the door and puts the key in his pocket.

'God, what a night,' he sighs. 'I don't think I've slept. Come on, let's go and chill.'

He leads me to the living room, where we sit together on the sofa with our coats still on because the fire hasn't been lit.

I look him hard in the eye. 'Remember when it snowed and we used to tell each other our confessions? Well, it's that time again. You tell me yours first. And then I'll tell you mine.'

He leans forward to hold his face in his hands for a while, exhaling loudly.

'Jay. You said we'd come back and talk, so tell me everything. I mean *everything*.'

'OK. Number one.' He inhales. 'Just go with me on this and don't overreact.' He reaches to brush his thumb across a mud stain on my coat. 'OK. I stalked you.'

My heart misses a beat. 'Stalked me?'

We'd always joked that it had been me who had made the first move at the point when I'd shouted 'love the shirt'; he'd said that I had chatted him up while I was standing behind him having a beer and wearing a bin bag. I'd told him that I had watched him make his way through the crowd: he'd caught my eye before we even spoke. Every time we talked of that first meeting we mentioned the words *fate, chance, destiny*.

'There was nothing *random* about our getting together. You'd seen me walking through the crowd and you'd been the first one to start chatting. But I'd been seeing *you* at every gig, months before the festival. I'd had my eye on you for a while.'

Fuck. There was me thinking I had been stalking *him* when all the while he had been stalking *me*.

Jay had been a fan of Cuckoo Spit for ages and had been to five of my gigs before the festival. Sheffield O2. Manchester Apollo. An intimate event in a marquee somewhere in Stafford-shire that even I couldn't remember the name of. A folk club near Oxford that had wanted us only in an acoustic format. A rowdy pub on the outskirts of Peterborough where the police had been called to a fight while we were packing up. At the bigger venues we had been supporting more famous acts: bands with shiny tour buses and boxes full of merchandise to sell; the smaller ones – certainly the pub gigs – were just us. Audiences were boisterous and the admission was cheap. But Jay listed them all.

I wouldn't have believed him had he not been able to mention some of the smaller details, like when the guitarist had broken three strings in the space of one song, or when a trio of drunken girls wearing neon unicorn horns had climbed on stage to complement our music with improvised Irish dancing. At the gig in Sheffield where we had supported Flogging Molly – it was my first proper gig playing fiddle with Cuckoo Spit – Jay, from that first time of seeing me, had become obsessed, had vowed to make me his own.

'Why?' But I didn't need to ask.

'You were gorgeous. Fit body, stunning face, lips: when you used to smile on stage it would turn me on so much. And being musical. And obviously your—'

'My hair. Because you wanted me to look like your last girl-friend. The perfect girlfriend.'

He turns quickly. 'No.'

'It's true. I've been and seen her.'

'Not the last girlfriend.'

Then I get it. Nell was the last one. Or maybe it was the woman that spoke to Lou in the pub toilets. Or someone else completely who had long black hair that got brought back here to be Ruth for a night.

'They all look like the last girlfriend, though, don't they? It doesn't matter which order they come in. Because the one before looks like the one before. All of them – including me – have to look like Ruth. She's the perfect one. Everything goes back in a circle to *her*.'

There's a sudden spattering at the window. Hailstones as big as marbles smash against the glass, and the wind whips up in the forest beyond. We turn our faces to see the commotion as the gale wails around the chimney.

'I know it looks that way, like I just wanted you because you looked like her, but it wasn't like that. *You* weren't like any of the others. I loved you. I still do, I love you. I really felt like we could have a proper relationship here and make something of it. I'll admit, between you and Ruth there were a few casual one-night stands who – coincidentally – had black hair, but they meant nothing. Absolutely nothing.'

'Tell me about the leaflets on the van. Who is putting them on?'

'That is some psycho bitch I met in a nightclub. Big mistake. I don't do nightclubs and it was just a one-off. Never again. But she was the one that came on to *me*, up for it and everything. I brought her back here thinking she was game for a bit of fun, and we took some gear, some MDMA, but then she just turned nasty. Weird. I drove her back to town and dropped her off and then she just started waging some kind of campaign against me every time she saw the van around. I mean, if she felt that I'd committed a crime she would have gone to the police, wouldn't she? But she didn't.'

I don't know if he's lying to me. But he's talking. At least he's doing that much.

'So. Who else?'

He swallows. Licks his lips and leans back into the sofa, stretching his arms to the ceiling. Outside, the hail has turned to rain and huge splats on the window make it feel like we are on a boat in a storm.

'Eleanor,' I say. 'Tell me about her. Tell me the truth.'

CHAPTER FORTY

'You want the truth? Everything?'

'Absolutely,' I reply. 'I'm done with lies.'

He lights up a thin cigarette and draws deeply on it. 'She wasn't what I'd call a proper girlfriend, not like you, not like Ruth. A few dates, a bit of fun. We drank together, shared a few spliffs, and on the odd occasion she would stay over. Once we did a barbeque for the gang to come round – that was all right – but that was the extent of our relationship. We weren't a couple. Not like us. She got on with Rick, but Maria never liked her.'

I wait.

'That's about it really.'

I smirk angrily to let him know that it's not about it at all. 'Everything. From the beginning,' I reiterate.

His hand is shaking as he brings the cigarette back to his mouth. Then he starts to tell me how it all started, how it all went back to Ruth.

Eleanor arrived at the end of September. According to her CV she was an experienced care worker, keen to take up the offer of a six-month contract, living in and looking after Ruth. Since the accident, Jay was a regular visitor to Ruth – every couple of days he would spend an hour or more with her – brushing her hair, massaging her shoulders, painting her fingernails, reading poetry and playing their favourite songs in an effort to elicit a meaningful response. So it was inevitable that he would meet Eleanor.

But it wasn't an instant attraction from his point of view. He didn't always agree with how Eleanor treated Ruth: she imposed strict routines such as getting dressed before breakfast and not being allowed chocolate after six in the evening. The sort of rules you'd put on a five-year-old. But they muddled along for a few weeks in a professional capacity, until Rick took Eleanor to Jay's cottage one evening with Maria, Phil and Patryk, to make up the numbers for a murder mystery evening. It was the usual situation: the game was abandoned halfway through and everyone had too much to drink. They ate a ferocious veggie curry that Jay had rustled up, smoked some weed, and Eleanor ended up in his bed for the night. No sex, he said. Not at that point. They were all too wasted. But the experience set some kind of precedent for Eleanor to begin occasional visits in the evenings, giving him the come-on. There were flirty looks when he went to see Ruth, which he didn't like: he didn't want to be cultivating a new relationship right there in front of his last girlfriend, even if she didn't fully understand what was happening. It didn't seem right.

'Did you take her in the locked room?' I ask, although I won't tell him about the note. 'Did she have special kisses?'

He raises an eyebrow. 'She was pestering for them all the time. If anything she got a bit addicted.'

I think of all the occasions I have pleaded with my tongue out, knowing the heaven that a special kiss would bring. So, Nell also got to that point. Was I hooked too?

'And what about Ruth herself?' I ask. 'Was the locked room

and the special kisses part of her life too, or were they just for the people that followed?'

Jay pauses, starts to roll another cigarette. 'It was different with Ruth. We both liked it a bit kinky, so we took turns with role play, dominating each other, that sort of thing. I would never have violated her. It was just a game for us and we didn't need drugs. Weed occasionally, but that's all.' He takes out his lighter, puts his cigarette in the flame and inhales. 'So, OK. There was afterwards, after Ruth, when I was able to get hold of ketamine and I met someone who looked a bit like her... well, I took advantage because I wanted to feel like Ruth was still there and things hadn't changed, that the accident had never happened. I'm sure you can understand?'

He's not going to come clean with the full story, is he? He will never admit that what he did was drug and rape innocent women just because they had black hair. So I have to continue with Nell, I have to find out what went so badly wrong that he killed her.

'Let's get back to Eleanor,' I say. 'Tell me more about her.'

Jay says that Eleanor started being unreliable with Ruth's mother. Even though she was living there she would sometimes feign migraines so that she didn't have to get out of bed and deal with Ruth's needs. It wasn't on, wasn't professional. And he didn't like the way that Eleanor talked about Ruth or her mother. So he tried to back off a bit, to withdraw from the relationship. He turned cold, standoffish, often being out or unavailable when she turned up in the evenings, trying to send a polite signal that he was no longer interested. She was insistent though, wanting something permanent, wanting to move into the cottage. But Jay had no feelings for her, no interest in a long-term affair. He used her as a plaything when it suited him: it was a way of dealing with his anguish over Ruth's accident and Amos's death.

My belly churns with what feels like boiling acid. Anger –

pure hot rage – shoots through my veins as I hear him describe my dead best friend as a *plaything*. I dig my nails into the palms of my hands. Still, I have to maintain my composure and can't risk giving anything away yet.

'But when Eleanor died,' I say carefully, 'how did that make you feel?'

He looks at me with his eyes ablaze. 'You know what? It made me feel fucking great.'

All the breath is knocked out of my lungs. I clench my back teeth, trying to blank the image of Nell's body at the bottom of the quarry. Something is on the verge of being tipped over, broken beyond repair. I almost daren't ask...

'Did you push her?'

His jaw juts forward; his nostrils flare. I see his hands shrink into fists as tension surges through his body. He stares into the fire grate even though there's only cold ash in it.

'Jay? You said you'd tell me the truth.' My voice is hardly more than a whisper. Everything inside my body is shaking. 'Remember? We're doing our confessions.'

He interlaces his fingers and balances his chin on them. There's a tic at the side of his left eye. Something clatters on the roof – maybe a thin branch that the storm has brought down – but it doesn't stir him. He bounces the wedge of his right heel on the laminate floor.

'Yeah,' he says. 'I pushed her right over the edge.'

There is stillness in the room. Outside, the gusty whining of the weather continues. We don't speak for three minutes, four minutes or more. We don't look at each other. Jay's heel is still bouncing at the same speed.

Someone has to say something but it's like neither of us knows what ought to be said when a murder confession has just been made. It will have to be me. I don't want him to think that my silence means acceptance.

'But why? Why didn't you just tell her the relationship was over? OK, sometimes people can be persistent...' I remember all the times I had followed Martin to work, begged with him not to give up on me '...but you don't kill someone just because you don't want to go out with them any more, do you?'

'It wasn't just that.' His foot stops still.

'What was it then?'

'It was something she said that just made me flip.'

'What did she say?'

'She thought her job was pointless. She said it would be best for everyone if she just tied a bag over Ruth's head and put her out of her misery.'

'Shit.' I wince.

'Yeah. I was pretty fucking angry.' He stands up and goes to the window to press his forehead against the glass.

I examine my clammy hands, wishing that I had my phone so that I could have recorded everything he said, so that I could have taken it to the police and got the justice that I want for Nell.

He turns abruptly. 'You don't know what it's like. All that grief bottled up, and I'm trying my best to get on with life and deal with all my shit, and then someone comes out with something like that and it's like... boom! Revenge is the only answer.'

I squeeze a smear of sympathy onto my face. 'Sometimes it seems that way, doesn't it?'

His body relaxes. I've said the right thing.

I check my watch, but it doesn't matter whether it's eleven in the morning or four in the afternoon, does it? There's a plan forming in my mind.

'Let's have a beer. Or wine or something.' Jay goes out to the kitchen. He thinks we're back to normal. He thinks that we can have one of our confession sessions and then follow it with drinks and a shag.

Well, he's going to be in for a shock, isn't he?

Because he's right about revenge. It *is* the only answer.

CHAPTER FORTY-ONE

'Tell me your confession now.' Jay pours us both a glass of red wine then sits back like we're about to watch a classic film.

'OK.' I pick up my glass and take the tiniest sip. 'You were talking about grief and saying that I don't know what it's like. But I do. Remember, I told you before that my best friend died? Nell? It was an absolutely awful time. I didn't know how I'd ever get over it.'

'Hey.' Jay squeezes my hand to calm it from the tremors that have claimed it.

'But I'll start at a point before then, quite a few years before. I'd been in an abusive relationship with a married man. Martin, he was called. I don't mean abusive in that he beat me up or anything, but he'd groomed me from being fifteen years old and I'd carried on with him, trusting him, falling in love with him, believing all the crap that he told me about how he would leave his wife for me. I'd never known what it was like to have a proper boyfriend, to be able to go out to places without worrying about being seen. Or to live with someone and spend night after night with them, doing all the normal stuff like cooking and cleaning and things that everyone takes for granted. Even when I went to uni I stayed loyal to him. It was ridiculous, the way I was addicted to him. Looking back, I don't know how I didn't see what he was doing to me. I don't know why I didn't end it and find someone single, someone my own age. He'd obviously messed with my mind. But my family seemed to think I was the one at fault when all the rumours got out and his wife and daughter discovered our affair. Nell was the only one that stood by me instead of blaming me.

'I met her at uni: we did the same music course. Shared a flat for years, worked in the same burger bars and crap retail jobs because music doesn't really pay. I managed to get a job teaching violin and she did some shifts in a care home looking after the elderly, entertaining them with singalongs and all that. We wrote some songs and got an act together and planned to travel Europe. She convinced me that it would be good to have a break from Martin. I think she could see what was going on and thought if she could pull me away for a while then I'd be able to recognise for myself the harm he was doing.'

'So what happened? Did you go?' Jay is rolling a spliff.

I put my wine glass down on the floor next to his. 'Money was a bit of an obstacle. We needed to buy tickets and pay for accommodation. There was no guarantee that we'd make enough from music while we were there, even if we were busking or playing bars. I had about three grand saved from my teaching job but Nell had nothing really. Then an opportunity came up for her to earn some decent money on a short-term contract, if she moved away for a while. The bummer was, though, that while she was away I got pregnant.'

'Ahh,' Jay says, lighting up his cigarette. 'That explains the abortion.'

'You're jumping the gun a bit,' I tell him. 'I just need to rewind. Because three weeks before I found out I was pregnant was when Nell died. I never got chance to tell her.'

'Babe,' he says, pulling my head to his so that he can kiss my forehead.

I feel my eyes brimming and I know I need to hold it all together. Keep strong, I tell myself. I exhale. Focus on the task.

'Oh God, you know what I think I need at the moment?' I give that special look to Jay as I run a hand through my tufts of hair, remembering how he hacked it all off only a day ago.

'Really?'

I nod. 'Yeah. Really. A double-trouble dose.'

'What? Two pills? Are you sure?'

'Yeah, fuck it. My head needs a big hit.' I smile sweetly. 'Come on, don't be mean.'

'OK. Whatever you say.' He goes upstairs and I hear him opening the little door into the roof space.

There's a grin on his face when he comes back down. 'You're ready for fun times?'

'I certainly am,' I say. I lean forward for his kiss, my lips taking both pills from his tongue.

'That's my girl.' He winks.

This will be the last time that I go into the locked room to be Ruth. But this time I won't be under the influence of any illicit substance. I crush the pills lightly between my teeth, pick up my glass and swill my mouth gently with wine before letting everything seep back into the red liquid.

'You need a top-up,' I say to Jay as I put my glass back on the floor. I take the bottle and fill both glasses to the brim before picking them up.

'Cheers!' I take his glass and sip; he takes mine and swigs, suspecting nothing.

He looks towards the window. 'It's calming down out there. Storm's blown over now. I'd better check the shed roof later.'

I keep a grip on my wine glass, holding it against my chest. A mix-up wouldn't be good at this point.

'Just going back to Eleanor...' I say. 'So you just took her for a walk and pushed her over the edge? Was it literally as easy as that?'

'Yeah, pretty much. I was so fucking livid, just... you know, *raging*. I couldn't stand the sight of her, the thought of her, any more. It seemed the only thing to do.'

'But how did you get away with it? Didn't you ever get interviewed by the police or anything?'

'Well yes, they came round a couple of times. But there was nothing they could prove, particularly when I had a solid alibi.'

'Really? Who gave you an alibi?'

'Maria. She was never a fan of Eleanor anyway. She said that I'd been clearing some stuff from her garden in the afternoon and then stayed for a couple of drinks into the evening. I mean, I had been there for *some* of the time, but... well she stretched the truth a bit for me. That's what friends are for, isn't it?'

I clench my teeth to quell the anger that is racing around my body.

'Anyway. I thought you were in the process of your confession about the married man and your friend? You've sidetracked me. And I really don't want to talk about *her* any more.' He swigs from his glass and grimaces slightly, examining and swilling the liquid around.

I copy him. 'The wine's a little bit harsh, isn't it? We never remember to let it breathe, do we? But it'll be fine with a few more mouthfuls.' I laugh and touch the liquor to my lips, encouraging him to do the same.

'So. Tell me more.' He gulps again and tops up from the bottle on the floor.

'It broke my heart when her parents rang to tell me that she had taken her own life. I couldn't believe them – she just wouldn't have done it. They said she had been having mental health issues.'

'Well surely you knew that if you were her friend?'

'But she was away, working in Derbyshire. I'd heard less and less from her as time went on because it wasn't easy to get a signal apparently, but she'd never mentioned being depressed or anything. Details about her new job were a bit sketchy, but the last thing I knew was that she'd got herself a boyfriend.'

'Hmm,' says Jay. 'Maybe he was a bit dodgy.'

'Maybe,' I say with a tight voice and a quizzical eyebrow. 'She told me she was living in a posh house, caring for a woman with a brain injury. That's all she said. Never told me the woman's name or anything and I didn't think to ask. Nell just wanted to earn some money and get back so that we could buy our tickets and get on the road. Later she said she'd met someone and sent me a video of them together. All I knew about this boyfriend was that he was a big fan of Cuckoo Spit.'

Jay's face has stiffened. 'Are you... are you fucking kidding me?'

'I just knew there was something wrong about it all and I wanted to find the truth. Nell wouldn't have taken her own life. OK, so now and then she had bouts of being miserable about stuff – don't we all? – but it wasn't proper depression, it wasn't a mental health issue like everyone was saying. I mean, the police didn't properly look into it and it just seemed like nothing was being done about a death that was obviously suspicious. And I don't know why Nell's parents believed the suggestion of suicide. But it messed me up big time. Big time. There was all the other stuff going on in my life as well and everything got seriously fucked up. As I said, I found out I was pregnant, then ended up splitting with Martin and having an abortion. I went off the rails, lost my job and had to move out of my flat. I was left with nothing. The only thing that could motivate me was the thought that I could get some kind of justice for Nell. And then it came about when I saw an advert for a temporary fiddle player with Cuckoo Spit. Everything started from there. I recognised Nell's *boyfriend* in the audience at one of the gigs but didn't get chance to talk to him until I saw him at a festival. Then it all just fell into place.'

There is fury and darkness in Jay's eyes as he knocks back the rest of the wine in his glass. 'What a sly fucking fox you are.'

'Eleanor was my best friend,' I say. 'And you killed her.'

CHAPTER FORTY-TWO

The pills haven't had time to hit him yet. His reactions are sharp. He smashes his wine glass into the fireplace and jumps up to loom over me and grab me by the collar of my coat. I try to push his arms away but his anger has more strength and energy than my defences. He drags me up out of my seat, through into the hallway, where I know that I am going to be put into the room to be Ruth.

And then I see it: the door has been repaired and there's a new lock on it. It's ready for me. It's ready for my last performance.

We wrestle as he jiggles the key into the hole to unlock the door. He clamps a hand harshly across my mouth and I am dragged, stumbling and unbalanced, into the room. I struggle and kick out with all my might but it is nothing against the strength of Jay. I try to scream under the pressure of his hand but the feeble sound is powerless.

He rams me hard against the side of the wall. Suddenly his hand slips from my mouth. I gasp the air and make a run for it towards the door.

But Jay is fast. He's onto me: fingers clamping the top of my arm, a foot hooking under my shin.

I feel myself falling, sprawling, my hood sweeping the ground before me as I'm howling for someone, anyone, to come and help. My cheek hits the floor. My teeth slice into my tongue and I taste the sudden metallic tang of blood. Pain hits me from all angles. I will my eyes to stay open, to look closely at the weave of the carpet, the line of dust on the skirting board, the fraying of Jay's shoelaces.

But I can't stop myself slipping, dropping, unable to hang on to reality.

'Help me. Help me.' I can't tell if I am actually saying the words. I might just be thinking them.

But no one helps me.

And everything goes black.

At first, I can't remember where I am. I expect to see the roof window and the newly furnished bedroom but I am somewhere else. My head aches and my belly is filled with queasiness. I'm groggy and confused, and somehow hanging from something. There are chubby candles flickering ominously in two corners of the room. I look around and take in the speakers, Jay's guitar, Patryk's amplifier: I'm in the studio, although it has now become a locked room once more. Only Jay has the key. My shoulders burn with pain and I realise that my hands are strung up above my head. Rope digs into my wrists and is threaded through the hooks so that if I drag my left hand down it pulls my right arm higher and vice versa. My throat is sore and prickly: I must have been screaming, although out here in these backwoods there is no one to hear me but the owls and foxes and mice.

Something feels familiar, but it also feels different. I am wearing the purple dress but this time there is no sense of elation to accompany it. My head is cold. I am alone. The place is silent, waiting for something. I remember yesterday, how Jay hacked my hair off over the sink. I managed to get away then.

But today, if I don't escape, he's going to kill me.

Another wave of nausea engulfs me and I convulse my weight onto the rope. The room spins and I feel myself slipping away from consciousness. There's no one to help me. All I can do is put my faith in the cottage itself.

Please, I say to the wall that I am hanging from. I lean my cheek to the aubergine paint. *Please keep me safe.*

The next time I come round, there is only blackness. Rustling. Shoulders ablaze with pain.

'Help!' I try to shout, before realising that there is a loose bin bag over my head. I struggle and writhe my head against the wall in an attempt to worm out of it. My bare feet and the carpet under them are cold and wet and I realise that I am standing in a patch of my own urine. How long have I been here? How am I going to get out?

I finally wrestle the bin bag off my head and yank once, twice, three times on the ropes as hard as I can. But the hooks are solid, cemented in, they're not going anywhere.

Please, don't let me die here, I cry to the wall again. My head and throat are jammed with sobs, with fear, and I drive my heels against the wall over and over and over and over until everything returns to black.

Later, I wake to the sound of the key being pushed into the lock. The handle dips but won't open the door. He keeps trying, turning the key again and again, but something isn't catching and the door remains shut. Maybe he's not fitted the lock properly. Maybe he's so stoned from the pills and the wine that he's trying to turn it the wrong way. Then there's a banging, a shouldering, a kicking on the door itself.

'Fucking let me in,' shouts Jay, his voice slurring.

I stand and hold my breath, begging the door to hold, hoping that he will pass out, hoping that he will relent and just go to bed, or drive away in the van or something...

Click click click. The key turns again. Suddenly, the door is flung open. He locks it behind him and puts the key in his pocket.

'Don't kill me,' I whimper.

'You've doped me, haven't you?' He blunders against the wall as he approaches. 'You spat the pills back in my drink.'

'Please, just let me go.'

A dull laugh. *Har har har.*

'Please.'

'Like I'm just going to let you out after you know everything about Eleanor?'

'I won't say anything. Really, I won't.'

Har har har.

He comes up close, grabs me by the beaded bodice of the purple dress. 'I don't even want to shag you any more. You're nothing like Ruth, your hair is fucking horrible, so I've decided that I'm just going to finish you off and bury you in the garden. I'm getting some new chickens next week. Your body can go under their shed. I'm going to get a knife and stick it in your heart. Let you bleed slowly to death while I watch.'

His body wavers in front of me, and I seize my opportunity. I grab the ropes and haul myself up, kicking both of my feet at him with all the force I can muster. He staggers backwards, then topples, his head hitting the opposite wall before he crashes to the floor.

I wait. His body is still, unmoving. I can't tell if he's dead or stunned. My heart hammering, hanging from my rope, I realise that if he wakes up then any small opportunity for leniency will be gone, and I will definitely, certainly, be dead.

Five minutes pass, ten minutes pass. Jay's body is still on the floor; I'm still hanging from the hooks in the wall. The door is locked. I remember that the studio window catch is broken, that it doesn't require a key: all I need to do is push it and slip outside.

But there are no tools within reach for me to use to cut the rope or smash the hooks from the wall. I pull myself up again and try to gnaw at the strands with my teeth. Maybe if I could weaken the rope it might snap. My shoulders burn and my body isn't strong enough to hold up for more than a few seconds at a time though, and I slump, exhausted, back to leaning against the wall.

'Please,' I whisper to the house, because there's no one else listening that will take notice. 'Let me get out.'

I reach up with my right hand to pull at the hook, to try with all my might to twist it, to claw with my nails at the plaster around it so that it can be freed. Did it move just then? Even just a millimetre? Hope spurs me on: I cannot be defeated or I will die. I yank my weight again and again and again and again until I black out once more.

CHAPTER FORTY-THREE

There's a crash and a shooting pain in my thigh and my side, and suddenly I'm awake. I've fallen to the floor in a heap with the ropes still around my wrist. I have pulled the hooks out of the wall, scattering brick and plaster onto my face and hair. I push up onto my hands and knees, watching Jay who is inches away. He's not dead. His chest moves up and down: he's still unconscious or stoned.

I have to get out, and quickly. There's no time to try and remove the rope or the hooks that jangle along its length: I may be able to untie it when I have found a place of safety. My shoes are nowhere to be seen and I need to move fast. Barefoot, I climb onto the windowsill and shove the side window open as far as it will go. I'm sure I can just about squeeze through the gap.

But then there's a moan from behind me. Jay squirms on the floor as I cram my head and shoulders through the thin rectangle of space.

'Hey!'

I hear him bashing into one of the amplifiers, knocking his

guitar over. It rings out like it's going to start playing 'Hard Day's Night', but I can't dither, I have to dive hands first to the ground, pulling my body and legs behind me.

My body thwacks onto the concrete at the front of the house. Jay is moving around in the room, shouting, disorientated by my disappearance. My wrists are still connected by the rope and I have to loop the spare length around my shoulder to stop myself tripping. What next? If I run down the lane he will follow me with the campervan or motorbike. I have to hide, to keep to the dark places as I make my way to where he won't find me. I know that the kitchen door is locked and it's not easy for him to open it without making a lot of noise. Maybe the best plan of action would be to creep round the back of the house and through to the end of the garden, over the wall and into the forest. I'm sure that if I can find my way through, it will take me to the main road where I can flag down a car.

I ignore the pain from my shoulders and hips and my bare feet on the cold gravel as I run down the garden path to the wall that holds back the forest. I scramble over the stones, trying not to tangle the rope as I hear Jay hauling open the kitchen door, shouting my name into the darkness.

The ground is icy-cold, wet from all the rain, and I skid in patches of mud as I sprint into the cover of the forest. Carefully, I make my way through the undergrowth of ivy and bramble from tree to tree, listening for the sound of Jay starting an engine to go out and look for me.

But he doesn't use a vehicle. I hear his footsteps slap the concrete, crunch the pebbles. I hear him yelling in the distance and I know that I need to make the gap between us bigger. He's coming after me on foot. How far is it to the road? A mile, maybe more? There is no proper path and I have to pick my way over the exposed roots and foliage, dodging from the wispy branches that claw my face. I can do it, I tell myself, I'm out here and not locked up any more, I just need to keep going and find the road.

Tree by tree, in the darkness I weave my way, not knowing if I'm going round in circles, just keeping moving in the hope that he won't reach me. He has stopped shouting now. Perhaps he has gone back indoors. Or perhaps he's gained ground and doesn't want to give himself away. I don't know if he's still stoned from the pills, or injured from me kicking him against the wall.

My feet are numb from the cold, but adrenaline is flooding through me, taking me further from the house, deeper into the forest where I am struggling to adjust my vision in the blackness.

There's a noise. I crouch and listen. A torch beam flickers between the trees; the crack of twigs showing he knows I'm here and he doesn't intend to let me go. He will be stalking, scanning the ground for signs of my presence. He will be following my desperate trail.

There is a smattering of stars above the canopy of trees, but I cannot work out which direction leads to the edge of the forest, to the road where I can let my lungs rip open and scream for help.

I can't afford to be reckless. Every movement matters in this cat and mouse situation. The longer it takes for him to find me, the angrier he will be. We are past the point of kissing and making up now and I know for certain that death will be the only outcome. Slowly, cautiously, I gather the skirts of the purple dress and stand up, keeping my eyes pinned to the wavering beam of light. Stepping silently towards the nearest tree, then the next, I ignore the pain from every stone and thorn that embeds in my bleeding feet, my mission only to reach some place of safety.

'I know you're there! I'm going to get you, however long it

takes!' His voice rings through the trees, bouncing on every trunk like a pinball.

I wait again, my heart hammering, forehead pressed against papery birch-bark.

Then the torch goes off. Where is he?

Nothing. Stillness and blackness. Then the rustle of under-growth, the flap of an owl above. Sharp quick breaths and footsteps.

Should I run for it now? Should I stay? I twist and turn my head to listen, trying to decipher the direction he's coming from but I can't hear anything above the bashing of fear under my ribs.

Suddenly he's there, behind me, his fingers clutching at my sleeve.

'No!' I tear away from his grasp and sprint clumsily through the trees, stumbling in rabbit holes, and whipping my cheeks on tendrils of overgrown ivy.

'Help me!' I shriek to anyone who might hear, but I know that it is futile: the nearest houses are over a mile away and even the most committed dog walkers don't come out at three in the morning.

Ragged sobs escape from me as I run pointlessly like a trapped animal. Is this it? Is this how it is going to end? His booted feet thunder behind me and all he will need to do is reach out and his hand will be on my neck...

He's down, tripped by a root, slewing face-first into the rough bracken. A new burst of stamina boosts my speed, my impetus, and I dart to the right, to where the trees are sparser and inviting me to potential open ground. Zigzagging through, I cling to the hope that the tiny wink of lights I can now see might be the road, and I can get there, I can make it.

The velvet dress catches and rips on something thorny, but I drag it away. I can't let anything slow me down. It's not far now, surely it can't be much further, my lungs are burning and bursting but I stumble on and on until there are no trees left and I hurtle out onto flat, open land edged with thick tree stumps. Which way? I can't hear any traffic, but I can still make out two small white lights in the distance, so I run again towards them.

But my ears are tuned to the quirks of resonance, and my panting breaths and pained moans are different out here. Ringing, lingering like an echo. Oh my God, I know what this means.

I am near the edge of the quarry.

I slow my limbs and turn to see if Jay is following. It's still too dark to see properly, but there is a moving shape in the distance behind, the spiteful thud of his dogged footsteps, the clumsy sound of his every exhalation. There's a tree stump, hip-height, beside me and I lean onto it to gather my strength, horrifyingly realising that three steps further and I would be over the precipice. I understand that this could be my final moment or it could be my pinnacle.

It's time. I have to do it, because it's either me or him and God knows I haven't come this far to fail.

I have to act fast. I unwind the spare length of rope from my shoulder and wrap a loop around the base of the tree stump. Venturing as close to the edge as the rope will allow me, I put my trust in its knots and fibres.

He's nearly here, close enough for me to see the rage on his face.

'You bitch!' he howls. 'You're fucking dead now.'

I face him squarely as he lunges towards me, and just at the point where he reaches to shove my shoulder I swing on the rope to the right, to where I overbalance and hit the ground, my left leg dangling over the rim of jagged limestone.

There's a shriek behind me, the sound of scrabbling hands and boots, and loose rocks scurrying, bouncing, chasing down the cliff, preparing the way for a falling man.

I freeze. I hear the smack of his body hitting the bottom. Then nothing.

It feels like ten minutes or more that I have held my breath, held my rigid body at the edge with my hands locked around the rope. Finally, I pull myself up and crawl to the tree stump where I wrap my arms around it and cry my heart out.

CHAPTER FORTY-FOUR

There's the sound of an engine ticking over. There's an intermittent *pum-parrr, pum-parrr* as windscreen wipers stroke away gobs of rain. There's the squeak of weight being adjusted in the seat beside me.

My body is stiff; my neck cricked. Bits of me are sore and stinging but it's hard to identify exactly which bits apart from the soles of my feet, which are in agony. I carefully stretch out my legs in the footwell and dare to open my eyes.

I am in the passenger seat of a car, parked up in a lay-by. I don't recognise the location. The road is flat and empty with straggly hedges. A lorry thunders past and the car quivers around us. Fat fingers squeeze the steering wheel. It feels like afternoon.

Rick turns to me. 'Are you OK? I didn't know what to do... I just knew that I had to get you away somehow...'

'What's happening?' My tongue is swollen, bitten, and it's painful to speak. 'Where are we?'

'You need to get away. You can't go back to Jay. He would have killed you. He *was* killing you, slowly, and you didn't realise. Believe me, I'm doing you a favour.'

'What? I was...' I struggle to remember what has happened. Was it all a sick dream, like all the other dreams that happened in the locked room? I examine my wrists. No rope, but thick red welts, the skin worn off. 'How did I get here?'

'I found you, unconscious, in front of the cottage door, about eleven o'clock this morning. You were freezing, with rope around your arms. Feet scratched to pieces and covered in mud. Looks like you'd either been out and couldn't get back through the door again or escaped and only made it to the kitchen step. There was no sign of Jay anywhere; it's like he's gone missing although the van and bike are still there. I took you indoors and lit the fire and got blankets on you to warm you up: it took a good couple of hours before you stopped shaking. I cut the rope off. Washed the cuts on your feet. Honestly, I didn't know whether to take you to A&E or something.'

I stare at him as the memories of the night start to creep back into my mind. The locked room. The escape through the window. The chase through the forest. The edge of the quarry.

'You came round for a bit but got quite confused. Although you did go upstairs and get changed yourself: I didn't do that.' Rick rubs the red patch of embarrassment at the back of his neck. 'I asked if I could take you somewhere safe, somewhere away from Jay and you said *yes*, but I didn't know where to go. You sort of passed out as soon as you got in the car. Exhaustion or shock or something. He's made a fucking mess of your hair, hasn't he?'

I shiver and laugh. Tears are running down my face, stinging my grazed skin. 'Well, I tried to test him out, but... He only ever went for dark hair, didn't he?'

Rick passes me a tissue from his pocket. He really doesn't look the type that carries tissues, but I don't refuse it. I pull down the passenger sun shield to look in the mirror and dab my eyes, my bloody grazes, my snotty nose.

'I know you've never liked me...' says Rick.

'What do you mean *I've never liked you*? It's always been the other way round: *you've* never liked *me*. You've always wanted me out of the way, right from the start.'

'Lauren, listen. Let me tell you something. I need to take you back – to your parents or your sister or something. You can't stay with Jay. He's dangerous. He's got you hooked on ketamine, dependent on him. You know before, when you asked me about someone called Eleanor? Well, this all happened to her, too. It was the same pattern of events. Until he killed her.'

'You're a bit behind the curve with all this,' I tell him bluntly. 'I know everything about Eleanor – Nell, as I called her. She was my best friend and it broke my heart when she died. So I came here to find the truth about her death. I didn't know if she *had* taken her own life or if she'd been murdered. I suppose I wanted to believe that it was suicide, because a lot of the time it felt good here and I thought that I could make a go of it with Jay. But then I started to discover little things that worried me, and I looked around at you and Jay and Maria and you all ended up being suspects at some point. Even Ruth was, before I found out how she'd been damaged in the accident. And when it became more and more obvious that Jay was the killer I got him to confess, and then I had to get revenge. It wasn't easy or fun, as you can see from the state of me. But I'm pretty sure that last night I succeeded.'

'What?' Rick looks me straight in the eye. The heaters in the car seem to have stopped working; a chill blasts around us.

'Jay is dead,' I tell him. 'He fell over the edge of the quarry.'

'Fuck.'

'Fuck indeed,' I reply.

CHAPTER FORTY-FIVE

I cup my hands around the mug of tea that Rick has paid for and blow gently at the steaming liquid. We are in a grubby 24-hour transport café where lone diners have left their trucks outside and are scooping food – pies, burgers, gammon and eggs – into their hungry faces.

The young waitress chats with the chef: an old lady with a face grizzled like tortoise skin who is lowering a basket of chips into a hissing fryer. I hear them mention Brexit and *The Great British Bake Off* in the same sentence, but my mind is too numb to work out their train of conversation. The chef has earlobes stretched long and thin with heavy hoops of gold that swing precariously every time she mentions Paul Hollywood.

We must look like an odd couple, Rick and me. I have my hood up to hide my hair and the bruising that has started to exhibit on my face. One of the truckers catches my eye and looks quickly down again to shovel thick gravy onto half a sausage. I check the clock above the counter: ten to five.

Rick slurps his tea. The grim, yellowy light in the café stains his skin, making him look ill. To be fair though, I must look worse.

He puts his mug down and presses his index finger on some stray granules of sugar at the edge of the table. 'Did you push him over?'

'No, I didn't need to. But I wish I had,' I say drily. 'I jumped out of the way to save myself, and he fell over. If he hadn't he would definitely have killed me. I'd spiked his drink with the ketamine that was meant for me, so he was pretty wasted.'

'He had it coming for a long time.'

We sit in silence, inhaling the oily air, watching the waitress wipe tables and scrape plates in between nudging the startings of a runny nose with the back of her hand. Another lorry pulls in front of the window: a clunking hulk of a vehicle that shrugs its load back and forth, before the driver climbs down and comes in to order a mixed grill.

'I'm getting a bit peckish,' says Rick. 'D'you fancy anything to eat?'

I shake my head. Rick holds his arm up and calls to the old lady who is tossing more chips into the fryer.

'Chuck a portion in for me, love. I'll have a chip butty.' He squirms in his plastic seat as he fishes coins from his jeans pocket.

'Do you think the police will want to speak to me? Have I committed a crime? I didn't physically push him.'

'They'll want to interview you. And I'd be willing to give a statement about what's been happening, to back up everything you tell them. But you shouldn't have anything to worry about: it was obviously self-defence. Look at the state of what he's done to you. Maybe you should take photographs of your injuries.' Rick stacks up four pound coins and slides them to the edge of the table where the waitress can collect them on her next round of table-wiping. 'I'm pretty sure he did this to other people too, not just you and Eleanor. There will be a lot of evidence against him.'

'Someone kept vandalising the van in town,' I tell him. 'A

woman who warned my sister about him. She said that he'd done it to her.'

'There you are then.' He looks up at the waitress as she collects the cash and drops a knife and fork onto the table with a thin paper napkin. She has the plumpness of a sweet-toothed childhood, and lank mousey hair that has been dip-dyed turquoise. Who am I to judge, though? I pull my hood tighter and lower my eyes.

'What I can't understand though,' an acidic inflection has crept into my voice now, 'is that you knew about a lot of this but you did nothing about it. You kept on being his friend. You kept it from your mother who lets him live in the house she owns. Why didn't you *do* something?'

'You don't know how complicated it all is. I was being his friend to try and *manage* the situation. It seemed to help Ruth when he visited, so obviously I didn't want to disrupt her rehabilitation. I needed to keep him around but keep some kind of control over him. To see the warning signs and get people to safety. Like I have with you. Because I knew that you and Jay weren't going to last much longer, believe me.'

'Get people to safety? You were too late with Nell, weren't you? And you were too late with me. I could have been killed too. How much longer were you planning to *manage* him for?'

Rick is pensive. 'Oh fuck, it's such a mess. You wouldn't understand how it all is with Ruth.' He looks around the café and up at the ceiling. He rubs a small circle in the steam on the window then wipes his wet hand on his jeans.

Then he turns to me. He scratches the back of his neck and sighs.

Out of the corner of my eye I see chips being tipped in a mound onto the buttered roll.

'Let me tell you something,' says Rick, his gaze still locked onto my face. He separates his knife and fork as his chip butty arrives and is set down between the cutlery. 'All these relationships with black-haired women: Eleanor and you and the others. He was just biding his time.'

'We were her replacements.'

'No. Not at all. You were just temporary tributes, just filling a gap.' He pops a chip into his mouth and gestures for me to have one too.

'No, you're wrong. I mean, I know originally I came to find out what happened to Nell, but something happened – I don't know, something good and positive – and I even ended up thinking that Jay was a nice guy and perhaps Nell *did* take her own life. Me and Jay were getting on, we had all sorts of plans, music stuff, doing up the house and garden. He could have got away with killing Nell if he hadn't been so secretive about Ruth, if he'd come clean in the first place, and I wouldn't even have minded him visiting her. The condition she's in: well, she's not a threat to anyone, is she?'

'Ruth's not a threat?' says Rick. 'Let me tell you: Jay still loved her as much as he did three years ago, or six years ago, or when they first got together. You can't possibly think that she's not a threat.'

'But it wasn't like she was ever going to be moving back in with him, was it? How could he feel true love for her when she was damaged like that, physically and mentally? He couldn't possibly have loved her in the same romantic or sexual way. Empathy, pity, regret, sadness: those are the sort of things he would have felt. Not love.'

But Rick is nodding his head up and down, up and down, up and down, and a wry smile is embedded on his face.

'Ruth is getting better. The last couple of months have been remarkable. With the physiotherapy she's expected to make a full recovery; already she's taking a few steps on her own every day.

'And Mum is flying out with her to America at the end of the month for some new miracle drug treatment that's been trialled over the past year with brilliant results. It will target the brain inflammation that's impaired things like her speech and co-ordination. Mum has had Skype conferences with the doctors out there who have studied all Ruth's medical details. They're saying that she's the perfect candidate for the treatment. We found out about it a few weeks ago but didn't know exactly when it would be offered. We've basically been waiting for the doctors to give us a date. Obviously, Jay was over the moon when he heard about this new drug. Because it meant that at some point Ruth could be back to normal. He thought he was going to be taking her home again.'

The new drug.

The overheard conversation in the kitchen where Jay had been hammering the table with excitement.

I'd got it all wrong. It was nothing to do with him dealing or getting high. Nothing to do with the special kisses.

It was about getting Ruth back. The real thing. Not having to make do with a tribute any more.

CHAPTER FORTY-SIX

My throat aches. A film of sweat wraps my face and neck. I'm shaky and hot and starting to feel sick. I need to take off my coat, my hood, but I can't because everyone will see the state of my hair.

'What's up?' says Rick as I rise and kick back my chair, lurching on the painful soles of my feet towards the toilet sign.

Inside the Ladies', I stand in front of the cracked mirror tiles and splash cold water on my face. I reel as my vision swims and doubles. I feel ill, really ill. I want to be snuggled up in bed with someone stroking my hair. But I don't have a bed now. I don't have hair either.

I sit on the toilet for a while and hold my head in my hands, taking deep breaths. Perhaps it's the shock of everything catching up with me. Perhaps I need to eat something. Perhaps Rick spiked my tea.

Where did my new life go? I just don't know what to think about it all. All I have now is Rick, the person who I thought was my worst enemy for the past seven months. I will have to deal with questions from the police, questions from my family, and return to the place that I ran away from.

I pull down my hood and self-pity overwhelms me. I cry but it makes me feel worse, makes my throat and ears swell with pain. The graze on my face feels like acid is being poured into it. My head throbs and stabs and screams with every tiny movement.

I start to shiver uncontrollably and have to pull up my hood again. My heart is rampaging like a machine gun in my chest. Snot and tears and sweat mingle and drip off my chin. My body wants me to sleep but the cubicle walls are too manky with graffiti and other dubious substances for me to lean my head upon.

The door squeaks open. I realise that I haven't locked the cubicle. The innocuous face of the young waitress peers around the edge.

'Are you all right? You've been gone ages and your friend wanted me to check on you.'

I hurriedly wipe my face onto my sleeve. 'Yes, yes I'm OK.'

She backs away and pulls the door shut. 'I'll just give you some privacy.'

I pull up my jeans; pull up my mindset. Tell myself that I must deal with all this. I can't just sit in a café toilet and cry and expect to come out and everything be solved.

'You don't look well,' says the waitress when I emerge with a wad of toilet roll wound around my hand. She hasn't even seen my hair.

'I think I'm getting flu or something.' I blow my nose and dab at my wilted eyes. 'Have you got any paracetamol? My head is killing.'

'I'll go and ask Joan. She's always got stuff like that in her bag.'

I rinse my face again while the waitress goes to find me some drugs. Minutes later, the door opens. Rick fills the space, a pack of ibuprofen caplets in his hand.

'Come on out.' His voice is placid, as if he is trying to cajole a dangerous dog. He extends his arm to shepherd me through. 'There's a glass of water here for you.'

We return to our table and I swill two tablets down with the water.

'You're supposed to have food with them,' says Joan the chef, who has come to retrieve the remaining pills.

Rick looks at his empty plate and shrugs. 'I did offer...'

'You can get ulcers if you take them on an empty stomach.'

'I'll be fine,' I say.

But Rick has succumbed to Joan's medical advice and got another pound coin from his pocket. 'Give us a packet of crisps and we'll get going.'

We sit in the car watching the diners, blurry through the viscous glass.

'Did you spike my drink?' I ask. I can't trust anyone any more.

Rick holds up his palms. 'What? What do you take me for?'

I look at his fleshy face. It seems sincere and I am inclined to trust that he didn't. I open the crisps and nibble the edge of one.

'I need to take you somewhere,' says Rick, getting out his satnav. 'So, tell me where.'

Rachel won't want me turning up like a bad penny again. There is no room at my parents' house: their tiny box room is always piled with stuff intended for the charity shops and even the sofa is only a two-seater. I remember them saying at the time of their downsizing that they had got a place where it would be impossible for the kids to move back into. It seemed like a joke back then: as if I would ever actually *need* to move home!

I begin to half-wonder about asking Rick to lend me money for a sleeping bag so that I can camp down in a shop doorway or a park bench. Because I really don't want to have to go to the most obvious place, do I?

'Your sister?' says Rick.

I relent.

'I suppose it will have to be Lou, if she will have me.' The humiliation will be horrendous even after everything that's happened. If it gets too much, I tell myself, then I will leave and go to a hostel or something. But right now, I need a bed; I need things tucked around me that feel nice and smell nice. She has those things. I will have to find a way of dealing with her comments and superiority.

We set off again. The satnav tells us that Lou's house is an hour and twenty-three minutes away. I force myself to eat four more crisps.

'You'll be OK,' says Rick. 'I know it's all been a bad experience for you.'

He's wrong. Until the last few days it has been good. I've had a focus in my life with all the DIY, and the outdoor environment has gone a long way with healing my mental scars. I have fallen in love with the cottage. Even being with Jay gave me hope at times – the sex has been amazing – and those indescribable feelings of pleasure: how am I going to cope with leaving it all behind?

'The accident really messed up Jay's mind. Amos had died and he couldn't do anything about that. But he still had Ruth, different versions of Ruth. The real one that he could visit and carry on loving, and the other ones that could satisfy his sexual needs. In his mind it was just his grieving process, it was just his own way of dealing with his PTSD, as sick as it was. But he's got his comeuppance now. And at least you've survived. You'll be able to start again.' Rick reaches over and pats my hand. 'Keep your chin up, girl.'

The pain in my head and my body is subsiding from the ibuprofen. But my soul is being tortuously crushed. No medication can relieve it. I press my face against the window, close my eyes and sleep once more.

CHAPTER FORTY-SEVEN

AUGUST

It is five months today since Rick pulled up on the wide, block-paved drive with his headlight beams bouncing back off the immaculate windows. He squeezed my shoulder as I dragged myself out of his car. Lou was out on the front step in her fluffy white dressing gown before I'd even made it to the front door. It was as if she had been expecting me. She held out her hands and moulded her face in a crinkle of sympathy. A light breeze frisked with her glossy black hair.

'No baggage?' she asked as Rick manoeuvred back onto the road and drove away.

I'd left everything behind in the cottage.

I shouldn't bitch about Lou. I try to think positively about her. She's done her absolute best to help me since I turned up, going straight to the salon the day after I arrived, to get her hair dyed blonde as a show of solidarity – 'we can be the honey sisters now: black hair is so last season anyway' – but obviously hers looks fabulous because it wasn't done by a student and then hacked off into tufts by an angry boyfriend. She insisted on taking photographs of every inch of my body, from every possible angle, and getting advice from a senior detective friend of hers before accompanying me when I had to give a statement at the city police station.

I hole up in her spare bedroom, which would probably be rated five stars if it was on Airbnb. Quality furnishings and décor, spotless en suite with roll-top bath and separate power shower, fresh-smelling white bed linen, and flat-screen television on the wall. But it is only a matter of days before I sully my quarters by weeping mascara all over the pillowcases and splashing vomit on the carpet.

'It must be difficult having to go through cold turkey,' she says as she hands me a scrubbing brush and bucket of stain remover.

Cold turkey? Of course, I deny it vociferously but it is clear that I am ill. Irregular heartbeats, burgeoning nightmares that alternate with insomnia, bouts of persistent tearfulness. All the special kisses that my body pines for.

I refuse to come out of my new accommodation or see anyone apart from Lou, who brings me food – pastrami sandwiches, dishes of noodles, Caesar salad, crackers and goat's cheese, and a plate of spring rolls and prawn toasts arranged around a bowl of sweet chilli dipping sauce. Sometimes I leave it on the tray, untouched, until Lou returns to take it away; other times I demolish the meal within minutes, craving more.

I go on eBay and buy a second-hand book which arrives in three days. I take it upstairs, rip the parcel open and hold the book possessively to my chest. The inside page has no inscription this time. I flick through the pages and stare at the illustrations of vegetables in rows, of bread being baked, of a pig being bled and butchered. It isn't the violence to the animal that makes me cry, but the opportunities that I've had and lost, the love and fun and new life that's been and gone that I will never get back. I pine for the ramshackle little house with its lush gardens and smoky stove and my stamp all over it...

'What are you doing?' Lou is in the doorway. My sobs are too loud for me to hear her return.

She steps towards the bed and grabs the book from my hands.

'*The Complete Book of Self-Sufficiency.*' She fans through the pages. Scorn creases across her face. 'What on earth do you want with this?'

I snivel even louder as I reach for the book. 'Please. Please just give it back.'

She holds it up in the air out of my grasp. It was the sort of thing she always did when we were children. She laughs and tosses it onto the bed. 'Don't get any silly ideas about having chickens here.'

'Don't fucking worry,' I snap as my anger cuts in. 'I'll be out of here as soon as I can, and I'll have what I want at my own place.'

She sits gently on the bed and tries to stroke my hand, before I pull it away. 'Come on. Let's not fall out. I just want you to be happy. All the self-sufficiency thing isn't really you.'

But it *had* been me for a while. I can't help yearning for what I have lost. Surely, I can get it back: there must be a way for me to sort all this out and return to my perfect life.

My mind swims constantly with memories and dreams of me and Jay together: laughing, drinking, dancing, fucking, getting wasted. I don't want them here but they turn up, uninvited. My body is excruciating with our separation despite my head reminding me of his depravity. At one point I link my bouts of sickness to the thought that I am having his baby and for nine days I cling to the bold desire that I could be pregnant, until my period arrives exorbitantly one night, messing up my absurd hopes and Lou's sheets.

'You might need medication or counselling,' Lou says as she

watches me rip the bedding off. 'You're still dealing with a lot of stuff and need to get your mind sorted out. And start thinking about getting back into the jobs market. You know, there's finances to deal with too, and you've basically been left with nothing.'

My ears prick, hypersensitive to the arrogance in her voice. Here is my sister, with everything *she* ever wanted – everything she doesn't need or deserve – still telling me how I should live *my* life. Furious, I throw the bloody sheet onto the floor.

'Who do you think you are?' I scream at her. 'Living here with your perfect house and perfect husband and your flash cars. All the fancy clothes and gadgets and everything that you can just have anytime you want it. You haven't earned any of these things; you don't have to worry about paying for stuff or holding down a job. So don't start spouting to me about what *I* should be doing when you've always had *everything* you've ever wanted.'

My body is shaking with vehemence, and Lou comes towards me and puts her arms around me tightly, gripping onto me like care workers do with kids who are kicking off. We stand, pressed hard together in silence, and some kind of chemistry takes over. When my tremors subside we sit on the bed and Lou puts an arm around me.

'Let me tell you something,' she says.

Surely, she's not going to attempt another rant about how I can sort out my crap life, I think, bracing myself for more super-ciliousness.

'On the surface, it might look like I have everything,' she begins. 'But that's not the case at all. The thing that I wanted most of all was the thing I will never have.'

I look at her, at the sadness and tears in her eyes that will spill out and make her face red and swollen and impossible to present to an outside world.

'Ever since we got married, I have wanted a baby. I stopped

the contraception straight away, thinking that it wouldn't take long. But a couple of years passed and nothing happened. We went for tests, they suggested IVF so we tried that and it failed. We tried and it failed again. And again. And again. It went on and on and we kept paying out and waiting and praying that it would work next time, but next time would come and we still wouldn't get a baby. Plenty of embryos but no actual babies. At first when they implant a few you dream that you might get twins. I would have loved twins, a boy and a girl. I would have called them Sebastian and Sophia. Remember me telling you about sibling names? Well anyway. All we got were years and years of cycles of hope and hell. Twelve times we tried and it wasn't to be. So you see, just because we have money doesn't mean we have *everything*.'

She sniffs and wipes her tears with her hand. Runny nose, shrunken bloodshot eyes, make-up streaked and striped down her face. No wonder she hates me for getting rid of my baby.

'I never knew.' It is true. I didn't ever suspect her deep secret. She kept it all to herself, just like I did with the abortion.

She gives a hollow laugh. 'I was so jealous of you, of your ability to get pregnant when you didn't even intend to. And then... for you to just *dispose* of it like it didn't matter. What I would have given if I'd known before you made that decision.'

I don't know what to say. We look at each other. The state of our faces, our wrecked lives.

'Maybe it's a lesson for us to talk more. Be honest with each other.' She squeezes my hand.

Then she is up on her feet, flattening her hair, swabbing the splodged mascara with her fingers.

'Come on. Let's have a glass of wine. I've got a nice bottle of Chardonnay in the fridge.'

CHAPTER FORTY-EIGHT

Rick turns up one Wednesday evening. I'm not expecting him and peer out of my bedroom window as a confident rap on the front door attracts my curiosity. The sight of his car on Lou's drive, and his familiar chunky body at the front door sets my heart galloping. I feel shaky, faint. What does he want? Surely it isn't something else to do with the police? I gave them information about everything straight after Jay's death, and although they put me on file as a witness, they released me as a suspect.

I listen and watch as Lou answers the door, then Rick ambles back to his car, to open the boot and take out my fiddles, my amplifiers, some bulging carrier bags, a holdall and a muddy rucksack.

He carries everything in four trips to the hallway. I can't make out their conversation until I hear Rick say, 'That's it then.'

I don't want to go down to him. Not really. It is as if my feet take me there of their own accord, pushing past Lou to get outside to the front step and stand face-to-face with him.

'Hey,' he says to me. 'You're looking better.' He squeezes his hands into the pockets of his too-tight trackie bottoms.

'How are things?' I ask as casually as I can.

'Lauren...' Lou warns me from behind.

'They're... OK,' says Rick. He looks at Lou instead of me. 'Well, not great actually.'

'Can I have a word?' I am out on the drive – barefoot – and pulling open the passenger door of his car before anyone can stop me.

Lou is gesturing in bewilderment; Rick is shrugging and following me as I shut myself into his vehicle.

'I brought your stuff back.' Rick flomps into the seat beside me and pulls his door only half-closed, as if he might need to make a quick escape. 'I expected you'd need it. There's your phone and everything, clothes and whatnot.'

'How's everything? What's happening with... you know, everyone back there?'

He shrugs and pulls a face. 'Maria's gone.'

'What? Gone where?'

'Phil kicked her out. She was drinking all the time after Jay died: his death basically did for her. I think she secretly had a thing for him and he used to supply her with gear on the side. But – you probably noticed – her parenting skills weren't great anyway and so she just kind of gave up doing anything for Lolly. Social Care got involved again, not because of the not speaking issue, but because Lolly was being badly neglected. But then Phil managed to grow some balls and decided that his daughter had to come first. Maria didn't like it, obviously, but Phil had had enough. So she's been gone about three weeks now and – would you believe it – Lolly is doing great and has even started talking again at school. Just goes to show.'

'Wow, that's amazing.' I smile at the thought of Lolly and how she trusted and befriended me. How I still owe her for her piggy bank savings. 'And what about...' Even now I have trouble saying her name. 'Your sister?'

A rosy flush spreads over Rick's face and he shifts his

weight around. 'Well... the trip to the States – you know, with Ruth – and her treatment and everything... well, it was all a big disappointment in the end. Not the miracle cure we were all hoping for.'

'So it didn't work then? She hasn't improved?'

'They've just about given up on the physio now, and the drug treatment made no difference. Her speech and co-ordination and memory have deteriorated, if anything. We've all had to accept that she'll never get better. So she's gone into a respite place. They have trained staff and equipment to deal with her needs, and we can visit anytime. The thing is, Ruth seems happier there. Maybe Jay's visits were too disruptive for her, I don't know.'

'What happened about Jay? And the cottage?'

'The police were all over the cottage after Jay was found. They seized his stash of drugs; identified the same substances in his bloodstream and basically concluded it was a drug-related accident. The place has been empty and locked up ever since.'

'I bet the garden needs weeding.' I think of the broad beans that I pushed into the soil back in March.

'You could say that.'

'Do you think your mum would talk to me?'

He looks puzzled. 'Yeah, why?'

I shrug. 'Just wondered.'

We stare at each other for a few seconds and something sparks.

'I'll give you her number,' he says.

'I'm going to get my life back,' I tell Lou. 'I've made a decision and I'm definitely doing it this time.'

I reorganise my stuff that Rick has returned, reminiscing wistfully as the scent of my old existence stirs and strays into my nostrils with the shaking and folding of each dress and T-shirt and elongated jumper. Lou insists that I throw away some of the ethnic stuff – 'the neighbours will think I have activists living here if you're seen out in that!' – then she bundles the rest into the washing machine with a double dose of fabric conditioner.

I pack everything into the walk-in wardrobe, and as an afterthought shove the self-sufficiency book in, too. It's all temporary though, because I'm not going to be here much longer.

It's three days later, and a mobile hairdresser-cum-beautician turns up, to snip at my tufts and give me a makeover. My hair has been getting longer and is half blonde, half black now that my roots are showing through.

'What colour?' asks the woman whose name is Corinna. She has fake eyebrows and a gold stud that looks like a dimple in her cheek.

'Silver-blonde,' I say. 'With a red flash in the fringe.'

So, I go through the whole rigmarole again of lightening and waiting and rinsing and blow-drying and mousse applications and backcombing and tweaking the ends, until I am allowed to look in the mirror from various angles.

And it actually looks quite impressive! A bit spiky in places, but volumised to give the impression of attitude and confidence. Which is what I definitely need at this point.

Corinna waxes my eyebrows and applies make-up. She dabs things on and uses an excessive number of sponges and brushes from a huge wooden box that Van Gogh would have been proud to own. I can't ever remember being so pampered.

'You look fantastic,' Lou tells me after I have been preened for hours.

It gives me a boost, it really does. Because I am at the point where I am finally going to get almost everything I ever wanted.

CHAPTER FORTY-NINE
OCTOBER

The clocks go back tomorrow. And I go back, too.

To the cottage down the lane where the keys are all mine and I have signed a proper rental agreement. There is a landline and wi-fi, and the newly fitted door doesn't stick.

Rick and his mother were only too happy for me to formally take over the tenancy.

It's strange how destiny works. How Nell's death brought me here and a certain kind of fate wanted to keep me here. How Rick's mum has managed to get me a job doing music therapy in the respite home where Ruth spends most of her time. I sit with her and play my fiddle, watching how she enjoys the tunes, and I tell her about how I have varnished the bedroom floorboards, and what vegetables I intend to plant in spring, and how I am going to get some rescue chickens to put in the orchard, and how Lolly is looking forward to having violin lessons with me every week, and how we go together sometimes to take flowers to Amos's grave. Our lives have overlapped and although I am not Ruth's stand-in any more, I feel like I owe her these moments. Chance, providence, serendipity: it all seems to be a circular thing that exists within good and bad and it can heal or it can harm.

I am the lucky one.

* * *

I put the key in the door. It's a red-grained composite with top-notch security locks and doesn't need to be kicked open. I step into the kitchen, onto the old floor tiles that I used to scrub and polish every week. The cupboards are empty and the table and chairs have gone. There are plenty of second-hand furniture shops in town though, where I could get myself a small pine table: I never liked that wonky Formica one anyway. The terra-cotta walls are looking a little tired now and I wonder if a change of colour might be a good thing. Maybe a vibrant blue, with some Moroccan-themed crockery and accessories? I will check what is trending in Homebase.

I pass through the hallway, noticing that the door to the studio has been replaced. No lock this time, just a simple brass handle. The living room awaits. Laminate floor still looking good. But there is mould and soot on one of the throws and the old three-piece suite definitely needs to go. Leather would be the most practical option, even though I have flirted with the idea of a mustard-coloured velvet sofa. Expensive, though. I flick the light switch on to check the aubergine wall. Something catches my eye. I move around the room and pull the curtains fully open to let the light in, so that I can properly see the wall that months ago I stripped and sanded. The angle of my sight; the light on the wall; the density of the paint; maybe rising damp has exposed it? Or a combination of them all. But, like a geophysical photograph, the secret below has risen to the surface and bled through the purple paint so that the words are visible once more.

Jay loves Ruthie.

Aubergine is a last-season colour anyway. No one on *Grand Designs* ever uses it now. It's all about wallpaper at the moment. I will go tomorrow and get four rolls.

A LETTER FROM HAYLEY

Dear Reader,

I want to say a huge thank you for choosing to read *The Perfect Girlfriend*, my debut novel. It's both terrifying and immensely exciting to release my first book into the wild.

If you would like to keep up-to-date with all my latest releases, including my next book due out in November, just sign up at the following link. Your email address will never be shared and you can unsubscribe at any time.

www.bookouture.com/hayley-smith

The Perfect Girlfriend began life some years ago as a 2000-word short story, an assignment for my Creative Writing course with the Open University. On the advice of my tutor, and with the characters Lauren and Jay refusing to leave my head, I began to weave a more intricate plot around the bare bones of that story and it eventually became a novel.

I would love to hear what you think of it. I really hope you enjoyed it, and if you did, I would be very grateful if you could write a review. It makes such a difference helping new readers discover my writing.

You can also connect with my Facebook profile, through Twitter or Instagram. I would love to hear from you.

Thank you again for reading.

Love,

Hayley

facebook.com/Hayley.Smith.Writer

twitter.com/WriterHayley77

instagram.com/HayleySmithWriter

ACKNOWLEDGEMENTS

Firstly, a massive THANK YOU to the wonderful team at Bookouture, and in particular my editor, Susannah Hamilton, whose ideas and insight are what has brought this story to life. You took a chance on me and gave me the opportunity to do my dream job and become a 'proper' writer.

Thanks must go to Ajda Vucicevic, my former agent, who rescued me from the slush pile and put so much into shaping this novel. Your enduring belief that this story would make it into the world was what always kept me going.

To my creative writing tutor at the Open University, the author Ray Robinson, who read the earliest version of this as a short story and told me to go and write a novel: thank you for your inspiration and advice. Here it is.

To my fantastic children, Nicola, James and Joel who always encouraged me and never questioned the amount of time I spent at my computer. Anything is achievable if you keep at it. Thanks especially to Nicola: you deserve a huge amount of gratitude for your enthusiasm and patience in developing my social media skills!

To Philip Gray who gave me the most comfortable office chair in the world so that I could write for hours without doing my back in – thank you.

And most important of all, the biggest thanks go to Michael for his love and support. He hasn't read a word of this novel but knows instinctively when I need wine.

Printed in Great Britain
by Amazon

37952696R10189